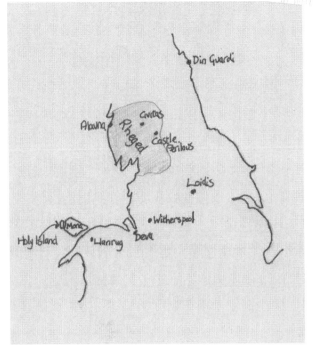

# Part 1

# The end of Rheged

## Chapter 1

**Civitas Carvetiorum Yule 593 A.D.**

It had been a year since King Urien of Rheged had been treacherously murdered by one of his body guards, Llofan Llaf Difo. Although his murderers had been killed by my warriors and me, it still rankled that the man who paid them to do this, King Morcant Bulc, still lived. That was not my doing; I would have slain him on the spot and his oathsworn but the dying king forbade it. Since that time I had been counselled by Queen Niamh, King Ywain, my wife Aideen and my healer and confidante, Myrddyn, not to kill him. Although I told them I would not I knew that, one day, the snake would die at my hands. He had ordered the murder of the last great king for he was jealous of King Urien's success and now he suffered because of his own actions, *wyrd*. The Saxons, under Aethelric had made steady gains up the east coast and much of Bernicia was now in Saxon hands. We now called it the Saxon name and not the old name Bryneich. King Morcant Bulc still held his fortress of Din Guardi and Metcauld but the lands to the south were now ruled by Saxons and its people were slaves to the men from the sea.

As yet the voracious Saxons had avoided conflict with us. It made sense for we had never been defeated and there were easier targets for them. King Urien and the men of Rheged had never lost a battle and the Saxons were wary of us. Besides they still had much to do to conquer the kingdom of Elmet where my brother, Raibeart, now a prince of that land defended the besieged people of Elmet effectively. In the old days I would have led a force from Rheged to aid our ally but these were parlous times and we could not afford the luxury of helping our allies for we knew that King Aethelric of the Saxons would take the opportunity to invade us. My brother and his father in law knew that they had a sanctuary in the north west and I also knew that Raibeart would not risk

4

his family on a dangerous journey. When he felt that they had finally lost he would join me and our young brother Aelle, defending the last free part of the old Roman province of Britannia. We had ensured our safety by building up our defences and our armies. We were a rich people; the wisdom of King Urien had seen to that, and while the rest of the island was subject to anarchy and war, the peace of Rheged meant that merchants still sought us out to sell their wares and we still sent our goods abroad. The privations of the Hibernian pirates might end that soon but we had survived well after the tragic death of King Urien.

King Ywain Rheged was my friend and I had fought with him, shoulder to shoulder on many occasions but he was not the king his father was. He was brave and he was fair but he did not have the strategic mind his father had had and I knew that one day, the inevitable would happen and the Saxons would come in such great numbers that they would overwhelm us. We had a sanctuary ourselves; a place to which we could flee. It lay further north, the King of Strathclyde was King Ywain's father in law and he would protect us but I knew that would only stave off the eventual end of the line of Rheged for even Strathclyde could be taken by the huge numbers of Saxons who had fled their lands to conquer ours.

My son, Hogan, now had a young brother, Urien, as well as his sister Delbchaem and, along with their mother, they were now my prime concern. I had fought long and hard for Rheged but I knew that it was a lost cause. Despite the fact that I, too, had never been defeated and was the one warrior the Saxons feared and hated; the Wolf Warrior. I was a realist and knew that there would come a time when I would have to run. The Saxons were like fleas- there was no end of them. My healer, Myrddyn, had been sent to aid me by the spirit of my dead mother and his arrival and support gave me hope that my family, at least, would survive for he was a pagan and steeped in magic and lore. Even the followers of the White Christ, like my own castle priest, Brother Oswald, respected his skills. Myrddyn and I believed that I would not die at the hands of a Saxon. He dreamt the future but, so far, he had not dreamed my death. I did not know if this was good or bad but, until he did dream it I would live.

I had been gratified, when we had returned with the dead king's body and buried him with all honours, that Riderch, the former champion of Bernicia, and his brother Ridwyn brought a hundred Bernician warriors to join me. He had looked ashamed as he had bowed to me. "My

5

lord these men have joined with me and left our king, Morcant Bulc, for we feel he has no honour."

"You have broken your oaths?" As warriors an oath was more binding than blood.

He had looked me in the eye. "The oath meant nothing once our king betrayed the oath he took to Kling Urien." He had shrugged. "We will deal with that in the afterlife but for now we would serve you."

Although I was pleased to have such doughty warriors, my castle and my lands could not afford to support another hundred warriors but King Urien's adviser, Brother Osric, came up with a solution. My brother, Raibeart, had been the defender of the fort at the end of the old Roman wall. Since his departure it was an invitation to the Saxons to attack Civitas Carvetiorum which was but fifteen miles to the west. The solution pleased everyone and we were all now much more secure.

This was the first time we had all gathered at King Urien's old fortress since he had died. Earlier celebrations had seemed wrong somehow but, as King Ywain now had an heir, the Dowager Queen Niamh had ordered us to attend. As I had brought my family through the gates I had felt a sadness I had not felt since my own parents had been killed by the Saxons. I had already paid them back for that loss and I knew that Aethelric and his men would also pay, as well as the Bernician king, for the loss of King Urien.

There was a subdued atmosphere without any of the normal banter and good humour. I was, of course, saddened by the fact that Raibeart was still in Elmet. The Dowager Queen had made a great fuss both of me and my family. She had a close attachment to all of us. When I had arrived she had embraced me and whispered in my ear. "Each time I see you, Lann, I am grateful to God for sending you to us. You could not save Urien's life but you made the end of his life valuable and I thank you for that." Then she had swept my daughter into her arms and taken my family away. "Come, let us see what cook has made for three good children!" I was very fond of the queen but I had noticed how frail she was. This time next year she would struggle to lift up my little girl.

As was my usual practice I first sought out Brother Osric who was the steward of the castle as well as being the brains behind many of the strategies. I knew that Myrddyn would have joined him immediately he had arrived for the two enjoyed each others company as well as common wit and ideas. As I entered the priest's office, which also doubled, sometimes, as his bedchamber, they were poring over another of the maps Brother Osric made. I knew that this one had been some collaboration with Myrddyn for he had added places he had encountered when travelling from Wales to Rheged some years earlier.

"And what will you do with all these maps priest? Most men cannot read them anyway."

He sniffed, somewhat imperiously. "My collaborator here can as can my Brothers in the church. If you warriors cannot read them then it is your loss."

"Oh I didn't say I couldn't read them. I take it this is a gift for me?"

"Do not be ridiculous; I daresay Myrddyn will copy one for himself which you may read." He leaned back and gestured towards a jug of the red wine he favoured. I often thought that the old priest had engineered the trade just so that he could get his hands on the fortified wine which came from the Iberian Peninsula. The room reflected the old man. It was very plain without a window and only a table and a case for his precious parchments. "Have you heard from your brother lately?"

We suddenly all became serious. I shook my head. "Not for a while but it is winter and he will have more things to worry about than keeping his big brother informed of events in Elmet." I took a small drink of the wine which I knew had a kick like a mule. "I suspect that the Saxons are busy consolidating their gains in Bernicia; after all Morcant Bulc is not as tenacious as Raibeart."

Osric snorted. "If I were to compare him to any animal it would be the creature they have in Greece, a tortoise, like the one which killed the poet Aeschylus." Even Myrddyn looked blankly at this reference. Osric waved his hand in front of his face impatiently. "An eagle dropped one of these creatures on his head as the poet had a bald pate and the eagle took it for a rock."

"What creatures?"

"A tortoise. Oh do pay attention Lann. I thought you were brighter than this. A tortoise has a hard shell and can withdraw into it when enemies are about. It thinks it is safe but, as Aeschylus and the eagle discovered, there is always a way to break through any defence. "He sat back exhausted by his explanation. "That is Morcant Bulc. He hides in his castle thinking that no-one can get in. But they will."

Silence fell until Myrddyn offered, "But they will defeat King Morcant Bulc will they not and then what?"

"And then they will turn their attention to Elmet and my brother and his family will be defeated."

Osric shook his head, "Perhaps not."

"You forget old man that I sat in with you and King Urien and helped plan our campaigns. We all agreed that it would take the combined armies of the four allies to defeat the Saxons. We do not have that army. In fact, even Rheged's army is smaller now than the one which defeated Aella and you can bet that the Saxon one is larger. They have more men than we do."

"Perhaps we need to use the gods and magic to help us."

I saw Osric shift uncomfortably in his seat at Myrddyn's mention of these pagan ideas. He had seen them work but it did not sit well with his Christian beliefs. "How?"

"We use nature as your brother does." Aelle had made an almost impregnable stronghold by combining a lake with ditches and cunningly built walls; his domain may be captured but his home would be safe. "The Romans used nature; just look at their wall where Riderch now rules. They divided the country from coast to coast to keep out the barbarians."

"Are you suggesting we build one too?"

"I am saying that there may come a time when we do build such a defence and then, of course, we can use stealth as I did once." Myrddyn had infiltrated the Saxon camp as a healer and helped to rescue Ywain when he had been but a prince.

I found myself nodding. "Now that is easily achieved. We have many men who can speak Saxon and many cunning and clever men. That may be something we can think about."

Osric took a deep breath and stood to ensure that the door to his office was, indeed, closed. "I am afraid that it will be you, as warlord, who has to make these decisions. Left to himself our new king will vacillate and wait for some divine intervention. His wounds, and his father's death, have made him think of his mortality. I would make those decisions and then tell him later. As we learned from Bladud and the assassin we cannot always trust those who are closest to us."

I had accepted the role from King Urien but this was different; would King Ywain back up my decisions? Myrddyn did his trick of reading my mind again. "Do not forget, my lord, the men with Riderch owe their allegiance to you and the majority of the men of Rheged would follow your banner. The warriors of this land look to you and not to King Ywain."

"Would that not be treachery on my part if King Ywain did not agree?"

"Myrddyn is correct Lord Lann. King Ywain would not oppose you; he might disagree with you or not wish to fight himself but he would not oppose you. Those decisions would be yours and I know that Prince Pasgen and his men would follow you anywhere." I smiled; Prince Pasgen was like the old Ywain. He was aggressive and enthusiastic. He had led one of the charges which had destroyed Aella's hopes of defeating us and he would be a valued ally. "And of course there is Lord Gildas." Lord Gildas had been a young warrior with Ywain and me. He had been responsible for the defence of the realm when we fought Aella and would have been given Raibeart's domain had the king not been murdered. Instead he was given the northern lands to rule while the king ruled from Civitas. "He has a powerful army and can lead your equites. No, I do not think that King Ywain will pose a problem but you, my young warlord, need to make your plans now while you have time." He nodded to Myrddyn. "This young man can aid you and we can now communicate quickly."

I gave them both a questioning look. Osric looked self-satisfied but Myrddyn was still my man and he said, "Birds, my lord. We have homing pigeons and we can send each other coded messages which, if intercepted, would yield no useful information."

It was obvious that they had both been planning this for some time and that gave me comfort. I was a warrior and not a thinker. "Well I feel happier now. I will see you at the feast."

King Rheged had definitely grown more portly since I had last seen him. He obviously enjoyed a comfortable existence but he also looked much happier. I suspect the birth of his son had done that. His wife, too, the daughter of King Rhydderch Hael, looked happier. The loss of their first born in the wolf winter had made her thin and tearful. Aelle had definitely grown more portly, but that was to be expected for with only one arm he was no longer active but he kept his mind active and had the most productive part of the realm. Freja, his wife and a former slave, had grown to be a lady of some standing and she frequently met with Queen Niamh and my wife. They provided assistance to those who had lost warriors in our wars. We were a family and life would have been perfect had it not been for the constant threat from without our borders.

After the feast we just sat around the huge fire and drank. Prince Pasgen sought Aelle and me out. "Have you had to deal with many Saxon raiders? You two, along with Riderch are the frontier now that Bulc has lost so much of his country."

Pasgen shared our antipathy towards the Bernician and he supported my belief that he should die at my hands. I shook my head, as did Aelle, "There are a few but I suspect they are just adventurous bandits rather than part of Aethelric's army. We leave their heads on a spear to discourage others." He smiled at the punishment. "And the Hibernians? What of them?" Pasgen had begun to use a few ships built in the Saxon style to patrol his waters to discourage the pirates who disrupted trade.

"We have had some success but they are too heavily armed for us to take on."

I suddenly remembered Angus, the Strathclyde warrior and his war hammers. "Do you remember when we fought Aella at the Dunum marshes? Angus and his warriors hurled their war hammers at the ships and burnt them."

Aelle shook his head. "That was from land brother, there would be as much danger for the prince's own ships as to the enemy."

"True but the hammers crushed metal; imagine what they could do to a flimsy boat."

"It is a good idea Warlord but we have no men trained to use them."

"Then ask King Rhydderch Hael. I am sure he would loan you some men to train yours and it would aid him for he, too, is troubled by the Irish."

Pasgen grinned. He had grown from the lithe young soldier into a powerful warrior who was capable of standing in a shield wall. "I am glad my father made you Warlord. So long as you rule the armies then there is hope. My equites long to ride behind the wolf banner."

"I fear that will not be for a long time. We will need just to hang on to what we now hold and our equites must discourage the Saxons."

And that was what we did once spring came and the land thawed. We kept three forces of horsemen constantly riding the borders seeking any sign that the Saxons were coming. Gildas led the equites of the king and Pasgen and me our own men. We had over two hundred mounted equites. We used mail, as did the warriors of the shield wall, but it was split at the crotch to protect the rider and his horse when fighting. Some warriors, Pasgen, Gildas, me and a few others also had a mail hood for our horses. This was not vanity for we would be at the point of the attack and our mounts would be immediate targets. My men still used the round shields of the shield wall, emblazoned with my red wolf but Gildas and Pasgen used the oval shields favoured by the Romans. They were better when used on horseback but my equites sometimes fought on foot and we compromised. We used a long javelin. We had found that the Saxons had taken to lying on the ground to avoid our shorter, throwing javelins and the longer spear prevented them from doing so. Finally, we all used a long sword which Brother Osric told us was called a spatha by the Romans. Our equites, along with our archers were the difference between us and the Saxons and, perhaps, the reason why we had survived for so long.

I was leading the thirty warrior patrol on that fateful day. Pol, my squire, and Scean, my standard bearer rode behind me. Despite the disparity in their ages, Pol was a boy and Scean was the oldest warrior who served me, they had both grown close to me having watched my back and fought to protect me so many times. When I had fought in the shield wall I had the confidence of knowing that Garth was there to protect my right but on horseback I had these two and they were just as comforting. Our scout that day was Aedh, the younger brother of my best ever scout Adair who had died fighting Aella. He too wore a wolf skin as I did and I had helped him to kill the wolf. He was determined to justify its wearing but I knew that he deserved that honour.

We were heading south east. There was a high ridge of land and below it, towards the land of the Saxons; the land became flatter and less hilly. We usually visited it once a month to see if there were signs of the Saxons. That particular day there was a thin mist which drifted into cloud on the ridge tops. It made visibility difficult but that did not bother us. The land was open and the chance of an ambush by those on foot was slim. We had paused at noon, although without the sun it was a guess, and Aedh reported that he had seen no signs of the Saxons. The news did not disappoint us; the longer we could go without seeing the enemy the better.

As we mounted and I prepared to send Aedh off, we heard the noise of a whinny. It came from down the valley and it was not one of our horses. Without a word being spoken my men drew their spears and

Aedh left us to see what had caused the noise. There was a possibility that it was a stray, it did happen, but it was unlikely as horses were so valuable and I had yet to see a stray. We remained where we were just listening for the sound to recur. It seemed an age before Aedh reappeared.

"My lord, there are ten riders; they look to be from Elmet."

"Ride beyond them and see if they are being followed." I turned to my men. There are riders and they may be from Elmet but they could also be Saxons. Be wary." I knew that they would acquit themselves well; we had become accustomed to treachery and tricks. We rode slowly down the slope and I began to see vague shapes ahead. They were too regular to be rocks and I knew that they must be horses with riders. I checked that my thirty men were in a half circle. I had no doubt that Aedh was correct and there were just ten riders; we would not be outflanked. I called, "Riders you approach Rheged land. Identify yourselves."

"I am Geraint of Elmet seeking Lord Lann the Wolf Warrior."

"Then you have found him."

The ten lumps emerged from the fog and I relaxed as I recognised Geraint whom I had fought alongside in Elmet when we had defeated and killed Wach son of Aella. I could see that the ten riders had suffered for all of them bore wounds. Geraint's left arm hung limply by his side. Their horses looked about ready to drop. I wished that I had my healer, Myrddyn, with me. I turned to Scean. "Take ten men and form a skirmish line down the valley." As he rode off I shouted, "Feed these warrior's horses and see to their hurts. Pol, see to their leader's mount, he is a friend."

I dismounted and was just in time to catch Geraint who almost fell from his horse. "Pol, water."

Geraint's eyes were closed and I wondered if he had died. I leaned in to see if he breathed and his voice whispered, "I am not yet with the gods Lord Lann, but it was close."

I sighed with relief and Pol poured water down his parched throat. I checked his wound and saw that he had lost much blood. Myrddyn had made us all carry pieces of torn cloth and I took some from my saddlebags. Using the water I cleaned the wound and then bound it tightly. I hoped it would stop the bleeding but Myrddyn would have to work hard or this brave warrior would die.

Aedh galloped in, "There are no Saxons my lord."

"Good. Ride to the castle and tell Myrddyn and Garth that we have ten injured warriors from Elmet. He is to bring carts and the rest of the equites." The resourceful young rider kicked hard and he was gone in the mist in an instant.

Geraint opened his eyes, "Your brother sent me, my lord, Elmet has fallen and much of our army was slaughtered." He relapsed as though the effort had been too much. My heart had almost stopped when he said Elmet had fallen but then I remembered he had said that my brother had sent me which implied, I hoped, that he was alive still. "He and the king and the ones who survived fled north west. We all fled but we were pursued. Our horsemen made charge after charge to delay them and they bought the time with their lives. When we could go no further we took refuge on a high rock above the river Raibeart called The Swale."

"I know it." It was a good place to defend but there was no escape route. The river wound around a steep rock seemingly placed there by the gods. There was water but little food.

"He sent twenty of us to find you." He waved his arm at his men. "These are all that is left of King Gwalliog's horsemen."

"And the archers?" Raibeart was a renowned archer and had made the archers of Elmet almost as feared as those of Rheged.

"Many of those still live but they are short of arrows."

"When did you leave him?"

"This morning."

Then we still had time. We could be at the river bound rock by nightfall but we would have to leave now. "I will have to leave you and your men here Geraint. Garth will bring warriors. When they come they will take you to my castle and you will be safe."

He struggled to rise. "We will go with you my lord."

My voice hardened, "Think Geraint, you and your men are wounded. You would slow us down." I put my hand on his shoulder and my voice became gentler. "You have done your duty and now I will do mine." He nodded. "Pol. You are to bring Miach and all the archers. Garth will know the place my brother has taken refuge you must come there and tell Miach to bring every arrow he can."

Pol looked torn between his orders and his duty to serve me. "What will you do my lord?"

I laughed, "I will annoy the Saxons until you arrive. Now go and tell Lady Aideen that we will have the survivors of Elmet as guests. She will know what to do." My wife and my steward, Brother Oswald, were

13

resourceful people they would have a comfortable welcome waiting for whoever we brought. "You will be safe Geraint. Wolf Warriors, we ride to fight the Saxons, mount."

The men of Elmet gave a weak cheer as we rode down through the mist to see if we could reach the last free men of Elmet in time.

Scean rode next to me as we steadily rode towards my beleaguered brother. Scean had served with me as long as Garth and knew me as well. He was a veteran and had stood at my side with the wolf banner since I had become lord of Castle Perilous. He knew he could speak his mind. "Do you have a plan, my lord, or do we just charge in and kill as many as we can?"

"I have a vague plan but it needs the others. What we will do is frighten the Saxons."

"Frighten?" I could tell I had piqued his curiosity.

"They will be camped close to the river, they have to be. We will make them think they have displeased Icaunus."

"It does not do to take the gods in vain, my lord."

"I know which is why we will make a sacrifice first and then we will make them think the spirits of the river are there. All we need to do is to distract them until Garth, Tuanthal, Miach reach us and then we can use real weapons to destroy them." I could tell that Scean was relieved. None of us wished to offend the river god but I felt a special bond with the river god, he had saved me on a number of occasions and I believed his would on the side of those who were born into the land and not some thieves come to steal it.

We knew that the gods were on our side when we found a deer which emerged suddenly from a copse. We killed the beast which appeared to gallop in front of my spear-*wyrd*. I saw the look of awe on my men's faces and even Scean appeared to be surprised. We cut out its heart and took that to the river which thundered nearby.

"Great river god, Icaunus, take this offering as an apology for what we are about to do."

The men all looked relieved as we continued on our journey. They had all heard and echoed Scean's sentiments but we had averted any danger to us and could now terrify and kill the Saxons below.

The high pierce of rock was visible from miles around and we halted some distance from it. Leaving one man to guard the horses and keep watch for Garth and the reinforcements, I led the men towards the distant fires which marked the Saxon camp. They had most of their men, from the number of fires we could see, on the southern bank. The northern bank had less room for them. There was a small waterfall which afforded them the opportunity of crossing the river as well as a ford I knew was further downstream. We had no idea of numbers but, from their fires it was a mighty host. I had assumed it must have been a large army to have driven King Gwalliog from his fortress stronghold of Loidis. We had left our shields with our mounts for this would not be a battle but a terror attack and we need to move swiftly and be unencumbered. My plan, devised and disseminated on the trail was simple; we would capture their sentries, kill them and then float their bodies down the river one by one. I hoped that this would make the Saxons fear the river and have to delay while they made a sacrifice to Icaunus. I knew that Garth would arrive by dawn and, although he would be tired we would be in a better position to fight, especially with Miach's forty mounted archers. The rest of my army would not arrive for a day; I knew that much for certain. We had to buy a precious day and hope that my brother and his men could hold out in their rocky refuge.

We spread out in pairs and skirted the periphery of the camp. I hoped that the Saxons would not be alert. I hoped that complacency would make them think that as their enemies lay at the top of the rock and had no escape save through their camp that they did not need to keep a keen watch. The noise of the waterfall hid our approach quite well. I could see that they had erected a barrier on the northern side to prevent my brother and his people from rushing through their lines and escaping.

We progressed very carefully and I saw a wave from the nearest pair as they saw their sentry. At the same time Scean and I saw ours. He was a veteran with scars visible in the moonlight and he had his cloak about his ears to keep warm; a sure sign of someone who has campaigned before. He had no helmet and wore no mail but he carried a spear and a short sword. We waited, patiently, for him to face away from us again. As soon as he did so we pounced. Scean had a thick wooden branch which he used as a cudgel and he struck him on the back of the head. The crunch and the pieces of bone told us he was unconscious or dead. We picked him up and went back to the river bank. Once we were there we drowned him as my men had drowned the other six men we had found. When the Saxons saw them they would see men who had been nowhere near the river, drowned, and they would put that down to magic or the river god; either worked for us.

15

We then waited with the stiffening corpses, watching for the first faint light of day. Scean had really sharp ears for the oldest man in my army and he suddenly hissed. "Someone is coming!"

We spun round, weapons in our hands and I was relieved to see one of my men. "Captain Garth is here my lord with forty horsemen and forty archers."

"Good, tell him to bring them forward silently." I turned to my men. "One in two of you get some sleep. Scean, sleep."

No one argued. We would need our strength in the morning. Garth and Miach ghosted next to me. "I ordered all of our warriors to come and I sent despatch riders to your brother Aelle and the king telling them that Castle Perilous was without warriors."

He looked at me fearfully, as though I would chastise him. I put my arm around his shoulder, "You did exactly as I would have wished." Besides I knew that the old warriors who could no longer fight in a shield wall, all twenty of them would defend my home as well as any. "When the first light comes we will let one of these bodies slip down the river and then all the others." They both gave me a look which showed that they were intrigued rather than perplexed. "I want them to think that Icaunus has taken their sentries. When we attack them I want them to believe that it is the spirits of the wood and not the warriors of Rheged. We will use the warriors who have a wolf cloak to increase the illusion."

I was pleased that they both looked pleased with the idea. I had not been sure that it would work but their approval was vital. "When dawn comes we will move towards their camp. I want the archers behind my wolf warriors so that when we retreat the Saxons can be slaughtered. The wolf warriors will attack silently," I gave a wry smile, "perhaps a wolf's howl from those who feel up to it." They both chuckled. "We are here to stop the Saxons attacking the men of Elmet. I want to draw them off towards our army. We have a long day to buy. Today will be the longest day. I want no heroics. It will be the Saxons who bleed and not us." I suddenly saw Pol with his wolf skin and felt guilty that my young squire would be putting his life in jeopardy and then I remembered, he would be doing so to save my brother and his family and I felt proud of him and all my other wolf warriors.

The sun began to peer over the eastern horizon and we carried the bodies to the waterfall which marked the western end of their defences. I turned to Scean, "The first body." I mentally counted and said, "The second." In no time at all the Saxon sentries were floating down stream, slowly on the current. We heard a yell as the first body was seen in the slow-moving eddies below the waterfall and soon we could hear the hubbub from the camp. "I grinned. "Now, wolf warriors, now, we go." There were thirty five of us with wolf skins and we slipped through the woods covered by Miach's archers.

Approaching as we did, from the west meant that we were in darkness while they were silhouetted against the lightening sky of the new day. The attention of the warriors was also on the river and the bodies which were being fished out. The warriors whose backs were to us died silently and quickly. I wondered how long we could continue as the third Saxon fell to Saxon Slayer. One of the men on the end of our line was seen and the Saxons turned to see the wraiths from the dark. We still had the advantage as their eyes widened in horror. They saw creatures that looked live wolves but held swords! However when I heard their leaders order them forward I knew that it was time for a retreat. "Fall back!"

The men were expecting the order and, killing their opponents, they turned their black cloaked backs on the Saxons and moved quickly west towards Miach, his archers and Garth with the rest of my men. The sudden move took the Saxons by surprise and it gave us a head start. We knew where our warriors were and they did not. As soon as Miach saw the line of cloaked warriors coming towards him he ordered the archers to loose a flight. Although aiming blind the rain of arrows could not fail to find bodies and many Saxons fell. Once again, they halted. Dawn had now fully broken and we could be clearly seen. Our wolf cloaks signalled who we were as much as my wolf banner and they formed a shield wall and came on. By the time they had organised themselves we had reached our horses and mounted. Miach ordered a third and final flight and then his lithe and nimble archers sprinted back to their horses and we all withdrew. I made sure that we withdrew in good order and at a pace which gave the illusion that they could catch us. Indeed, they probably thought that they would as it was scrubby bushes and trees through which we escaped but my men were used to such terrain and half an hour later as our horses climbed the gentle slope of the hills to the south they gave up and withdrew.

"Well done men. Tuanthal, take twenty of your men who have the fittest horses and follow them. Do not let them get close to you. I merely want to know if they intend to attack the men of Elmet today."

Grinning, my young captain of horse said, "With pleasure my lord. My men were a little bored awaiting your return."

We all dismounted and checked our horses for wounds and then ate and drank a little. I looked around for the young despatch riders. "I need someone who can swim and climb." A forest of hands went up from the boys and riders. I saw Aedh and Pol amongst them. I pointed to them and their joy was matched by the disappointment of the rest. I took them to one side. "I want you both to swim the river and then climb up into the camp of my brother. I am sending two of you in case there is a problem. Do you understand?" They both nodded eagerly. "You do not have to do this and I will not lie to you, it may be dangerous. We know not if the enemy has warriors hiding in the bushes on the far side."

"We are happy to risk it." Pol was the more confident of the two.

"Then take off your cloaks and just burden yourselves with a seax or dagger." As they began to rid themselves of anything which could drag them down I gave them their instructions. "Tell my brother and King Gwalliog that Lord Lann is here and his army will arrive on the morrow. When they reach us we will attack the Saxon camp. I will sound the buccina as we attack so that they can attempt to break out at the same time. One of you can stay with my brother in case he needs to send a message and the other can return to me. You may decide which it will be." I put an arm around each of them. "May Icaunus watch over you." We walked to the water's edge. The river did not look deep but I knew that the current was deceptively quick. "Swim upstream and the current will bring you to the shore opposite. Miach!"

"Yes my lord?"

"Bring your best five archers and kill any Saxon you see appearing on the other side of the river."

We watched, with bated breath, as the two brave young men began to swim across the river. I had already known that they could both swim and I suspected others who had volunteered could not. I scanned the opposite bank for any sign of danger but I saw none. Once they emerged from the water, they disappeared in the undergrowth. There were tense and nervous moments as we waited for them to appear on the scrubby and rocky cliff. Scean had the oldest eyes but also the most effective. "There they are!"

They looked like dark brown specks on the other side of the river. There was a heart stopping moment when Aedh slipped and slithered back down the twenty paces he had just climbed. I saw Pol turn his head and his mouth moved. I wondered what my squire was saying. Whatever it was it helped Aedh to carry on. As they neared the top I hoped that there would not be an over eager Elmet sentry. I had told them both to shout that they were from Rheged as soon as they neared the top but I also knew how a tense situation could make a man behave. There must have been a path of some kind near to the top for first Pol and then Aedh disappeared.

Everyone visibly relaxed until we heard the drumming of hooves as Tuanthal and his scouts returned. My young captain of horse sprang lithely from his mount. "My lord, they are erecting a wooden wall to hold us."

I breathed a sigh of relief. "Thank the gods for that. They think we are more than we are. Miach, mount your archers and annoy them. Make it hard for them to build the wall." He laughed as he led his men away. "Garth I want a defensive camp building here. I do not want to be surprised by a sudden attack from the enemy. Tuanthal, get some rest but send scouts out to see what the land is like to the east and the south as well as trying to discern their numbers but we have achieved our objective; they are no longer attacking the men of Elmet and, if the army reaches us tomorrow then we can attack."

# Chapter 2

I had one of my men watching the summit of the rock and, at about noon, he suddenly shouted. I ran towards him and he pointed to the crest of the rocky refuge. I saw my brother's standard being waved. My boys had made it and Raibeart still lived. Now it just depended upon the numbers of the enemy we would face for I only had five hundred men at my disposal. While my men were the best trained and armed in the land I would find it hard to dislodge a large army. I was on tenterhooks awaiting the scout's report of the numbers.

Scean had organised cooking and some of Miach's hunters had managed to kill some game. Scean was an old soldier and knew the value of a full stomach. Myrddyn and Brother Oswald would have done the same but our hasty departure had meant that we had not planned for this eventuality. It was late afternoon when the camp was finished. We had some hot food and the scouts returned. Tuanthal had a serious look on his face which did not bode well. "My lord, they know there is danger and they have patrols out looking for whoever killed their scouts. They stopped about half a mile away. We approached as close as we dared to their camp. There are three thousand Saxons encamped by the river and more than half are armoured in mail."

It was, potentially, the worst news we could hear. "Any horse or archers?"

"A handful; nothing to worry us."

Garth stroked his beard. "We will be outnumbered then but we can be more mobile."

Scean handed me a rabbit leg, dripping with gravy. "Of course we don't know how many men your brother has with him."

As I gratefully ripped the meat from the bone I pondered his comment. Until either Pol or Aedh returned we would be in the dark but if the Saxons had driven them hence it seemed likely to me that they would be in a sorry state.

I was satisfied. If we had not left Rheged immediately then the Saxons would have been free to attack my brother. This way we could add our weight to his defence. It would still be a bloody day but we had a chance. "I want as many men rested as we can. Those who fought last night have the priority and I want every guard to be doubly vigilant. If we can approach their lines quietly then there is no reason to suppose that they cannot do the same."

By dusk I was convinced that they would not attack. Our defences were, at least as solid as the Saxons and we had cleared thirty paces of scrub to give us a killing ground. I was relieved to see Pol emerge, dripping but smiling from the river. I thrust his cloak about him. "Well?"

"The men of Elmet have lost many warriors, my lord, and can field but six hundred although they still have a hundred archers. There are many women and children there and that is why Lord Raibeart said they had to halt. Their horses are not ready to use but when the buccina sounds he will lead out the men of Elmet to attack those before him."

I clapped him about the shoulders, "Well done Pol. Now get some food inside you and get dried out." It was as good a report as I could have hoped. We would be outnumbered but the Saxons would not expect an attack from two sides. "Miach, when the rest of the army arrives I want some quivers of arrows sending across the river for Lord Raibeart."

The army arrived, silently, after dusk and they were led by Myrddyn. His young face beamed at me. "We brought more men that we hoped. Riderch sent fifty of his warriors to guard the castle."

Old friends never let you down. "Good. Did you bring arrows?"

He pointed to the carts behind. "We brought four thousand."

"Miach, get some men to build a raft and we will ferry across a thousand arrows for my brother."

While the raft was being built I gave Myrddyn all the information we had. His mind was as sharp as any and I hoped he could see something we had not. I was disappointed when he said, "I think you have done all that you can my lord but I suspect that they will come this night."

Myrddyn always seemed to be able to see things which other men could not. However I had had the same thought which was why I had rested so many of my men. "Make your men rest then for I feel we will need them ere long."

It was pitch black by the time the raft was built and Miach's four men ferried the arrows across and began the difficult climb in the dark. I had rested enough and stood with Garth and Myrddyn close to the killing ground. It was silent and, as Myrddyn said, that was unnatural. There should have been the noises of the animals and birds in the wood but all that we heard was the waterfall. It confirmed that there were Saxons in the close by and our arrows would not help us; we would have to rely on my warriors.

They came in the darkest part of the night. We had forty sentries peering into the dark but it was Myrddyn who alerted us. "They come."

"Rouse the camp but quietly. We will hold them here until you return." I hissed in the dark to the men around me. "Stand to! They come." As I drew Saxon Slayer I heard the other blades as every warrior drew his weapon. Pol and Scean appeared, as though by magic and I felt much safer knowing that my two protectors were standing to protect my back. Even though we knew they were approaching it was nerve wracking; the first warning we might have would be a blade in the dark. The fence before us would not stop a wedge, merely slow it up and give us the chance to kill some of their warriors as they destroyed it.

I caught the glimpse of a white face and I picked up the javelin which was in the ground before me and hurled it. I heard a scream as it struck the face. Others threw their weapons and the Saxons screamed their war cry as they raced towards us. Numbers were hard to estimate for it was dark but it didn't matter; we just had to kill as many as we could until the rest of my men reached us. I slashed my blade at head height and felt it jar into bone as it ripped a warrior's face in two. Scean's spear stabbed over my right shoulder and I heard the death scream of the axe man who had swung his weapon at my sword arm. I sensed a sword on my left and automatically raised my shield. More in hope than expectation I stabbed forwards with my sword and it slid under the arm of the warrior I had struck. Suddenly I heard a shout of, "Wolf Warriors!" from a hundred throats as the first of my men rushed to support us. Although our wooden wall had gone it had done its job and the disorganised Saxons had no order. While we also lacked a solid line we were better trained and it began to tell. Inexorably the Saxon bodies piled up although it was hard to tell if we were winning or losing for we fought and died in darkness.

And then there were no more Saxons before us. There had been no order to retreat but they had had enough and had returned to their own camp. I glanced around to see if Pol and Scean were alive and I was relieved that they were and were uninjured. I could see some of my warriors had fallen but there was a satisfying wall of enemy bodies before us. We waited until Tuanthal's scouts had returned and told us that the Saxons had returned to their own camp. I left some warriors to strip the dead of any weapons and armour and others to keep watch while the rest of us tried to get some sleep for the next day would see us fighting in earnest. I would not allow the enemy to dictate when we fought. Even though we were tired I knew that we had momentum on our side. We had bloodied them twice and I wanted them hurt before they regained their confidence.

Myrddyn did what he did best; he healed the wounded and saved many lives that night. The wounded men would not fight in this battle but they would fight again and we had too few warriors to waste them. We had lost twenty warriors wounded and dead but eighty Saxons were slain in the midnight battle. I gathered my captains and Myrddyn around me. They knew my strategies and they knew that they could voice an opinion. The scouts had reported that the land to the east was flatter than near to the rock and that would suit our horses.

"Tuanthal, if you take fifty warriors you can gather in that part of the valley. You will have time to get around their flanks unseen and you should be able to give them a shock. If you charge in an extended line they will see more horses than there are."

"Will we advance in a shield wall, my lord?" Garth knew that he would lead the shield wall.

"Aye with the slingers before us and Miach, and his archers, behind. We will be vulnerable on our right flank so we need some horse and archers there to discourage a flank attack."

"What about the other bank?"

We all looked at Myrddyn, not questioning his statement but wondering what his fertile mind had concocted. "The other bank?"

"Your men took the arrows across last night. If you sent archers across then they could give the Saxon defenders awaiting your brother another surprise. They will think they are safe on the river side and it will divide the attention of the defenders. It may also make them think that we are a larger army than we actually are."

I looked at Miach who nodded. "Scanlan is a sound leader. He could take twenty men across. I will need to begin them now."

"Good. See to it. Remember the signal will be the Roman horn. No one attacks before it sounds."

Tuanthal left with his men as Miach's men were ferried across the river on the fragile raft. Garth went to ensure that the warriors were prepared and Pol brought me my sharpened sword, gleaming in the sunlight. He now had a shield to go with his seax as well as a helmet. He was too valuable and brave to risk losing for the sake of a piece of metal and wood. As we gathered near to our wrecked wooden wall I hoped that the sudden appearance of my army would make the Saxons defend our side with all that they had; when Tuanthal, Raibeart and Scanlan attacked I hoped that the cracked confidence of the Saxons would be shattered. That was my plan but it hinged on the enemy being weak and I did not know the leader. If it was an Ida then I might win but a Wach or Aella could just tip the balance in their favour. The Saxons knew me and how I fought but, each time I fought them, it was with a different leader. I would need to use Myrddyn's mind and magic to help me if I was emerge victorious.

We had twenty slingers and they slipped through the undergrowth ahead of us. I would not sound the horn until we had started to fight. If I made the call too early then the Saxons would have time to shift their forces. I wanted them committed to killing me. Scean had my wolf banner already unfurled as we edged cautiously through the scrub towards their lines. Unlike us, they had not cleared the brush and bush so that there would be no open area in which we would be able to fight. Given their superiority in numbers that suited us but it made it a nervous time as we crept forwards, never knowing when the conflict would begin. My slingers would be the eyes which would save us and I heard a shout and a scream as the first of them scored a hit.

The noise from the Saxon camp told me that they were aware of our attack and the increasing screams that my slingers were having success. Garth's reassuring voice boomed out. "Lock shields and be ready!"

Although the terrain prevented a solid wall my well trained men were able to break the wall when they came against a tree or bush and then reform. We had two ranks and the second were armed with spears. When the Saxons came forwards there would always be one line which was solid and that would give my men confidence that they could withstand an attack. The archers formed a third line and they would not all loose together but choose their targets; this was dictated by the terrain. The first sign we had of the Saxons was the line of retreating slingers I quickly counted them as they retreated through our lines. They seemed to be intact and their grins showed me that they thought it a grand game.

The Saxons must have had an inkling of who commanded for they did not rush at us but came with a measured approach. An attack with the normal wedge formation was out of the question and they used a shield wall too. With one of our flanks anchored on the river they would try to outflank us and that, too, worked in our favour for it would draw their men into a long extended line and I was sure that my horse and archers could hold them.

"Raise the banner and let them see whom they fight."

As soon as Scean raised the banner the men began to bang their shields and chant, "Wolf Warrior!" over and over.

The Saxons responded by hurling their own insults back at us but, more importantly, they began to head towards me and the banner. They kept their shields together but all were keen to be the one to kill the killer of Saxon champions and the warrior Saxon mothers used to frighten their children. Inevitably some of them showed too much of themselves and my archers began to pluck warriors from the wall. Of course there were plenty of replacements but it began to impede the subsequent lines and disrupt their flow. Suddenly they were close enough to attack and they lurched forwards. They could not use their weight advantage because of the undergrowth. I thrust Saxon Slayer forwards to pierce the eye and skull of the first warrior I saw. He inadvertently aided me by rushing at me. A spear took out the man to his left and Scean's sword the warrior to the left.

I could hear the Saxon voices at the rear screaming for my blood and I smiled. My fame was a weapon and I used it; I know that it increased my danger and Aideen would hate to think of me placing myself in such a position but it was effective. I could now see that they were committed and I shouted, "Sound the horn!" The warrior with the horn was behind the spearmen and he was ready for the order. The wailing notes echoed against the rock and through the air. There was a slight hesitation in the Saxon attack which my men took advantage of striking at men who were distracted by the strange noise.

There was now a press of men locked in combat. My archers chose their targets and my shield wall did what it did the best, it killed. Suddenly a bloody warrior ran up to me. "My lord they have turned the flank!"

"Tell the men to fall back to the river." This was to be expected and we would be in a better situation than the Saxons. The enemy would have to spread his men thinner and we would still be compact with our rear protected by the river. "Begin to fall back to the right. Left flank hold firm."

The roar from the enemy showed that they thought we were beaten and they came recklessly on falling to our measured blows. They had the taste of victory in their nostrils, Disaster struck when one of their

25

warriors had, what we termed, the death dream. He deigned a shield and hurtled at us with the mad look of a warrior who would die and join the gods. He struck at me but the axe slid down my shield and ripped the arm from the warrior to my right. He was stabbed in the thigh with a spear but, such was the rush of battle fury that he did not even notice it and decapitated the next man in the line. Suddenly there was a gap in our shield wall and the Saxons poured through behind their madman. Pol bravely slashed at his hamstring and that did slow him up. He roared in rage and turned to destroy the flea which had dared to hurt him. I punched hard on the side of his head with my shield and heard his jaw and cheekbone crack but, more importantly it pushed him backwards. I stabbed forwards with Saxon Slayer and the sharp sword ripped through his throat and half severed his head. His eyes became blank; he dropped his axe and fell dead at Pol's feet. We had no time for self congratulations for we had a wedge of warriors attempting to split our lines. Brave Pol slashed and sliced with his seax, Scean chopped and hacked with his sword and I punched and stabbed with Saxon Slayer. Garth had seen our dilemma and sent men from the secure river flank to bolster our lines and they fell back.

There was a brief respite as the sudden rush was slaughtered and we dressed our lines. I glanced at Pol who grinned back at me; he appeared to be without wounds. I heard Scean say quietly, "I hate those mad buggers with the death dream. They never die quickly. You have to chop off the bastard's head!"

"Garth, how are we doing?"

"North flanks are now secure, my lord, but we lost some horses."

It now depended upon my horsemen and my brother. We could continue to be the rock upon which they fell but unless the other two could make inroads then it would be a stalemate.

"Miach, try a few volleys in their rear ranks; let us slow them up a little." We would waste some arrows as the trees would deflect and stop many of the flights but if only one in ten struck home then the Saxons would have to be wary.

Suddenly I noticed that they were no longer advancing but looking nervously over their shoulders. Myrddyn appeared at my side. He was smiling. "Let us use nature to destroy them my lord." He stood and opened his mouth; I had not noticed what a powerful voice he had until he intoned, "Icaunus and the spirit of the wolf destroy these invaders who have dared to treat your land with such scorn." It was only then that I noticed he had spoken in Saxon and his voice had carried across to the silent Saxons. He turned to me and said, "When I give you the word then order a charge."

Few men would have had the audacity to give orders to me; Myrddyn was one of the few. I turned to the men. "Prepare to charge on my command." They looked at me as though I had eaten the mushroom which makes you insane but they did as ordered.

Suddenly Myrddyn shouted, "Now!"

"Wolf warriors! Charge!"

We all lurched forwards and I saw that the river had grown in size and appeared in full spate. The terrified Saxons saw that at the same time as my wolf warriors charged and they fled in terror. We kept charging for there was no alternative but the Saxons did not stop. We reached their camp, filled with their wounded and their dead and we carried on until we met Tuanthal and his exhausted horsemen. He reined in, grinning although bleeding from a wound on his leg. "I have no idea what you did my lord but the whole army has gone. We killed many but my horses could pursue no longer."!

I looked at Myrddyn. "Tell me of the magic that made the river rise and roar as though alive. "

He smiled. "I used the despatch riders and the slingers to build a dam and hold back the waters. It was not a large dam but when we broke it then the waters flowed as though Icaunus had ordered it."

I clapped him about the shoulders. "Whatever it was, it worked. Garth, form a perimeter and despatch any wounded."

With Scean, Pol and Myrddyn at my side I headed for the waterfall which was the quickest way across the river. I hoped that my brother and the men of Elmet had fared as well as we had. I could see Saxons still fighting on the other bank, their backs to us. "Miach bring your archers."

Standing on the rocks above the small waterfall Miach and his archers slaughtered every Saxon who remained on the northern shore. They had nowhere to run and did not know that the rest of their warband had fled. I almost ran to get to the other side. There looked to have been more Saxons fighting there than I had expected. The faces of the men of Elmet looked drained and they could barely raise a wave. What was worse, I could see neither my brother nor King Gwalliog.

# Chapter 3

"Myrddyn get some of our men over and see to the wounded. Pol find my brother, you know their camp." I could see the two banners still flying but that meant nothing. The two men could have died unseen. Just then I heard a voice calling my name and I looked up to see Aedh racing towards me. It pleased me as much as anything that my young scout still lived. "I am glad that you still live young Aedh."

"Lord Raibeart is on the hill he sent me to find you."

"Lead on Aedh and tell me of the battle while you do so." I knew now that my brother lived but it was not like him to be in the rear of a battle.

"We watched as the Saxons attacked you and the men of Elmet wanted to attack but Lord Raibeart said to wait for your call and that you would not fail." He suddenly looked serious. "I knew that you would not fail my lord but I could say nothing." His trust in me was touching and a little worrying. "When you did sound the horn we all raced forwards. Lord Raibeart's men used our arrows and slaughtered many of the Saxons but when we reached their lines they had reinforced the men and we were outnumbered. That was when the king fell. Lord Raibeart rescued him and led the men back up the hill and then you appeared on the waterfall and your archers ended the Saxon's lives. I knew you would come, my lord but it was nerve wracking waiting for you."

I knew then that something else had urged me across the river; had we delayed then all might have been in vain and my order for Raibeart to attack might have been disastrous.

Pol looked serious as he found me. "My lord, the king is wounded. You must come."

"Find Myrddyn and bring him to me."

There were many wounded warriors but I saw that they had built a fort for the women and children who greatly outnumbered the warriors. Now I knew why they had been unable to outrun the Saxons; they had been encumbered with those who could not defend themselves. Raibeart saw me and strode towards me. He had wounds on him but none appeared serious and he embraced me. "Thank you for coming. I think that, had Geraint not found you, we would have been slaughtered. They outnumbered us greatly."

"There will be time for tales later now what of the king? Aedh says he is wounded."

"He is but the wounds which are killing him are in his mind. Only his daughter, Maiwen lives, his wife and his sons all died and he blames himself." He looked over my shoulder, seeking someone. "Is Myrddyn close by, for he is the only one who can save him?"

"I have sent for him."

King Gwalliog was surrounded by a sea of concerned bodyguards. They relaxed their weapons into their sheaths when they saw me. The king gave me a wan smile. "You have once again saved my people, Wolf Warrior, but this time I have lost our land." His face was wracked with remorse rather than pain."

"Do not worry King Gwalliog, we drove them from your land once and we can do so again."

He shook his head and I could see a tendril of blood drip from the corner of his mouth. "No Lann, this is all that is left of the army of Elmet. We could not even populate one town now."

"Out of the way!" Myrddyn bustled through the bodyguards and knelt down next to the king. He took out a small flask and held it to the king's mouth. "Drink your majesty."

I saw the outrage on the bodyguards. "This is Myrddyn and he is the greatest healer in the land; it was he who made the river rise and drives the Saxons away for he is a wizard too." Myrddyn gave me an admonishing look but I shrugged, the bodyguards stepped back so the lie did not hurt.

"Step back and give me room to work on the king."

I led Raibeart away from the press. "He is right, Lann, this is all that is left."

I bit my lip. I had a hard question to ask and I did not wish to offend my brother. "How did they manage to win so swiftly? Your strongholds were well defended and sound."

Raibeart slumped to the ground. "That was the problem; they were too well defended and, apart from Loidis, they did not keep a good watch. The Saxons struck at the same time one night. There was a warband to each of our settlements and the men were slaughtered and the women and children enslaved. They tried the same with Loidis but we repulsed them and they lost many men. The king and his sons left the next day with the horses to see where the Saxons were and they were ambushed. Geraint, the king and twenty others survived." He shrugged. "The strength of Elmet lay in their horsemen and they were destroyed in an instant. My archers were good but they could only defend. We were besieged and, although we had food, we had limited arrows. Then disease spread through the stronghold and we decided to flee towards you. We used all the horses we had left for the carts and the night before we left we sortied and slaughtered the Saxons who were watching the walls. It bought us a precious day but, as you know, carts move slowly and they caught us. Geraint and the horsemen fought valiantly to keep them from us but each day fewer returned. Then I remembered this place and I sent Geraint to find you and we came here. I knew we had water and food and that we could defend it. It was close brother, one day more and we would have all died." His eyes welled up. "Maiwen has taken the loss of her family badly. I think she blames herself for if we had stayed in Banna then they could have joined us and our children would not have been placed in danger."

"Brother, it is *wyrd*. These things are shaped by others and it is how we deal with them that mark us as men. You did well and you have saved many of the people of Elmet. But the king is right. If this is all that remains then you need a new home."

"Rheged?" His eyes pleaded with me.

I nodded. "The land close to Aelle is fertile and empty and, more importantly, safe. The northern half will become more dangerous as the Saxons eat up Morcant Bulc's land."

"My lord?" Myrddyn had approached us silently. "I have dressed the king's wounds. They are not life threatening but he appears to have lost the will to live."

Raibeart shook his head, "It is as I feared. Thank you Myrddyn, now could you look at those of my people who have the wasting disease. It has hit the old and the young."

"I will my lord." He looked at Raibeart. "You are without injury?"

He grinned, "Once again I have been spared. It seems all my wounds come from inside."

Raibeart's trouble was that he thought too much and worried about too many things. I did not worry, *wyrd* had seen to that. Too much had happened in my life which was outside of my control. If I was destined to die at a Saxon's hands then, so be it, but it would not worry me. "We will leave within the hour; those Saxons may regroup and follow us again."

Raibeart went off to organise his people and I turned to look for my own captains. Tuanthal rode up and dismounted. Pol handed him a water skin. "Thanks Pol, fighting makes a man thirsty. I cold drink the river dry." He pointed downstream. "The Saxons stopped two miles yonder my lord but they are spread over a large area." He saw my mouth opening and answered the question he knew was on my lips. "By noon they will be ready to come again."

"Good. Tell Garth to get the men organised, we leave within the hour. Mount up twenty of Miach's archers and then you can keep watch on the Saxons. We will try to make Castle Perilous before dark. You and Miach need to buy us the time."

"The men are tired, my lord."

"I know but if we are then so are the Saxons and they have already run further than we. Just do your best Tuanthal."

His smile told me he would. "Of course, my lord. Will you need the scouts or shall I take them?"

"You take them. Your need is greater than mine."

It was a short while later when the carts began to stream down the hillside to head west to safety. The remaining warriors of Elmet and Raibeart led the way while I remained with Garth and my men as a rearguard. When Garth reported to me he held in his hand the axe from the death warrior. The men are carrying the rest of the booty my lord but this is your prize."

The axe was magnificent and had inlaid silver and Saxon runes along the blade. I clapped my hand to Saxon Slayer. "I only need the sword from my home; the king killer." I saw Pol's eyes widen. "However, Pol, if you would like it as the warrior who helped me to fell the beast then you may have it. But I warn you the axe is not an easy weapon to master."

"I will learn my lord, and thank you." I knew that he had been aggrieved when I had allowed Aedh to keep the wolf skin from our hunt and this more than made up for it. Garth's approving nod also told me that I had made the correct decision.

We kept some eight hundred paces behind the carts and the men and women of Elmet. We wanted space to fight should the Saxons return. I knew that Raibeart would prevent an ambush ahead and we both knew the country well, having spent our childhood there. Once we had passed Stanwyck the journey would be harder but less hazardous as we would be climbing the long, grinding, slope towards home but it was, mercifully free from ambush sites and was easier going along the Roman Road. We had but ten more miles to worry about.

"Garth, did we lose many?"

"Twenty warriors and ten archers. They will be hard to replace." He peered ahead, "But at least we now have your brother's warriors and the men of Elmet."

Myrddyn had placed himself in the cart with those who had the most serious wounds but he had told me of the despair and despondency amongst the men of Elmet. "They will need time to heal, Garth, before they can fight again. They will need to own the land they will be given and that cannot be rushed."

"Captain Riderch and his men managed that at Banna, my lord."

"True but they had fought with us for some time before that and knew the country well. This is the first time the men of Elmet will have crossed the divide. The brunt of the attacks will have to be borne by us."

Pol's voice sounded afraid, "Will they come then my lord?"

"Having captured Elmet and defeating Morcant Bulc I would think that they will seek to achieve the prize they desire the most, Rheged. They will come but they will find us a harder nut to crack and I hope that we can prove to be too big for their bellies!"

We had reached the Roman Road when Aedh found me. "Captain Tuanthal says that the Saxons are pursuing. He and Captain Miach are holding them but there are many my lord."

"How many?"

"Captain Tuanthal says that they have been reinforced by a fresh band of warriors. There are more now than there were."

Garth looked behind as though he could see them. "There is nowhere now to ambush them."

"No Garth so we will head for the highest part of the road and await them there. As I recall there is a steep gully to the south which leaves just the north to defend. Pol, tell my brother what we intend and urge him to make haste to Castle Perilous whilst we delay them. Aedh tell the same to Captain Tuanthal and tell him to rejoin us. I want no more losses." The two young men galloped off. Only a pigeon would deliver the message faster. "And now, Garth, we push the men. I know that they are tired but we can rest when we reach the summit of the road."

Our men were hardy warriors and they were kept fit by Garth. We went much faster up the road having no wounded to slow us down. When I saw the place I had mentally chosen my rear-guard reached us. I could see from the empty saddles that they had paid with the lives of my warriors. "How long?"

Miach looked up at the sky. "Soon, after noon."

That gave us a long hour. "Well that is something. I want you two on our left flank to stop them surrounding us. Garth, I want a double ditch digging on either side of the road. We will use three lines of warriors and the archers can shelter behind them. Put the slingers on the left."

My men groaned and moaned as they dug the ditches but they were all veterans and they knew the benefit. One wag quipped, "All this digging and nothing to plant."

Scean shouted, "We will plant the Saxons and hope they do not grow!"

I was not worried, we were in good spirits. We had yet to lose although we had ceded the field on some occasions. I was worried that we were heavily outnumbered by over five to one. We just needed to delay them until nightfall and then we could slip away. My castle was but twenty miles hence and it was all down hill.

The Saxons could see a long way ahead and they knew we had halted. There was no place for an ambush but the road was steep and the gully to one side and the slope to the other narrowed the frontage and suited us. Their warriors would struggle to keep their footing if they tried to flank us and we had a compact frontage. They halted and began to form a wedge. It was the most sensible formation and their leader would hope to break our three lines. I wondered who it was and if he had fought me before; if not then we had the chance to surprise them for they would not know of my archers. The two ditches were not deep, just the length of a man's calf but there were rocks in the bottom and they were ankle breakers. More importantly they would disrupt their attack and make them arrive piecemeal. But they had plenty of warriors to fill any ranks behind. The warband which was before us was huge and I wondered if they had pulled men away from their invasion of Bernicia. If not then they had more warriors than I could have dreamed of.

My spearmen in the third rank had their weapons over our shoulders in the front rank and they would jab them forwards when the Saxons struck. The hill meant that the Saxons could not run at us for we were at the summit. It was our archers, however, who began our defence and sixty archers sent flight after flight towards the Saxons. They had expected that and their shields protected them but it also meant that their attention was not on the ground and the men on either side of the road crumpled and screamed to the ground as they struck the first of the ditches. The ones on the road came forward losing the support of many of their comrades. "Brace!" The point of the wedge struck our line. Not one of my warriors moved and the spears did their worst striking faces and, for those with the face masks, through their eye holes. I punched with my shield and that allowed me to swing my sword. I chopped through the helmet and skull of their leading warrior. The second ditch also did its job and my archers now managed to strike more warriors as they stopped their volleys and began choosing their targets individually.

Then they changed their tactics and the warriors from their flanks came onto the road and gave their weight to the squared off wedge. We began to edge backwards as their combined numbers forced our retreat. This would not do for we had to hold them. It was my job to lead the counterattack. "Garth, push them forwards! Wolf Warriors on! For Rheged!"

I punched with my shield and used the pommel of my sword to hit two men at once. Scean's sword took out a third and Pol's seax stabbed upwards to despatch a fourth. We had the space to step forwards. I felt Garth to my right and knew that we had a sound wedge again. We had stopped moving backwards as their attack faltered. Without crossing the ditches they could only bring ten men to face our warriors. It was a bloody battle with no quarter sought or given. Our spearmen in the third rank helped us to keep them at bay but we were tiring. I turned to speak to Garth, "Give a push and then rotate!"

I saw him nod and I shouted, "Push! Second rank, rotate!"

We had practised this manoeuvre many times and as we stepped to the right the second rank stepped to the left and took our places. The Saxons in their front rank who were tiring now faced fresh warriors and, inexorably, they were slowly pushed back. It could not last and I heard their leaders order a retreat. That afforded my archers the opportunity to kill men who foolishly turned the backs. We now had respite and my spearmen handed their spears to the men in the front rank and they became the front rank. When the Saxons came again they would face fresh warriors. I shielded my eyes to look at the sun. We had a couple of hours until dusk. It would be a close-run thing if they came again.

I looked to the left and saw my captains' wave; they still stood. "My lord, they appear to be debating."

I could see that he was right. Three warriors, they looked like leaders, were standing before their men and an argument was in progress. This was an unexpected bonus. Then the argument stopped and a warrior detached himself from the warband and deposited his sword and shield to the ground. He walked towards us with his arms spread wide.

"Looks like they want to talk."

"Shall I have him killed my lord?" There was no protocol about this sort of thing. Sometimes a talk would take place but at others the poor warrior chosen would be killed outright. "No Garth, for it will buy us time and we should be able to escape after dark."

The warrior stopped ten paces from us and spoke in Saxon. "King Aethelric would speak with you." The disdain in his voice told me that he would have rather fought me but I was intrigued to meet the new King of the Saxons.

"I will meet him in the middle."

"Shall I come with you my lord?"

"No Garth," I grinned. "I wouldn't want him to think we are afraid of one Saxon."

"All the same I will have an archer watch him."

I strode forwards and saw a warrior, about my own age coming towards me. He had, as I did, a scar on his face and he wore, as many Saxons did the amulets and bracelets which marked his successful combats. It confirmed what we had heard, the Aethelric was a warrior. We reached roughly the middle between our lines of warriors. Already the flies were settling on the corpses and gorging on the blood; they were the winners in every battle.

I took off my helmet and held it in my right hand as I waited for him to speak as he had initiated the truce. Eventually he spoke. "So you are the one they call Wolf Warrior. The one mothers use to frighten their children. You are the warrior my men wish to kill in single combat."

I remained silent and he switched to Latin. "You say nothing. I was told you spoke our language?"

I gave him my wolf smile. "I do but I was waiting for you to say something I did not know and to come to the point. I normally do my talking with Saxon Slayer;" I put my left hand on the pommel and I saw his men stiffen, "the sword which has slain Saxon kings and champions since I was a boy."

His eyes narrowed and I think he was adjusting his opinion of me. "They speak right of you that you are a man of few words and much action." He waved a hand at his warband. "It must be obvious to you that we outnumber you and we will, despite your horses and your archers, defeat you so surrender now and I will let you and your men live."

35

"In that case do it and do not waste my time making me listen to meaningless boasts."

He looked at me incredulously. "You cannot win."

"That is what you believe but my men and I believe otherwise." I smiled again.

He seemed nonplussed. "Then I offer you an alliance. Join with me and Rheged will still be an independent country which gives allegiance to me."

"I am not the king of Rheged."

"No but you are the warlord and, as such, make the important decisions."

He knew much and I wondered if we had another spy in the camp but then I remembered that we had many merchants and the Saxons traded with those. It would be easy to discover my role. I pointed to my men. "These men you see here are not the army of Rheged, they are my men, my Wolf Brethren and yet we have defeated your warband already and fought this one to a standstill. Why should we bow our knee to you when you have never defeated us? Until you do then do not presume to dictate terms to the men of Rheged and especially not to the Wolf Brethren!" I had raised my voice and my men heard Wolf Brethren and roared their defiance, striking shields with their pommels and cheering. "When you collect our bones then you can dictate terms, until then Aethelric fear me as Ida, Wach and Aella did. I promise you that you, King Aethelric, will meet the same fate."

He was white with anger but he had no reply. I waited until he had turned back to his men and then I too turned. Suddenly one of my archers loosed an arrow which appeared to be coming straight for me. When I heard a thud and scream I turned to see a warrior, axe in hand with an arrow in his mouth. He was but ten paces behind me. I faced the Saxons and roared, "I see that Saxons are as treacherous as always which is why we cannot believe your lies; you have no honour!"

Aethelric must have given his orders before he met me for the whole Saxon line leapt forwards as he reached it. I barely had time to reach my men and turn before they were upon us but my archers, who were infuriated and angry with the deceit did not miss their mark. My Wolf Brethren were so incensed that they hurled themselves furiously at the Saxons, seemingly immune to wounds, and within a few heartbeats there was a wall of Saxon bodies. I watched as they withdrew and knew that their attack was spent. They had lost too many warriors and too much face to fight anymore that. Aethelric would take the defeat and regroup- we were not worth losing too many men when the easy target of Bernicia remained. When it became obvious that they were making camp I began to withdraw the men. Tuanthal, his horses, and the archers were, once again, our rearguard but the Saxons, apart from a few desultory rushes by headstrong young men, appeared to be happy to see us depart. It must have galled them to think that they outnumbered us by so many and yet they could not shift us.

Raibeart had sent some of the Elmet horsemen on fresh horses to escort us the last couple of miles to Castle Perilous although it was not necessary. I was embarrassed by the tumultuous cheers which greeted us as we crossed the bridge and into the defended walls of Rheged's first and last castle. The emergency huts we had erected on the western side of the castle would be full for the first time and we could be a crowded castle until Raibeart and his army left us. I knew that Aideen and the other wives would not mind the over crowded conditions for they knew how close we all were to such a calamity.

Raibeart, his family and the king all stayed within the castle itself in the guest rooms. All of us were too exhausted to make much conversation and I was in my bedchamber almost as soon as we had eaten. Aideen lay next to me and her warm hands awoke me from my gentle sleep. "You have done well again my husband but again you have put your life at risk."

I kissed her in the dark. "War has come to Rheged for the first time, my love. I no longer fight in Elmet or Bernicia but here to defend our home and family. All of our lives are now at risk. The Saxons are less than twenty miles along the Roman Road." I felt her stiffen in my arms. The baldness of my statement had shown her clearly our danger. The next time I fought she would be able to hear the battle and she and the children would be close to the death and destruction.

"Will they win?" Her voice was small and thin and I could hear the tears which were a breath away.

I would not lie to my wife. "Eventually? I do not know. Soon? Definitely not. They will need many more men before they can do so. I faced off their whole warband with my handful of men. With the whole of Rheged behind me we could easily defeat them so sleep easy, at least for a while and Raibeart and Maiwen will be neighbours for they are going to settle the empty lands twixt Aelle's and ours." What I did not tell her was that once we were alone it would be a different story. She giggled her approval and her hand slipped down my body to ensure that I would not be sleeping, not for a while anyway.

King Gwallog of Elmet died the next evening. Myrddyn did all that he could to aid the king as did Brother Oswald but it was as though he had decided that, having lost his family and his land, then he should end his life. I was summoned by Raibeart when it was obvious he would not last the night. "The king is dying and he has said his goodbyes to his family. He wishes, now, to speak with you."

I liked Old King Gwalliog for he was a true friend and a fine warrior who fought ferociously even though he was a greybeard and a grandfather who should have been dangling grandchildren upon his knee. I could see that he was near to death for his skin had the thin translucent quality of the old. He gestured me over. His four bodyguards nodded but there was none of the smiles I normally received; we all knew that this was a momentous occasion.

"Lord Lann, I just wanted to thank you, for you have always been loyal and faithful to me. You saved my kingdom for me once before and you have saved my people now. Promise me that you will look after and protect my family. Raibeart is a good man but you have vision, my friend and you will survive the Saxons."

I held his hands in mine. "I so swear and you will be revenged. I will punish the Saxons for what they have done to Elmet."

He shook his head, "No Lann, it was *wyrd*. The only hope we now have is Rheged. Protect what you have." I did not argue with him but I did not agree either. He had waited for them and had been punished. We would not wait and if we went down then they would know they had fought in a war. "One last favour, Wolf Warrior, my sword."

I passed him the sword of Elmet and with a smile upon his face he went to the next world. We buried him in a mound with his sword, banner and armour. Elmet was no longer and its symbol lay with its last leader, King Gwalliog. For me it was doubly sad, this was the second king I had buried in the last two years and of the two allies who remained alive I wanted to kill one. The last loyal ally was King Rhydderch Hael and he too was old to continue the fight much longer. When he died then King Ywain would inherit his kingdom but I wondered if that day would ever dawn.

# Chapter 4

Leaving Garth and Brother Oswald to see to our people I went with Raibeart and the survivors of Elmet to the lands to the south and west of us. Aelle came to meet us and, what could have been a difficult meeting proved easy. Aelle ruled this land but he loved his elder brother. Luckily the bonds of family proved stronger and Raibeart was given a tract of land which went from the northern lakes to my domain. There were good valleys, clean water and secure flanks. Raibeart was grateful to us both.

"First I must travel to Civitas Carvetiorum to seek the approval of King Ywain. I know it was his father's wish that the people of Elmet be given sanctuary but we must see that all is done well."

"And I will begin a stronghold here." Raibeart looked grim. "I have been driven from two homes by the Saxons; this is where I will die!"

There was a terrible finality in his words and both Aelle and I were shocked at the tone but, it was understandable given what had occurred. "Take care brother and if you wish your family to shelter in Castle Perilous then it is there as long as you need it."

"Do not worry. Geraint is healed now and eager to find the Saxons; his patrols will ensure we are not surprised."

I took only Pol and Myrddyn when I rode to see the king. It was not bravado; I just needed Castle Perilous and its warriors preparing for the onslaught I knew was heading our way. Every warrior and worker needed to improve the already impressive defences. Word had reached the capital before I got there and the guards shouted encouragement, "Well done my lord!"

We have sent the Saxons packing again!"

"A great victory!"

I wondered how the report had been disseminated to the people for, in my eyes, it was not a great victory. We had escaped by the skin of our teeth. The king was not in the castle, he was visiting his brother and I sought out Brother Osric first.

"I hear that you sent the Saxon king away with a flea in his ear?"

"He had us and the only way I could extract my men was by bluff."

He gave Myrddyn a wry look. "And I hear that you are now the wizard who can control the waters."

"Just a little trick."

The old priest shook his head, "A dam! How clever. I do not disapprove for now the enemy believes we have magic on our side. We may not believe in it." He saw the stony looks on our faces and amended his words, "I may not believe in it but so long as they do then all is well. Is your brother returning to Banna?"

"I have had the presumption to allow the people of Elmet to settle twixt Aelle and me. I know King Urien would have approved." I added quickly.

"I have no doubt of that but King Ywain? We will see. One effect of your report will be that King Morcant Bulc will find the ravaging Saxons besieging his home sooner rather than later."

Myrddyn nodded, "That is good news for Rheged for it gives us time to build up for their attacks when they do come."

"And they will, believe me, they will. We are now the only outpost of Roman Britain left and when we and Strathclyde fall it will be a Saxon Britannia."

"That is a depressing thought, Osric."

"But true nonetheless. Saxon chiefs see this land as a place to become a king quickly. Aethelric was just a chief until Aella died and now he rules Deira, Elmet and half of Bernicia." He tapped each place on the map which was on his table. He shook his head. "You had better see Queen Niamh or I will in trouble and I will speak with your wizard here to discover more of his tricks."

The Queen looked very frail and tearful when I was admitted to her chambers. "I have lived too long, Lann. I have buried sons, husbands and now brother kings."

"No your majesty, your people want you to live forever."

"But I do not. If it was not for the grandchildren… well. Now then, "she brightened a little, "tell me of Raibeart and the others." She leaned over to pat my hand. "Well done, by the way. Urien would be pleased that we still have a hero whom the Saxons fear."

"We have settled my brother and the people of Elmet between Aelle and me. I came here to seek the king's approval."

"I think that it is a good thing. King Urien would have thought it wonderful for the three of you are a wall against which the Saxons will break. He always relied heavily upon the three of you. I will speak with my son. He will approve. And now tell me of your children. It is a year since I saw them."

I spent the rest of the afternoon telling the old lady of Hogan and his tricks and the two younger siblings' idiosyncrasies. The talk was good for me too. I did not see as much of my children as I would wish and telling the queen relived the memories. By the time we were called to food I felt better than I had in a long time. The king had returned when we reached the hall. He too was showing signs of grey and I wondered if I was too. I would have to ask Aideen. King Ywain was genuinely pleased to see me and I sat on his left to enable a quiet and private conversation. His wife, his mother, Brother Osric, each of them was ignored as he asked for the details of the short campaign we had conducted. After I had finished he then began to question me in great detail.

"This Aethelric what kind of leader is he?"

"He is rapacious your majesty; he wants Rheged."

"But he offered us an alliance did he not?"

"No, your majesty, he said we could be free as long as we were subservient to him. That is not freedom and it would just be a way in the back door. I am certain that he wants this land and Strathclyde and he is as clever as Aella and his sons."

"Perhaps an alliance would buy him off until we had gained strength again."

I was shocked at this attitude. It was not the attitude of his dead father. All the resolve we had built up before his father's murder had now been lost. "We will never be as strong as we are this day your majesty unless the Bernicians come over to us and so long as King Morcant Bulc rules that will not happen."

"Then should we not acknowledge him as High King and fight under his banner?"

The table had become silent as our conversation had grown louder. When the king spoke of serving the Bernicians I could see the shock on their faces. Queen Niamh looked at her son and said, coldly, "Serve under the man who ordered the death of your father? Listen to yourself my son and grow a backbone. Listen to the Warlord for he is the only hope you have of survival. When the Saxons do reach us then you and all of our family will be the first to die."

There was a stunned silence as the queen's words sank in. I think it brought it home to Ywain that he could no longer do as he wished. As the king he had to serve Rheged and it did not sit well with him. He laughed to cover the embarrassment, "Then it is a good job that the Wolf

41

Warrior is my oathsworn then, is it not?" He rose and took me by the arm. He led me outside to the ramparts where we stood and looked eastwards. "Lann you are the oldest friend I have and I can speak openly with you. " He hesitated. "Since I was captured and wounded I have been afraid of battle. I have been afraid I might die."

"All men fear death Ywain."

He shook his head. "I have seen you fight and you fear neither man nor death. I envy you that belief but for me I cannot do that. It is why my father made you Warlord, you know that?" I nodded my head. "Then promise me that the Saxons will not kill me."

It was, by any measure, a ridiculous thing to say but I understood him and I sympathised with him. "You know I cannot do that but know this, I will die before they can hurt or capture you. You have my oath on that."

He suddenly became happier and embraced me. "That is all that I ask for you will outlive us all. There is something in your destiny that marks you out. My father and Myrddyn know that."

It was my turn to be surprised. "Your father and Myrddyn both knew it?"

"You must have known that there was a prophesy of a wolf who would come to Rheged's aid, he would bring a magic sword and so long as he lived, wielding his sword then there would be freedom."

"I had not heard that. And Myrddyn too?"

"I did not hear that story but he told it to my father after he was wounded on the Dunum when he healed him." I would need to be having a conversation with Myrddyn and soon!

King Ywain formally gave the land I had identified to Raibeart and the survivors of Elmet. He also confirmed that all military decisions and the defence of the realm would be in the hands of Lord Lann, Warlord of Rheged. As we headed home I asked Myrddyn, "What of this prophesy of yours, the one you spoke of to King Urien but not me, the lord to whom you swore an oath."

He did not seem discomfited by my stern look. "The prophesy is about you and is not necessarily intended for you." My look changed to one of total confusion. "Let us say, for the sake of argument, that I told you that you die next month and the man who would kill you would have one eyed and a wooden leg."

"That is ridiculous how…"

"Nevertheless, if I told you that then the only man you would fear would be a one eye man with a wooden leg and you might be reckless and be killed by a young boy who stands besides you as you watch for one eyed, wooden legged men."

Pol burst out laughing and I confess I too was amused. I shook my head, "Whatever you tell me, I promise that I will not let it change me. I may not even believe it."

"Oh you will believe it for it came, again, from your mother."

I suddenly felt the world change; my mother speaking through Myrddyn, again."

"When?"

"It was when I spied on the Saxons. I hid in a cave north of the Dunum for a couple of days to make my arrival seem more believable. As I slept she came to me and told me to protect the man who would be the last of the Britons and that you would not die in the land of Rheged."

I was disappointed, as prophesy it seemed a little dull. "Is that all?"

"The king was more impressed when I told him for he said that it meant that you could protect Rheged and you would survive the Saxons. I think it was why he made you Warlord, to protect his family. As long as you live in Rheged and fight then the kingdom will be safe."

"When did you discuss this with him?" Part of my reaction was petulance; I had been the subject of a conversation as though I was an object and not a man.

"When I healed him I had a long time to speak with him and he was interested in you and the sword. When he discovered that I had these dreams he asked me about them." He paused, "I meant no offence my lord."

I relented, "I know; it is just that… well I want my mother to speak with me."

Myrddyn sadly shook his head, "You have a gift with weapons and as a leader but my gift is that of my mind and my ability to speak with the dead. We cannot change the way we are born. We just have to make the best of what we are given by the gods. I might to wish to fight as you do in battle but it is not in me to do so and you cannot talk with the dead."

The next weeks seemed to fly by as we trained new warriors, made new weapons but, most importantly, kept constant patrols along the high divide. Riderch now had a few horsemen of his own and, with the keen and energetic Prince Pasgen to the north, we had the length of Rheged patrolled by the finest horseman on the island on which we lived.

The reports were disturbing rather than worrying. The Saxons had built some camps across the Roman roads or close to them. They were penning us in. Garth, Myrddyn and I discussed shifting them but there seemed no reason at the moment. We knew we could rid ourselves of these nuisances but it would cost us warriors and they were in short supply. We decided, instead, to send scouting parties much further afield. We used Tuanthal's horsemen in twos with a slinger with them. This way they could cover large distances and yet we would still have enough horsemen for the patrols. What we needed, now that we were besieged, was intelligence and this was the best way to provide us with that intelligence and knowledge.

The worst part of the patrols was that they kept our men away for many days at a time and we had to suffer the anguish of not knowing if they had been captured or killed. As with most things, I would have preferred to be the one taking the risks rather than ordering someone to do it for me. I did, however, meet regularly with my brothers for we would need to act in concert when it came time to fight back or to defend Rheged. As ever, Myrddyn sat in with us and offered suggestions and ideas. He was now more of a counsellor rather than just being a healer.

When the patrols had all returned and met with Brother Oswald, Myrddyn and me it was a depressing time. They had had to hide the whole time; any of the people who had lived in the land of what had been Bernicia and conquered Rheged before the Saxons came now lived as thrall under the yoke of those oppressors. What was worse was that more and more Saxons were flooding into the Dunum and settling on all of the prime land of what had been Deira, Elmet and Bernicia. The worst news, however, was that Morcant Bulc had become a vassal of Aethelric and had acceded to the terms which meant he kept Din Guardi and was still king. Bernicia was now Saxon and we truly were isolated; we only had the men of Strathclyde as allies.

I struggled with the perfidious treachery of the act of this most self centred of kings. It was Morcant Bulc's fault that the Saxons had been allowed a toehold in our land. It was on his orders that King Urien, the last hope of Britannia, had been killed and it was his fault that he had not pressed home his advantage when we defeated Aella. I knew then that I should have killed him long ago. I became restless and reclusive. I knew that both Myrddyn and Aideen worried about me and so, one early morning I left to go hunting with Pol. We did not hunt animals but information and we rode to Banna to speak with Riderch. My friend had been told the news of the events in his homeland and I hoped that he could offer me an insight into this King of Bernicia.

He and his brother Ridwyn had made Banna into a formidable rock upon which any attacker would break. It had been a powerful Roman fort with steep cliffs and rocks surrounding it but they were not complacent and both were serious as they discussed their homeland with me. "Tell me, and please answer honestly. Are all your countrymen of the same mind as their king?"

"It shames me to tell you but, there are a great many, especially amongst the leaders, who feel the same way. I do not believe for an instant that many of the warriors will be happy with this turn of events but they obey and follow their leaders."

As soon as he said that I had the beginnings of an idea. "If the king died then who would become king? Is it the son or is he elected?"

"They normally elect the son but Bulc's is but ten year's old and I think they would want a warrior."

"Or King Aethelric could put his own man on the throne and that might upset the loyal Bernicians."

Riderch frowned. "What do you plan my lord?"

I sat back in the chair and half closed my eyes. "It is only the beginning of an idea but I was thinking of travelling to Din Guardi and killing King Morcant Bulc."

There was a stunned silence. The two warriors both knew me well and had fought alongside me in shield walls but I do not think they expected me to come up with that idea. Riderch was the first to speak. "You are warlord. Is it not irresponsible to risk your life like this?"

"And with no chance of success. You have been to Din Guardi and know that it is impossible to enter without being seen." Ridwyn knew me well and he backed up his brother.

"You may be right Ridwyn which is why this is just an idea. The next couple of hours will determine if it goes ahead or not."

Despite their obvious misgivings I could see that they were intrigued. "What do you mean, my lord?"

"I would not even dream of trying this was it not for the fact that you, Riderch had charge of the king's bodyguard and you must know the castle better than any other. I do not intend to storm the walls with an army. My aim is to sneak in, kill the snake and leave. Hopefully without anyone being the wiser." I smiled. "Myrddyn's little trick with the river made me think that we can use superstition and magic to aid us against our enemies. So, is there a secret way in?"

Suddenly he smiled. "Of course there is."

Ridwyn, who had lived in the castle said, "There is?"

"Aye. Close to the water's edge there is a cave. It is below the sea level but, at low tide it is accessible. It leads to a gate which comes out close by the kitchens. It was built when the castle was built as a way out in case of great danger. I do not think it has been used for years. The door may not even open any more."

"That is all very well, brother, but I assume it is locked. How would my lord get through a locked gate?"

Riderch suddenly looked deflated, like a jelly fish out of the water. "Do not look despondent Riderch. You have shown me that there is a way in. We now need to find a way to use that entrance."

"What we need is a Myrddyn who could gain access to the castle."

"But obviously not Myrddyn for he is too well known to all as my man."

We sat in silence, each of us wrapped in our own thoughts then Ridwyn brightened. "I could travel back to our homeland; return to the village as though I had deserted."

"It would be too obvious for you to try to enter the castle."

"I know my lord and I would not. I would go fishing as I did as a boy and I would find someone who works in the castle and enlist their aid."

"That is risky brother; suppose they betrayed you?"

"I would have to make sure of them before I told them aught. Think, my lord, this would give us the advantage that I would be on hand to get you away in my boat."

"And how will you get a boat? The one you used will be taken. You have no boat."

"I will have when I spend the money I steal from my brother with whom I have just had a falling out."

"It seems a good plan but how would you be able to let me know when you have succeeded? If we use messengers then they would be spotted as strangers and the castle alerted."

"Someone would have to come with me and then hide away close by so that I could give them a message." He looked at his brother. "It should be a Bernician in case they are seen."

Riderch smiled, "Then we have the perfect man. Bhru lost his hand in the last battle at the Dunum and he lost it because Llofan and the other traitors hung back. He hates King Morcant Bulc and yearns for revenge. We keep him here because he still wants to fight. We offered him a pension but he refused. He could go back with you and be a recluse, someone who is disillusioned by the fighting and wants to live alone. He could take a horse and the two of you could work out how to leave messages. It would work but, my lord, I am not certain it is wise."

I laughed and slapped the table. "You think all the times we fought overwhelming odds it was wise Riderch? I think that few of the things we do are wise but sometimes they are right. Sleep on it and then visit me at my castle to give me your decision for I will need to sleep on it too."

As we rode back Pol became inquisitive. "My lord what should I tell Myrddyn when he asks what we did? "

He had the innocence of youth about him but he was intelligent.

"Why, the truth of course."

"But we did not go hunting."

"No, instead we discussed important matters with two old friends."

We rode in silence. "My lord can I come with you when you go to Din Guardi?"

I pulled back so hard on my reins that my horse almost stumbled. "What?"

"I could not help it my lord. I was lying in the chamber next to the one where you spoke with the brothers and I heard all."

I was angry but at the same time it was my fault. I should have expected it of him. He was loyal and protective and rarely moved more than ten paces from my side. "In that case Pol you had better lie."

He grinned, "With pleasure my lord."

# Chapter 5

The message came back within a day of my return home; the plot was on and I now had to wait, quietly and patiently for the news which would take me across the country. Riderch would give Ridwyn the details of how to find the door and then they would engineer a falling out. I would have to be patient and wait. I am not a patient man by nature. Partly to stop me becoming too restless and partly to allay suspicion when I finally did leave the castle, I took to visiting various people such as Aelle, Raibeart, Pasgen and Ywain. As Aideen was pregnant again she took no offence at my regular absences for she knew I did not deal with such things as pregnancy well. I made sure that I was at home for at least three days before I took off again. Pol liked the intrigue and the fact that he knew something the others did not. He had a particular rivalry with Aedh; probably because he thought I had favoured Aedh when giving him a wolf skin. It was not so but it did not stop Pol having smug looks whenever we rode from the castle. Knowledge is power and Pol had the power over Aedh.

I had visited Ywain and Pasgen and was about to leave to visit Raibeart when Myrddyn approached me. "Do you mind if I accompany you, my lord?"

"Of course not but I only go to visit my brother."

"I know," with a knowing smile, "I thought I would see how some of my former patients were doing if their wounds were healing."

Although it seemed a plausible reason I felt there was an ulterior motive which was confirmed when I saw the smiles from Garth and Oswald as we left just after dawn. We chatted easily enough but the questions he asked were probing ones and, even though he did not ask me directly, I knew he was trying to ascertain where I had been journeying.

Raibeart had constructed a wooden fort already on the top of a natural knoll. Although there was no direct water supply I could see that he had defence in mind and the stream which bubbled close by could be used in an extended fort. Not far away was a lake which I knew abounded with fish. While Myrddyn checked on his charges, Raibeart took me on a tour. "The wooden fort at the top is in case anyone comes in the next few months but we will use stone from the same quarry you used and build a wall which encloses part of the stream. We will have a warrior hall and a hall for the people as well as a stable block." He smiled at me. "I will use your idea of a hall above the stables. When that is done we will make a stone building at the peak of the knoll where we can defend against any attacker."

"And Maiwen and her people are they happy here?"

"It took some days and they were always looking at the horizon for the Saxon hordes but, once we had the wooden wall erected and they saw how green and fertile the land was then they became happy." He gave me a rueful smile. "Of course the land they all wanted was to the west so that the Saxons would have further to travel to reach them."

I told him of the treachery of Morcant Bulc and the fact that there were now just two free kingdoms. It neither surprised nor worried him. "We always knew that he was a snake. Perhaps you should have killed him the day the king was murdered."

I took a deep breath; either Aelle or Raibeart would need to be in my conspiracy and Raibeart was the man I trusted above all others. "I intend to go to Din Guardi and finish what I started and should have done years ago."

He did not seem shocked but nodded, "With your army?"

"No brother, my army fights and kills Saxons. If I did take them to kill Morcant Bulc I would have to kill Bernicians. I would be doing the Saxon's work for them. King Aethelric would want us fighting our fellows. No I am going into his stronghold alone and I will kill him there."

"Murder him?" There was no outrage or disapproval in his words merely a need for clarification.

"I will give him the chance to fight me but I will have nothing on my conscience if the coward refuses to fight. The reason I am telling you is that I will tell my people that I am visiting with you. I will only take Pol with me. I have two men over there already."

"The Wolf Warrior telling a lie?"

"Not a lie, merely a distortion of the truth."

He laughed. "Do not worry I agree with some lies for this one will save Aideen and your people anguish and torment." He became serious. "But promise me that you will be careful."

"Of course. I have no death wish, you know that. Once Bulc is out of the way then his people may either join us or fight against the Saxons; either suits us for it weakens the enemy who is growing ever stronger."

49

"I know and that is the reasons why I have urged the people here to be profitable as profitable as Aelle and the rest of Rheged. We need trade so that we can have the best equipped army there is. I want my land to be as golden as their neighbours."

As we rode back, three days later, Myrddyn told me how well the people were doing. "I know he is your brother and you think well of him already but he is a great leader. The warriors and the people all say that but for him Elmet would have drowned beneath a sea of Saxons more than a year ago."

"I am fortunate in my two brothers for they are both sound leaders and well respected by their people. Rheged is lucky to have them guarding their borders."

He gave me, unusually for him, a very serious look. "My lord no matter how great your brothers are, without you Rheged would fall. Everyone knows that. You must be careful." He waved a hand at the three of us. "This is not wise. The Saxons are closer now and they would sacrifice many men to catch you alone and kill you."

"Thank you for your concern but I do not need my men protecting me. They are better used protecting the borders."

"Then promise me that the next time you go off on one of these little jaunts you take me, at least, as well as the redoubtable Pol."

"You would give orders to me Myrddyn?"

"You misunderstand me, I would never presume to give orders to the Warlord of Rheged. Perhaps it would be easier if I asked the Lady Aideen if I should accompany you. I know that she would worry if she knew of the danger you put yourself in." There was a hint of malice in his eyes. He knew he had me.

"No Myrddyn, I would not worry my lady in her condition. You may accompany me when I visit Aelle next week." I saw Pol's look of surprise and I gave a slight shake of my head. I do not know if it was my imagination or not but I am sure that Myrddyn saw it and a gleeful grin played about the corners of his mouth.

The journey to Aelle's land felt like a visit to another country. Once we had crossed through Raibeart's domain and over the col into Aelle's the land changed. The circle of mountains protected many large and small lakes. The valley bottoms were fertile and the hillsides dotted with grazing animals. Aelle had a small tower at the col; it would not stop an enemy but it would give warning and it showed how thorough a leader he was. The men recognised us and waved as we dropped down towards the lake with the reeds which teemed with fish.

When we came to the second lake I pointed up to a black hole on the hillside. "That is where Aelle quarried much of his rock and it is now a huge cave. It has struck me that it would be a good place to defend should one be attacked."

Myrddyn looked at me in surprise. "Are we likely to be attacked?"

"Not at the moment but it pays to plan ahead."

Aelle's stronghold was now all stone and slate. The contrasting colours and rocks made it both functional and beautiful at the same time. His guards saw us from a mile away as Aelle had cleared much of the land for agriculture and to give him warning. He rode out to greet us with two of his sons, Lann and Raibeart. They had grown much and would soon be learning to fight. The two boys threw themselves at me.

"Uncle Lann! Have you killed any more Saxons?"

Aelle shook his head, "Boys, your uncle is more than a killer of Saxons."

"We know father but you said that the Saxons all fear him and he is the greatest killer of Saxons."

Aelle looked apologetically at me. "Sorry Lann but you know how boys are. Take the horses to the stables and show Pol his quarters." The two boys eagerly led a bemused Pol into the castle which had twists and turns intended to deceive an attacker if they managed to break through the outer wall. Aelle took me by my arm, "It is good to see you. You are looking well and, perhaps a little less careworn than the last time I saw you."

I smiled, Aelle had a way of making you feel like you were the most important man in the world. "Aye, I suppose I am. Although with Aideen with child again I expect a few more grey hairs."

"You still look young to me."

"Then your eyesight is failing."

His stronghold had been converted from a Roman fort as had mine. The resourceful Aelle had renovated the hypocaust and, later, restored the bath house. "Shall we enjoy a couple of hours in the bath house?"

Myrddyn said, "I will check on my former patients, my lord. Have some time with your brother."

My wizard had the knack of reading minds. "In that case, brother, I will join you."

51

After we had undressed, we sank into the luxuriously warm water. It was as though the Romans had not left, save that there was no slave to oil and scrape our bodies. I glanced at Aelle's stump, a reminder of the first time we had fought Aella. He noticed my glance and smiled, "We both have scars now to show for our endeavours eh brother?"

"True and I am equally glad that our brother Raibeart has avoided such scars."

We lay in silence allowing the warm water to soak into our bodies. My leg wound felt less stiff than it did normally and I found myself almost drifting off to sleep. "He came to see me you know?"

I suddenly woke up and looked at Aelle. He had a knowing look on his face. "And?"

"And now I, too, will worry when you go to Bernicia." I looked around in case anyone was close by. "Do not worry. I gave orders that the building was off limits to all. We will both sleep easier if you tell us how you intend to pull off this feat. For I have been to Din Guardi and I think it cannot be done."

I told him the whole plan. I had no qualms about telling Aelle; he would never reveal my plans. I found it therapeutic to tell him because I saw a few flaws that might prevent success as I was going through it. None of the flaws was disastrous but their elimination would increase my chances.

"It seems a plausible plan. So you will have two Bernicians with you in the cave and one possible accomplice inside the castle. And Pol?"

"Guarding the horses; we need to have a quick way out."

"There are two obvious problems which I can see. One is that you may have too many men to overcome in the castle itself and three of you would struggle and secondly they will chase you down, having to cross the country diminishes your chances; especially as the Saxons will be looking for you. As soon as they realise the Wolf Warrior is in their land then every warrior will hunt you."

"We may be lucky."

"Oh you are lucky, believe me. As the Romans might have said, Felix is your middle name, but there is another way."

Aelle had this ability of seeing the same thing you did but in a different way. "I am all ears."

"You said that Ridwyn is going back as a fisherman with a small boat?"

"He is."

"Then that is your escape route. Sail down the coast and along the Dunum. Raibeart and I can have some horsemen on the Dunum to watch for you."

I thought about that but I had my doubts. "We would have to sail through the Saxon ships on the Dunum."

"You go through at night. You would be a small boat and would not have to worry about running aground."

I ran through the idea and found it as safe as mine. I had seen the Dunum estuary and there were mud flats on the northern shore. The Saxons ships would avoid them but Ridwyn's shallow draft would make it feasible. "You have convinced me and now let us get dried before my skin becomes as white as a jellyfish."

Freja made a great fuss of me for she knew how much Aelle thought of his big brother. Pol, too was feted as though a lord and he loved the attention. They were a kind and loving couple and it showed in their children who were well behaved, clever and full of humour. I enjoyed my two days with Aelle. He took me out in a small boat on the Wide Water and showed me the rudiments of sailing. Even with just one hand he showed great skill. As I managed to tack he gave me a knowing look. "Had you longer with me brother then I could teach you to sail even better."

"Do not worry, Ridwyn is a good sailor and I am a quick learner."

As we were about to leave he turned to Lann, his eldest. "Go and fetch your uncle his present." He ran quickly back with a young dog and I thought for a moment it was my old dog, Wolf. "No it is not Wolf; he died last winter, it is his grandson. He is the best trained dog we have and the one who is almost as good as his grandsire. He obeys the same commands his grandsire did. He is my present to you."

"And what is his name?"

"What would you expect? Wolf."

"I am indebted to you for I missed Wolf."

Aelle came closer to me. "Keep me informed and send me a message when you will be taking your next trip."

"I will, I promise."

As we headed north Wolf just trotted close to my horse much as his namesake had. It was only then that I knew how much I had missed having a dog. As we had crossed the col that Myrddyn finally spoke. "It will be another companion for you to take with you to Din Guardi on that fruitless quest for revenge."

I threw an angry look at Pol who recoiled in his saddle. "No my lord, I swear, it was not me."

"No it was not your squire nor your brothers, nor Riderch and Ridwyn."

"Then how did you know?" I felt a shiver run down my spine. Had he been reading my mind? Was he a real wizard after all?

"I could say that I had read your mind or I could make up a lie and say I had a vision but the truth is that you, yourself told me." He saw the confusion on my face. "Oh you did not speak it in words but you showed it in your actions. You have been reclusive since you visited Banna. Garth, Oswald and I have spent less time in the solar than we used to. Then there was your preoccupation with Brother Oswald's maps. When I examined the maps you had viewed I soon deduced that you were heading for Din Guardi and once I had deduced that then it was child's play to work out that you were going to kill Morcant Bulc in revenge for the death of King Urien."

I laughed aloud. "Excellent. You have most of it but not the reason. This is not revenge although I will gain some satisfaction from knowing that the snake is dead. Morcant Bulc knows too much about our defences and can aid the Saxons. H e is now a Saxon puppet and will do all that they ask of him. Allied to that is the fact that without him the people of Bernicia may well either join us or rise up against the Saxons. With Morcant Bulc at their head they will always do as Aethelric wishes."

"Then I have done you a disservice my lord but I would beg that you take me with you along with Pol and the dog."

"I think I risk enough with Pol and Ridwyn. You are too valuable to Rheged to lose."

"Well with all due respect to the two of them I think I might be of a little more use when we actually get to the castle. No offence Pol." Pol shrugged and grinned.

"I had thought to have you stay at home and watch over my family."

"Garth can do that and besides, I made a promise to the spirit of your mother that I would watch over you."

I was defeated and I knew it. "I take it Garth knows," he nodded, "and Oswald," he gave an apologetic nod, "please tell me that Lady Aideen knows nothing."

He spread his arms. "Do I look stupid, my lord? The last person in the castle who will ever know will be your wife for we will get the blame, not you, and she does have a rough edge to her tongue."

We all laughed at that and I spent the rest of the journey giving him the modified plan. There would be no more surprises and we only awaited a message from our two warriors in hiding. We had only had time to spend two nights at home when the message came from Riderch. I sought out Myrddyn. "We leave in the morning." Now that he was in the know it became much easier for me as someone else could do all the planning leaving me with the difficult task of giving a reasonable excuse to my wife for yet another absence.

I knew that I would have a problem when I saw her face. Normally pregnancy did not bother her but, just occasionally, she became hot, flustered and easily annoyed. This was one such day. I explained that Riderch needed my advice and that was going to visit him, taking Myrddyn and Pol with me.

"It seems to me that the Warlord of Rheged would be the one whom men came to if they needed advice rather than sending for him like a minion!"

"You know that is not my style my love. I need my eyes everywhere."

She was not mollified. "Then how about your eyes here for a change and take charge of your son Hogan. He is getting too big now for me to chastise."

That, I knew was a lie. "What I will do, my love, when I return, is to take Hogan hunting. I can train him better that way and I will ask Garth to give him some military exercises while I am not here. It will tire him out and give him some discipline." I stroked her hair and kissed her brow.

"I do not like to be so alone."

I patted her bump, "You are not alone you have our child."

That was the wrong reply and she struck me on the side of the head. "Fool! Take yourself away for you do not yet know how to talk to women!"As I left with my ears ringing I remembered the words of Queen Niamh who had said something similar. I had thought I had become better but I obviously had some way to go yet. I should stick to silence- that normally worked.

We had decided that I would take none of the items which marked me as Wolf Warrior. I left the cloak, the helmet and the shield in my chambers. I put Saxon Slayer in a plain scabbard and picked a plain horse from my stable. We would be leaving the horses in Bernicia if all went to plan and our regular mounts were too valuable to risk. I had lost my fist horse Blackie the previous year and my new horse Raven was the best horse in the stables. I would leave him in the care of Tuanthal.

As Oswald and Garth knew my mission I took them to one side. "Send a message to Raibeart and Aelle and tell them I have gone on a journey. They will understand. If anyone comes from the king then I am at Riderch's and then travelling to see my brothers. That should suffice. Garth would you keep Hogan occupied; he is making Aideen a little cross."

They both grinned, "We heard, my lord."

Oswald then nodded. "I will increase his Latin lessons!"

I felt sorry for my son. I would have to take him hunting when we returned to make up for the Latin lessons. If anyone noticed my attire, as we left Castle Perilous, they did not speak of it. The sentries waved and the workers in the field shouted our names as they always did but I felt different. I felt almost naked riding without my wolf cloak, helmet and shield. I still had a Saxon shield, a perfectly good helmet and a leather cloak but they were not mine and it seemed as though I was less of a warrior. When Myrddyn asked me what was amiss and I told him he nodded in agreement rather than pouring scorn on the idea.

"It is why your men fight so hard for you my lord. The Wolf Standard does not bring with it any secret power but they believe that its very presence means that they will win. So it is with you. Apart from the helmet, you have had those items since you left your home and they have almost become your lucky charms. Fortunately we go not to battle but to murder."

I ruminated on his words and they made sense but I wondered if it would affect my skills with the sword. I was getting ahead of myself. We had yet to reach Bernicia let alone the fortress of Din Guardi. We needed to take it one step at a time. The meeting place we had arranged with Ridwyn was the beach a mile from the castle. He would find us rather than the other way around. I had no idea how he had secured entry to Bulc's lair but I knew that he would not have sent for me if he was not sure that we could get into the castle. Until we reached the land beyond Dunelm we would be relatively safe. The Saxons deigned to use horses and stuck to the roads and tracks. We used little known ways for I had traversed this land for years. As we rode, I though of the word which still jarred- murder. I was committing a crime; the Christians would say a sin but it had to be done. I owed it to Rheged to avenge its king and prevent its demise.

The first night we camped close to the high waterfall which marked the high point in the land between Rheged and Bernicia. It was unlikely that any enemy would scale the falls for there was little reason to do so. Had we been travelling east to west then we would not have used it but west to east meant that we had a fine view of the valley and any potential enemies who might be below us. We were eating dried meats and fruit for our meals as we did not want to light fires and attract attention. It was autumn and the nights were growing shorter so it was uncomfortable sleeping without a warm fire but we only had two or three nights to suffer the discomfort and we wanted no-one to know of our arrival.

As we rode down the valley in the early hours of the next day the enormity of our undertaking hit me. We had to travel almost a hundred miles north east through country which might be teeming with Saxons. The quickest way would have been up the Roman Roads but the Saxons had commandeered them as a way to control the people. Luckily there were the old track ways of the Brigante and Votadini who had lived here before the Romans and we used those. Myrddyn had learned all that he knew from maps made by Brother Osric. I still did not fully understand how they worked but they did for he was able to steer us in the right direction, even in the middle of a forest despite never having set foot there.

Our first problem came during the afternoon of that second day. We had made good time and we reached the Tinea which the Saxons called the Tyne. There was a bridge but it was on the Roman Road at the old fort called Chesters where we had first defeated Aella. Myrddyn showed his wisdom that day. "Let us turn west and swim across the river. It will be narrower and shallower the further west we travel and we should avoid any Saxons."

We managed to coax the horses into the water and we kicked hard to the opposite bank. Wolf made rapid progress and, reaching the other bank shook himself dry before we were half way across. Pol and Myrddyn were upstream of me when my squire lost his grip on his reins. The current grabbed him and swept him towards me. I had no time to think and, keeping tight hold on the reins with one hand I thrust my spear haft towards him. Icaunus was watching over us and he grabbed the spear and then my horse's tail. He clung on for dear life. Pol's horse had reached the other bank first and was contentedly chewing grass having shaken off the water when we reached him.

Myrddyn looked up at the skies. "Thank you for watching over us." He glanced at me. "Your mother's power is strong Lord Lann."

I wondered then at the various events in my life when I should have died or come to grief and how I had survived. Could it be that someone was watching me from beyond the pale? If they were then there was a faint chance that we might just succeed. Pol angrily grabbed his reins, blaming the innocent horse for his fall. Having had a real scare, we pushed on and reached the forests. These huge wooded areas went from the eastern beaches almost to the high waterfall. Although they were dark and foreboding they afforded the best chance we had of staying hidden and we camped in a cheerless clearing where a lightening struck tree had died. We had no change of clothes and the smell of our drying garments was not pleasant.

Pol said quietly, after we had eaten. "I forgot to thank you, my lord. Thank you for saving my life."

I smiled at him and ruffled his hair. "We are warriors Pol and that is what warriors do, they look out for each other. You have come to my aid often enough in the shield wall."

Myrddyn leaned back against the huge bole of the tree. "I have never fought in a shield wall. Is it terrifying?"

"You have no time to think; you just have to fight and trust that the men around you will fight as well and hard as you do. Victory goes to the ones with the most resolve and the best training." I pointed to Pol. "Even an untried warrior such as Pol here can have an effect so long as he does not quaver and does not flinch. The moment you back a little then you begin to lose."

"You make something which is really brutal sound noble."

"It is in a way and I pray that you never have to suffer it for it is a terrible and violent place." With those happy thoughts we slept, knowing that the next day we would reach our goal and sight the castle of Din Guardi.

# Chapter 6

Din Guardi looked even more impressive than it had the first time I had seen it. We stared at them from the eaves of the woods having emerged out of the gloom and into the bright open beach. There the huge castle almost appeared to be sitting high in the sky. Myrddyn and Pol had never seen the like and they too were astounded. It was not just the fact that the sea surrounded three quarters as it was also the fact that the remaining quarter had a cliff to scale or a twisting ramp which would subject an attacker to withering missile attack. Even at low tide an attacker would have to negotiate either a slippery sea weed ridden swamp of sinking sands or sand dunes riddled with grasping marram grass.

Myrddyn turned to me. "No army could take that."

"I know and when Aethelric gets his hands on it he will make his kingdom the most powerful in the land."

Pol asked innocently, "Is it greater than Civitas Carvetiorum?"

"Rheged's castle is powerful but it can be attacked on all sides. An attacker can use rams and onagers. If enough men attacked then it would fall." I exchanged looks with Myrddyn. That day would come one day and we both knew it.

"We have to get to the north of the castle we have arrived too far south." I pointed to the collection of small huts which were across the narrow harbour. "There are boats there and I assume that Ridwyn will have one. He will be watching for us. The problem is that the sentries will also be watching for strangers. Myrddyn you will leave first and head due north. Pol will follow but veer closer to the coast, not to close but a little closer than Myrddyn. I will follow you."

"I assume there is a reason for this plan my lord?"

"Yes Myrddyn. It will look less suspicious to the sentries, should they see us. And it gives Ridwyn three chances of seeing us. The one most likely to get caught is the one in the rear. As I am the most competent warrior…"

"Brother Osric would be impressed my lord; impeccable logic."

"Wait for us in those sand dunes north of the fishing boats. Be careful!"

Myrddyn trotted off and I rode next to Pol. "Remember that everyone you meet is an enemy and yet to fight might bring disaster. Today, my young squire you will be using your mind and not your seax."

"Perhaps when we return from this, my lord, I will use a sword and then, who knows, the axe we took." His enthusiasm was infectious.

I waited until Myrddyn was about a mile away and said, "Head towards the castle for about a hundred and fifty paces and then head for Myrddyn. It will look as though you are going in a different direction." Smiling he urged his horse on. I slid Saxon Slayer in and out of my scabbard. I hoped that I would not need it that day but I had to be prepared. I set off towards the south, through the woods. I lost sight of Pol but I was not worried. There had been no-one near to him. When I emerged from the forest, with Wolf sniffing next to me, I saw that was closer to Din Guardi than I had expected and I headed north along the edge of the forest. Soon I passed the place from which Pol and Myrddyn had left and, as I cleared the forest I saw the dot in the distance that was Myrddyn. He was close to the sand dunes and Pol was about half a mile behind.

Wolf growled and stiffened and suddenly I saw two men approaching from the west. They appeared to have come from the dunes themselves and they were approaching Pol. This was the worst event which could have arisen. Myrddyn would not know the dilemma he was in and I took the decision to act. I kicked hard and my horse responded. I could see that they had spoken with Pol and that he had stopped, which was a wise thing to do but it put him at their mercy. The soft ground over which I was riding made little sound and I glanced to my right and saw that the castle was hidden by a promontory of rock. From my previous visits I knew that the dunes were in plain sight and I wondered if the sentries could see the meeting ahead, as I could. I watched as Pol's horse reared when one of the men grabbed it and then the other pulled Pol from his saddle. I galloped hard. "Wolf, follow!"

By the time I reached them they had a sword at Pol's throat. I glanced over my shoulder and saw that we were still hidden by a blind area and invisible to the castle and its sentries. One of the men turned around aggressively to me with his spear pointed at my horse. I spread my hands innocently and said, in Saxon, "What is going on?" I waved an impatient hand at Wolf who had begun to growl; and bare his teeth.

The man relaxed when he heard my words. He replied in poor Saxon, "This is spy from Rheged. We take to the king."

I grinned, drew my sword and dismounted. "Excellent. I hate the men of Rheged. They killed my brother at Dunelm I will make the spy talk. Hold his arms and we will see what his manhood is like."

They put down their swords and, laughing grabbed Pol's arms, spreading them as though he was the White Christ. There was one on each side. I saw the terror in his face. He was not looking at me but at the two men. I held Saxon Slayer in two hands and with two swift blows decapitated both of them. Pol jumped to his feet as though he had been struck himself. "My lord! I am sorry they just came at me and I didn't know what to say."

"We have no time for that Pol. Help me to put their bodies on our horses." Poor Pol's horse almost sank under the weight. He would have to walk. I went over to get the heads. They both had long hair and it was tied at the back making it easier for me to carry them. I saw Pol whiten. "And we have no time for you to be sick either. Lead your horse slowly, as though we are merchants with bags of goods on our horses."

The walk to the sand dunes was the longest mile I have ever walked. I was glad when I saw Myrddyn's worried face peer through the marram grass, I deliberately avoided looking towards the castle. That would have aroused suspicion but I desperately wanted to see if the alarm had been raised. The two men were obviously from the castle and they would be missed. We now had less time to complete our task. Finally, we reached the path in the sand dunes and we disappeared from the castle's view. Myrddyn almost pounced on us when we reached his horse.

"What happened? One minute Pol was alone and the next time I looked there were two men holding him down."

"They were Bernicians and when Pol spoke they recognised him as a warrior of Rheged." I smiled at the still petrified youth. "I think we will teach you some Saxon. It may make life easier. And now let us get rid of these bodies and the heads. First search them to see if there is anything of value about them." While I saw to the grisly task of burying the heads the other two took weapons, money, rings and, most importantly a key. I had no idea what the key was for but it could be a useful object. "Now bury them but make sure they are some distance from each other and I will watch the castle."

I peered through the grass and could see no discernible movement along the walls. It was a mile or more distant but I could see the sentries, moving along the wall. There was a steady flow of carts and visitors to the castle. It all looked normal. When I returned my two comrades had buried the bodies and I could not see where. Inevitably nature, in the form of the wind, would uncover the bodies but it would not be in the next few days. "Pol, you are the lightest, when we have moved away then make the sand smooth so that no-one can see our tracks."

"And now, where to, my lord?"

I pointed to the dells and hollows above the beach. "Ridwyn will look for us up there. He said to look where the sand becomes rock and that looks to be the place to me."

Ahead of us the land rose a little at the natural outcrop of the rock beneath the soil. The wind and the tide had formed the dunes at its base and, as I remembered it, there was a huge bay on the other side. All we had to do was find somewhere which was hidden and await the Bernician.

We found a flat hollow which hid us from view. I sent Pol inland, with Wolf to guard him, to find water and we unsaddled the horses. It occurred to me that we might have finished with the brave beasts which had carried us hither and it pained me to think that we might be leaving them. It was, however, a sacrifice which would be worthwhile if we succeeded.

Night fell. Pol had found some water and. Although it was slightly brackish, the horses didn't seem to mind. It was harder for us to lie there waiting either to be discovered or for Ridwyn to appear. We kept a constant watch on the castle but there seemed to be no disturbance there which might indicate that their men had been missed. Perhaps the men had not been from the castle. The wind whipped in from the sea and chilled us to the bone. Myrddyn tentatively asked, "Should we light a fire?"

I shook my head. "I would prefer the cold to fighting curious Bernicians or Saxons. Wrap your cloaks tighter about you."

The moon had just risen when Wolf growled. I held my hand to silence him and slipped my sword out. The other two followed suit. It was with some relief that Ridwyn's face appeared above us. He strode over to me and bowed. "I would have been here sooner my lord but I was confused at the three riders and a dog. It was only when I recognised Pol that I knew who you were. I was expecting you alone."

"It matters not. Before we go there is something you should know. We had to kill two Bernician guards. These are their belongings." I showed him the key, the amulets and the swords.

"That would be Dagda and Sayer. They are guards from the gatehouse. The key is the key to the side gate." His face became serious. "They will be missed, my lord. They both command warriors."

"It cannot be helped but we now have another way, if we need it. Have you been to the cave yet?"

"Not yet my lord."

"Then let us go there now."

"That means going back the way we came."

"It cannot be helped. If the cave is not there or is guarded then we will need a different plan and you can fill me in on the details as we go."

"I have no horse."

"It is only a mile or so is it not and we will be less conspicuous if we go afoot, leading the horses." For all my confidence I felt exposed and naked as we left the dunes to cross back to the forest. I expected men searching for Sayer and Dagda to fall upon us but we reached the safety of the woods without incident. As we went through the pine carpeted forest, Ridwyn told me that he had found a young girl of seventeen, Anya. She had been captured in the wars in Elmet and given as a slave to King Morcant Bulc. As she was pretty she had been used and abused by the king and his bodyguards. When Ridwyn had seen her she was weeping as she collected mussels at low tide. After befriending her he had found that she was thinking of ending her life. She had been unable to run as there was a guard always watching her.

"Then how did you speak to her?"

"I was fishing quite close to her, lowering crab pots into the sea, takes time. The conversations lasted a couple of days and were as brief as we could make them. She told me that she has the run of the castle for there is but one way in and out. I asked her to find the door and she told me, last week that it is there where my brother told us it would be. She managed to open it and she said she saw a dark cave beyond. It was when I had that news that I sent the message."

"When will she open it?"

"I will see her tomorrow and so it could be tomorrow night."

"If the cave still exists."

He added cheerfully, "Oh it will be there my lord. I grew up near to the castle and know it well."

We left the horses in the woods and Pol and Wolf guarded them. The three of us scampered through the dunes. We could see lights in the castle but they did not illuminate the outside. We would have to watch for the guards but they appeared to be gathered on the landward side. There was a high rocky outcrop which hid us from the view from the seaward side and the crash of the waves on the rocks disguised any sounds which we might make. The tide was well out and Ridwyn led us confidently to the cleft in the rocks which he assured us led to the cave. When I saw him frantically look around in panic I knew something was amiss.

"What is it Ridwyn?"

"It should be here but it is gone! Is this magic Myrddyn?"

Myrddyn shook his head, "No Ridwyn, it is nature. Look the sea has deposited sand. Stand where you think the entrance should be." Ridwyn walked four paces closer. "Right, let us dig."

We began to scrabble and scrape like rabbits building a burrow. Suddenly Ridwyn's arm disappeared and he turned with a grin. Myrddyn just said, "Let us get inside before we congratulate ourselves."

It took another hour before the hole was large enough to peer into. Had we had Pol he could have wriggled inside but we had left him with the horses and we had to dig for a little longer until Myrddyn was able to disappear inside. The wait seemed to be interminable but finally he reappeared. "I found the cave," he paused, "and the door. There appears to be no keyhole."

"There isn't. It is a bolt on the inside. It is an escape route and not a way in and out."

"Good. Let us rejoin Pol."

Ridwyn looked shocked. "But all our hard work. We may have to dig again tomorrow!"

Myrddyn laughed. "The sea does not work that quickly. It will merely mask our work and will take moments to undo."

By the time we reached Pol the first thin line of the false dawn had arrived. "Come we will go to Bhru. He has a hut close to where we met." We were able to ride through the forest to avoid detection and soon smelled the comforting aroma of wood smoke. Bhru appeared behind us as we dismounted. He had a few teeth missing and when he grinned at us he looked terrifying. "I thought it was you, my lord, but I weren't taking any chances. There is a stall behind the hut for the horses and I have a bit of stew on. I thought as you would be hungry."

We were ravenous and wolfed down the food quickly. Pol quickly fell asleep and Ridwyn took his leave. "I will need to find Anya and tell her it is tonight after the moon has risen." He paused. "I promised her that she can come with us."

The question hung in the air and my immediate reaction was to say no but then I remembered Aelle's mother and the horror of captivity and

I nodded. "But you should know that we will not be returning by horse." Both Bhru and Ridwyn stopped what they were doing. "It was pointed out to me that they could easily catch us on the one hundred and thirty mile journey but they will not expect us to go by boat."

"Which boat my lord?"

"Your boat Ridwyn. Is it big enough for all of us, Bhru and Anya included?"

"If we hug the coast and do not run into a storm then we might survive. But what then?"

"We sail along the Dunum. My brothers are meeting us with horses and warriors. All we need to do is slip into the estuary at night and reach the Roman Bridge."

"It is risky my lord."

"Life is a risk Ridwyn. Let us see what *wyrd* has in mind for us. So far it has not been all bad has it?"

Laughing he said, "No my lord, but it has been most interesting."

After he had left I said, "We will need to turn the horses out before we leave I want them to wander. They will be discovered and the false trail will buy us time." Although well trained, if the reins were tied on the pommel of the saddle, then the horses would walk until tired if given a slap on the rear. It would not fool the Bernicians for long but we did not need long for us to disappear. "And Myrddyn put your mind to coming up with a trick which makes them think that we entered and left by magic."

When I awoke it was afternoon and Ridwyn had returned. "You have stirred up a hornet's nest my lord. They are searching high and low for those two men you killed. They think they may have been deserted but some think it was Saxons who had a falling out with them. They were both known to be gamblers."

"But Rheged's name has not cropped up then?"

"No, my lord."

"And Anya?"

"Game and ready to go. Last night three of the king's men had her. She cannot wait to leave."

"Then all we can do is to wait until dark. Bhru, you had better cook whatever food you can. We can fill our bellies for I fear we will get little until we reach the Dunum. We also need water skins filling."

Myrddyn smiled his enigmatic smile. "Already done."

"And the magic?"

"Ah well we are in luck for Ridwyn has a wolf's head in his hut."

The warrior who had stood with me in my shield wall looked embarrassed. "I knew that I could not bring my cloak but the head seemed to be a good luck charm."

"Do not apologise Ridwyn although I am intrigued as to how my wizard can use that."

"Well when we leave I will put the skull next to the dead king with a bloody dagger in the skull's mouth."

"Is that it?"

"No I will lock the door after you leave and let myself out with the Bernician key."

"Is that not risky?"

"Not really, for the ones who know me should be dead by then and I can pretend to be a lost Saxon in the castle. Ridwyn said there are many there. I will then lock the gate and join you at the beach."

"I think I would prefer just the wolf skull."

"Then they will find the unlocked door and know how we escaped. This way they will search the castle for us and then suspect each other."

I could see that it was a good plan. I would have to trust in the spirits which had protected us until then. We waited until dusk and then saddled the horses. They had been faithful companions and it grieved me to let them go but I hoped that they would find a good owner. We slapped them hard on the rump and they galloped west. I brightened myself with the thought that they might make their way home to Rheged. Perhaps I was deluding myself, they were, after all, just animals.

We went swiftly and quietly to the beach. As Myrddyn had predicted the sea had only filled in a small part of the entrance and it took the five of us a short time to clear it. Ridwyn and Bhru left to bring Ridwyn's boat around and Pol and I cleared more sand to make the exit from the cave easier. We then went into the cave. It was pitch black but we had flints and two torches we had made in Bhru's hut. When we lit them the cave was shown to be enormous. It could have swallowed my warrior hall twenty times over. A rough path could be seen and, leaving one torch for the others, we made our way upwards through the natural tunnel. As we climbed I wondered if the gods had made this just for us. I knew that Myrddyn would have an answer; I decided to ask him, on the sea voyage home, if we ever managed to complete our quest. There were steps cut into the stone. They were a little slippery since we had opened the entrance again but all the seaweed we could see looked dead. The cave had been dry for some time.

Pol raced up the steps and shouted, "The door! I have found it."

Myrddyn shook his head and said, angrily, "Shout a little louder. The guards in the gatehouse didn't quite hear you!" I smiled at the look of horror on his face as he realised what he had done. I waved my hand to show that it was not a problem.

My healer made the top and tried the door. He glared at Pol and then said, quietly as I arrived next to him. "It is shut but we may still be too early."

"We just sit and wait. Check your weapons."

We had left our shields outside the cave. They were there in case we were pursued. I had Saxon Slayer and a wickedly sharp dagger. Pol had his trusty seax and the sword he had taken from the dead Bernician. Myrddyn had a cudgel and a seax as well as the wolf skull. When I had asked him about the cudgel he explained, "We need silence from our enemies. We need to surprise them. I will leave the sword play to you warriors and I will hit anyone I see just as hard as I can."

We waited in the silence, with just the faint sound of the surf outside of the cave. I knew that we had a finite amount of time we could spend in the cave. When the tide returned we would be trapped. It seemed likely that part of the cave remained dry but it was a worrying thought. Suddenly we heard the sound of a reluctant bolt being opened. Our hands went to our weapons although I rationalised quickly that the only way it would be an enemy would be if Anya was a traitor or had been compromised. I nodded to Myrddyn who pulled on the rusty ring which was on our side. The door swung open and revealed a frightened young girl. The fact that Myrddyn smiled at her and said, "Anya?" made her smile.

"You are the wolf?"

He shook his head as he controlled his laughter. He pointed to me, "No he is Lord Lann, the Wolf Warrior."

Her eyes pleaded with me, "You will take me?" She suddenly realised there were only three of us. "Where is Ridwyn?"

"Do not worry. He is bringing his boat." I turned to Pol. "Pol, take her to the entrance and you can wait there for Ridwyn. Wolf, guard Pol."

67

She gave a half bow and almost ran by me. I suppose if I had been abused by the warriors as she had then I would make the speediest exit I could manage. "Now what, my lord?"

"We could go in but I would rather wait for the other two. Bhru can guard this door and three of us should be able to deal with most eventualities."

He looked relieved, "And I am in agreement. I thought for a moment you would hare into the castle and kill the garrison all by yourself."

I laughed but found myself worrying that perhaps I was becoming too reckless. As long as King Urien had been alive then I felt I had a point of reference; someone to whom I could seek advice. Now I had no one and others sought advice from me. Would I become a reckless despot who acted on a whim? What was I doing in this dank cave? Did I really think that I could sneak in and kill the King of Bernicia and get away with it?

Suddenly I heard a voice in my head and it was a female voice. "Think with your heart and be true to yourself."

I looked at Myrddyn who shook his head and smiled. "Her voice comes to me too my lord. It is a surprise when it happens, is it not?"

"You heard too?"

"She speaks to me often but it is always in dark places in the depths of the night." He spread his arms around the cave. "Like this."

We heard voices and we held our weapons before us but it was just Ridwyn and Bhru. Ridwyn's face was filled with joy and I wondered about him and Anya. "The boat is here. Pol and Anya have loaded it with the supplies and are waiting for us."

"Good. Bhru, guard this door."

"Aye my lord."

I looked at my two companions. "Well let us get the deed done." I led the way for I was the most familiar with the castle. I suspected that the kitchens would be empty but we took no chances. When we came to the end of the tunnel I peered around the corner. The smells and the heat told me that it was, indeed the kitchens and that meant I knew where we were. Two floors above us were the main hall and the quarters of King Morcant Bulc. I hoped that the guards would be outside and not inside. We drew our weapons for surprise was vital.

I paused at the next stairs and listened but I could hear nothing. We slowly made our way up. The guard, presumably on his way to the kitchen was more shocked than we when we met. My sword was out and I stabbed him in the neck. Although it caused a river of blood, it ensured his silence. Ridwyn carried the body and disposed of it in the kitchen. I was warier now; where there was one warrior there could be two. I heard voices and I paused. They appeared to be coming from the guard room which I knew was to my left. Beyond it was the gate. I quickly climbed the next stairs which I knew led to the king's chamber.

There would be a guard outside the door that much I knew. The question was, would he be alert or not. I signalled Ridwyn. He was a Bernician and could use the local dialect to lull the guard. I whispered into his ear, "Pretend you are drunk and say you have a message for the king. Use you local words, I will be close behind. I want his back to us; you must stop him falling." He moved ahead of me and I gestured for Myrddyn. I took his cudgel and he gave me a smug smile. I would make him pay for that.

Ridwyn staggered a little and gave a hiccup, with a silly grin on his face. He mumbled something and the guard gave an irritated wave of his hand. Ridwyn half fell forwards and the sentry automatically reached out to grab him. Ridwyn cleverly twisted and fell on his back so that the sentry had his back to me. In two steps I was behind him and, as he sensed my presence and began to turn I smacked the cudgel against the side of his head. Half of his skull caved in and I saw grey, wet matter dripping to the ground. He was dead. More importantly for us he fell, silently, on to Ridwyn. We rolled him off. I returned the cudgel to Myrddyn. We moved the body away so that we would not trip when we made our exit.

Our new problem was ascertaining how many men were within with Morcant Bulc. It was late and I assumed there would not be many but it would take only one to raise the alarm and make our exit impossible. Myrddyn saw my problem and held up his hand. He moved towards the door and I wondered, as I drew my sword, what magic he would be performing now. He put his ear to the door and listened. He held up one finger, then two and, finally, three. He waited a little while longer and then held up three fingers. There were a small number of men in the room then and it could be three, four or five. We had surprise on our side which should take care of at least one. If it was four or less then we had a chance. Five would make life difficult. I extinguished the torch making the corridor black. At least we would not be highlighted against the torchlight.

I approached the door and gestured for Myrddyn to open it. He was less skilled than Ridwyn with a sword and had a quicker mind. When he opened it he would be planning our next move. I took a deep breath and nodded. He opened the door as quietly and slowly as possible. It was with some relief I saw the quiet glow of a room lit by the fire in the far end of the room. I could see that there were chairs with their backs to the door. We entered and began to creep towards the chairs. Suddenly a girl appeared from Ridwyn's right. He had no time to think and he swung his sword at her, it took her head off but not before she had begun a scream. Morcant Bulc and two of his men leapt to their feet. Myrddyn was the quickest off his feet and with his mind. He took a step forwards and swung the club at the surprised warrior whose head was crushed like the sentry's. Ridwyn smashed his bloodied sword at the second man who barely parried it and then I forgot all else as I face King Morcant Bulc.

In some ways he had a slight advantage, he knew the layout of the room and he had seen me fight. I had never seen him fight. I surreptitiously pulled my dagger from my belt.

"So you are a murderer in the night now, vaunted Wolf Warrior. How far have you fallen?" The sarcasm in his voice oozed.

I realised that I had to kill him quickly before he could raise the alarm. Had he shouted rather than gloated then his guards might have come. Myrddyn must have read my mind for he closed the door. I had no time to play with the king and I stabbed forwards with Saxon Slayer. I have quick hands and the king had been drinking. Even so I think the sword would have beaten his defence anyway. His feeble deflection just took the blade to slice through his side. I saw the look of horror on his face as the blood gushed out. I could see his mouth forming the words which would summon the guards and I jabbed my dagger at his throat. "This is for killing the king who could have saved our land. Die you treacherous snake." There was life in his eyes as I spoke the words and then I watched the life leave King Morcant Bulc, the king who made possible the conquest of Britannia by the Saxons.

We had no time to congratulate ourselves and Myrddyn went to the door to scout the exit. I saw Ridwyn now taking in that he had killed a girl. "You could do nothing Ridwyn. It was *wyrd*. Do not let me down now."

"Sorry my lord."

Myrddyn then said. "Let us seat them at their chairs?"

"What?"

"We have time and it will add to the illusion that they died magically. Clean their weapons and replace them. We need to make it look as though they did not fight their killers."

"And the girl?"

"And the girl."

When we had seated them they did look as though they were still alive. He then took out the wolf skull and put it on the table with the dagger I had used to kill him. It felt macabre but I could see what effect it might have. We made our way down the stairs. The noise from the warrior hall had died down to the snores, belches and farts from sleeping drunken warriors. Myrddyn paused at the door and I wondered if he was regretting his idea. "Are you sure you want to do this?"

"It is a risk but I think we can manage it, now let us go down to the gate and let you out." The lower parts of the castle were empty and we saw a relieved Bhru sheath his sword when we arrived. "I will see you on the beach." With a nonchalant wave he shut the door and I heard the bolt slide shut with a deadly finality.

We had extinguished our torch but we still had the one Bhru had used and we hurried out into the chill night air. Ridwyn sensed my air of apprehension as I looked back into the lair of the snake from which we had just escaped. We had succeeded but my company was incomplete. "Do not worry my lord. If anyone can escape it is Myrddyn the wizard."

# Chapter 7

Pol and Anya, too, were relieved to see me and Wolf jumped up to lick my face, or perhaps it was the blood which covered me, I do not know which. Ridwyn carefully loaded us in the boat putting the lightest, Pol and Anya at the front with Wolf and then the bigger men, Bhru and me in the middle. He seemed happy enough although he fiddled on with the water skins until he gave a satisfied grunt and turned the boat so that the bow was pointing out to sea and he was holding the stern. "Bhru when Myrddyn is aboard then raise the sail and tie it off."

I was glad that one of us, at least, had an idea of how to aid Ridwyn. "Is it done, my lord?"

"Yes Pol. Morcant Bulc is dead."

"Was he alone?"

"No, there was a girl," I heard the intake of breath from Ridwyn, "and two big warriors."

Anya gave a triumphant snort. "Then I am pleased that all four are dead for those were the men who used to rape me each night."

"And the girl too?"

"No she was worse for she held me down and said things to me while they soiled me. She said horrible things. I am glad she is dead and pray she roasts in hell."

The girl was obviously a Christian too. "Well Ridwyn it looks like your blow with the sword was ordered by someone other than you. *Wyrd*!" Ridwyn smiled from ear to ear. True warriors never like killing innocents and I knew that he would sleep easier knowing that she had deserved it. Now we had to wait. I peered at the castle watching for a sudden flurry of lights which would show that we had been discovered.

Ridwyn said, "The tide is turning, my lord."

I snapped irritably, "And?"

"And the sea will cut off Myrddyn's route to us soon my lord, sorry."

I sighed, "And I am sorry too. I should not have snapped. Where is that infernal magician? Why could he not have just left with us rather than trying to beguile them with his cleverness."

"Because I am Myrddyn and that is what I do!"

He appeared next to the boat as though by magic. I saw Anya cross herself in that annoying way the Christians have. "Then get in the boat, you annoying little man."

72

He was not bothered by comments and happily jumped in the stern of the boat with Ridwyn. "Do you not want to know how I escaped?"

"Not yet!" I snapped peevishly. Let us get out to sea. The tide is turning and it is not as easy as it would have been."

Ridwyn began to steer and then said, "Get the oars out, we need to fight the tide. " Anya held on to Wolf, not that he needed the support, while the four of us hauled on the oars until, after what seemed an age, Ridwyn said. "Ship the oars we are past the worst." He smiled and seemed happy for the first time. "You can sleep if you wish. I can steer by the stars."

"Before I do I would like our magician to tell us how he escaped."

We all looked at Myrddyn who smiled and said, "I walked out." My mouth must have dropped open for he laughed and continued. "The men in the warrior hall were asleep and I walked through them to the side gate. The two sentries asked me what I was doing and I tapped my nose and said the king had asked me to do something for him. They, too, had had a drink and when they saw the key in my hand they assumed, I suppose, that it had been sanctioned. They said they would watch for my return."

"They didn't ask who you were?"

"No. I suppose if I had looked furtive or suspicious then they might have done but I walked and talked with confidence. Besides I was leaving the castle and as I locked the side gate after I had left they would have felt secure."

I shook my head. "You truly do have powers Myrddyn." I then addressed them all. "We have succeeded tonight but no-one can ever know that we did what we did. I want the Saxons and the world to believe that their king was killed by magic. Myrddyn has given us the chance to fool everyone. I want you all to swear silence."I held out Saxon Slayer. They put their hands on it and all solemnly agreed. I could see that Pol was the one who regretted this the most. I imagined him telling Adair of his role in the adventure but I knew that, having sworn, he would remain silent.

Despite my misgivings about the proximity of the water and the alarming way the boat seemed to bob up and down, I eventually went to sleep. When I awoke I had a salty crust on my lips and I felt stiff. The others were still asleep and a red eyed Ridwyn still steered. "Good morning my lord."

"Are you not tired Ridwyn?"

73

"I am fine but as the only one who can sail a boat I will have to forego sleep until we reach the Dunum."

"When will that be?"

He shrugged. "I am not sure. There is one major river between the Tinea and the Dunum. We may have passed it in the dark. But we will know when are close to the Dunum, there will be sand dunes and marches and the seals. The land to the south towers high above the river, if you remember. We will not miss it."

I peered around and found the water skin. I drank for a long time, mainly to rid the taste of salt from my mouth. I noticed that I was not hungry. "It is strange. I have not eaten for many ours and yet I feel no hunger. Why is that?"

"I know not my lord, perhaps it is the motion of the boat but I rarely eat when fishing. We have food if you are hungry."

"No. I will survive."

We sailed in silence. Bhru's snores made me smile. "The gods were with us my lord. We have shown them a clear pair of heels and we escaped without their knowledge."

"It was intended that it should be so. A man, even a mighty king like King Morcant Bulc cannot get away with treachery and perfidy. There is always a reckoning."

"Is that why you value the truth and honour so much my lord?"

"They are principles worth cherishing. In a dark world they are a beacon of light."

Gradually the others awoke but it was only when Anya's smiling face looked around the small vessel that I realised we had forgotten nature's call. We men could easily cope but the young woman looked uncomfortable. I glanced at Ridwyn and saw the light of understanding upon his face. "Anya, if you change places with Myrddyn I can show you how to steer." Myrddyn looked less than pleased that he would have to negotiate the pitching little boat but I had an idea what was in Ridwyn's mind.

"Myrddyn, just do it!"

He shrugged and complied. The boat pitched a little more than previously and the side looked perilously close to the water's edge but they managed to change places. "Just keep steering with the coast on your right hand and we will be fine and," he added, as though an afterthought," if you need to, you know, then just sit on the back of the boat and, well just go. We will all look ahead."

Anya glanced at us all and every one of us looked studiously south, she giggled, kissed Ridwyn on the cheek and said softly, "Thank you."

The day passed pleasantly enough but I found that I was bored. I could not be a sailor. As dusk fell Ridwyn said. "We are getting close to the Dunum. I am going to head further west. Pol, keep your eyes peeled for a river to the right."

Eagerly Pol leaned over to stare at the coast. "Just don't fall in!"

"No, my lord!" I could almost hear the excitement in his whispering voice.

Once the sun set the sea became a threatening and dangerous place once more. The worry was exacerbated by the fact that we have to negotiate an estuary filled with Saxon ships. I, for one, would not be sleeping until I was on dry land once more. "I see the river my lord, there!"

"Do not shout Pol. There may be sentries. We can hear you!"

"Sorry, my lord."

"Now we need to be alert. Everyone." Ridwyn's voice carried the authority of a king on that tiny boat. I did not even dream of arguing with him. Our lives were now in his hands.

It was fortunate that it was dark and we were such a small boat; any sentry would struggle to see us. But equally, as I was discovering, shapes on the shoreline merged and blended into each other. What was a ship and what was a bank? A low mist appeared to hang over the water and I thanked the Icaunus for the protection she afforded. We were now invisible.

Suddenly Pol's voice sounded sharp and strident, "A ship!" Moments later we bumped into the prow of a Saxon ship.

There was no time for recriminations; Ridwyn shouted, "Oars!" We each grabbed an oar and began to row as fast as we could. At first we thought we had escaped unseen but then lights appeared on the ship and we heard the hubbub as Saxons crowded the sides to peer down at us. A spear hurtled across our bows and we rowed even harder. And then just as quickly we were in the mist again and hidden. "Keep rowing. It will not take them long to set off in pursuit of us. Anya, come and take the helm. I will row too."

Ridwyn joined Pol's side and we soon stopped crabbing. It was not Pol's fault; he was just weaker than Myrddyn. I could see Ridwyn looking over his shoulder and I suddenly realised why; he was looking for the place that we had fired the Saxon ships. Their rotting timbers would still be below the Dunum and could rip out a Saxon boat. I recognised the bluff on the south bank. "There Ridwyn!"

Ridwyn almost shouted with glee when, he too, saw the place we had hidden. "Anya, push the helm over to your right as far as it will go."

Alarmingly the boat went at right angles to our previous course and I saw the prow of the Saxon ship less than fifty paces away. "Now put it in the middle. You are doing well my girl!" The praise made all the difference and we straightened up. Our manoeuvre took the Saxon steersman by surprise and we gained a little. I saw that the bank was less than ten paces away. If the Saxon ship continued on this course then it might run aground anyway.

The Saxon boat had more men and I could see that it was gaining on us. I contemplated taking my bow but I could not see the steersman and the loss of the power of my oar would mean we would be captured. The Saxon ship seemed to stop in midstream, as though it was a horse and the rider had jerked back on the reins. It had struck something. If it was the bank then they would pull themselves off. A soon as it started to settle in the water we knew that it had been sunk by one of their own ships- *wyrd*.

Ridwyn left his oar and took over the steering of the boat. I noticed a tender touching of the hands as they exchanged positions. I could see Ridwyn joining the married men club very soon.

As we rowed westwards, upstream we could see the sky lightening behind us. It was slow but it was steady and soon we began to make out the features along the river and to recognise some of them. Of course we were now in Saxon country so the fact that we could see the bank did not help, it hindered. We were all tired now. Ridwyn had not slept for two days and the rest of us had catnapped in a rocking and rolling boat. It was a dangerous time and as the banks became clearer we sought any enemy who might raise the alarm. The trees which lined the river were a boon for it hid us from any who were some way from the river but we knew that we had to pass close to the Roman Bridge. Before then we should have been met by my brothers' horsemen but suppose they were not there? We could not travel across the land without horses and we were all uncertain where the bridge was.

Ridwyn took the decision for us. "Lower the sail Bhru. It marks us as a target. Rowing might be hard work but it is safer and, I am sorry my lord, but I am tired."

"My lord, why not pull in over there and hide in the bushes to allow Ridwyn to sleep. Pol and I can scout the bank and find where we are."

I nodded. "Except that it will be Pol and I who explore! You are a wizard and not a scout."

Pol and I slipped over the side whilst Bhru held on to an overhanging branch. We made our way through the tangle of undergrowth and emerged where the woods came down a shallow bank to the river. "Pol, get up to that clearing and see if you can see anyone. I know where we are." As Pol scampered up the bank I saw that we were close to the place where Prince Ywain had been held captive whilst wounded. If we had horses then we could be on the Roman Road north within the hour. But at least I knew that we were but twenty or so miles from the Roman Bridge. We could watch the banks for Raibeart's men.

Pol returned, "No signs of life my lord."

"Good let us get back to the boat."

Ridwyn was sound asleep when we reached them. His head was cradled in Anya's lap. She held a finger to her lips. I smiled. It would take a battle horn to wake a sleeping warrior as tired as Ridwyn was but I spoke quietly nonetheless. If did not do to upset a mother hen. "We are close to where we found the prince and you Myrddyn." I glanced at Bhru. "Could you sail the boat if I steered. I am loath to stay so close to the Saxons." Already the mist was clearing and I could not believe that they would not pursue the boat which had cost them a ship.

"With Pol's help, aye my lord." He held up his stump. "The river twists and turns my lord and we will need to use the sail more than when we sailed south."

I knew my limitations but I daren't wake Ridwyn yet. "We will just try it and see how far we can get. If I prove to be a bad captain I promise we will put in."

I put the tiller hard over and, as the wind caught the sail we began to move. At first it was easy for the wind was coming over my right shoulder but when the river curved then it changed. "You need to go across the river and back, Lord Lann. You will not be able to sail in a straight line."

"Thank you Myrddyn. Is sailing another skill you have?"

"I merely observed Ridwyn. Would you like me to try?"

"No!" I snapped. "I will manage." I saw the same smug smile he had affected before. My wizard needed taking down a peg or two.

Perhaps because of the smile I concentrated and soon got the hang of the infuriatingly slow progress upstream but at least we were moving. The mist totally cleared and blue skies appeared above us. After bobbing up and down on horses it was a tranquil and pleasant way to travel. The herons at the river side ignored us as they feasted on the abundant fish.

Suddenly Anya let out a scream. "The Saxons!"

I looked over my shoulder and saw a Saxon ship rowing up the river after us. "Ridwyn! Awake!"

Pol shook Ridwyn and he looked in horror beyond me to the rapidly approaching longboat. "We cannot outrun it. Head to shore."

I put the tiller to my left as the right-hand bank, the northern one, was closer. "As soon as we reach the bank then get ashore." I saw a small beach and we grounded. Everyone got off the boat and then Myrddyn said, "Turn it around and float it."

I was about to argue but remembered that he had not steered us wrong yet. "Pol, take Anya up the bank. Turn it round."

"Now push it into the stream." While we had been obeying his orders my wizard had started a fire close to the centre of the boat. As we pushed it began to head towards the Saxon ship. He looked at me and shrugged. "It may slow them down."

"Well done!" Grabbing my bow I strung it and notched an arrow. I aimed at the stern of the ship and loosed three arrows in quick succession. I had no idea if I struck anyone but the combination of the arrows and the boat made the ship turn and bought us some time. "Up the bank as quickly as you can!"

Pol and Anya had already reached the top with Wolf and I saw my squire scanning the top for danger and an escape route. Bhru, Myrddyn and Ridwyn followed in quick succession. I turned to see what had happened to the Saxon ship. They had halted in the middle and now had a row of shields protecting the steersman. I ran up the bank. "There is a dip yonder, my lord, and there are trees. They may not see where we are." We had delayed their pursuit but soon they would be after us.

"Good lad. You lead off." The problem was that we had to get away from the river but that meant leaving the one place Raibeart's men would seek us. It could not be helped. The most immediate danger was the boatload of Saxons. The dip was half a mile from the river but we reached it before the Saxons had climbed the bank. I pointed into the woods. "Wolf, scout!"

The dog ran off and we recovered our breath. I did not want us moving quickly and disturbing the undergrowth. At the moment we were invisible but, as we had not hidden our tracks, they would be able to follow us.

"I will lay a few snares, my lord. It may slow them up." Ridwyn was a good hunter.

"Be swift. I want to leave here in a few moments."

The three of them spread out and made snares and trips. It would not kill them but we just needed them slowed down and wary. I hoped that they would tire of the pursuit before they caught us. When Wolf returned I knew that the way ahead was clear and Pol led us again with the dog at his side. I remained at the rear, ready with my bow. As we jogged along I was aware that we had Anya with us and she would slow us down. Had I made the wrong decision in allowing her to accompany us? And then I thought of Monca and I knew that, no matter what befell us, I had made the right choice.

Suddenly Pol shouted, "Saxons!" And I knew that we had been led to our doom by my revenge.

Myrddyn raced back. "The Saxons are ahead. They must have landed some men behind us and then sent more to cut us off."

Pol, Anya and Ridwyn returned to join Bhru, Myrddyn and myself. Wolf stood growling at the invisible Saxons. Pol pointed to Wolf, "I would have raced into them had Wolf not growled. There are forty of them, at least."

For the first time in my life I knew not what to do. To go forward would be suicide. We could not fight forty. And what of going back? How many were there? There seemed only one choice. "Head south, back to the river!" It speaks well of my people that they just obeyed and trusted my judgement. It might have been the wrong decision but it was a decision. I gambled on the fact that the Saxons would assume we were heading in the same direction. Of course once we reached the river we would be stuck but, at least, it delayed the inevitable.

I waited until Pol had passed me and I ordered Wolf. "Stay!" His senses would be more acute than mine. I notched an arrow and held three in my hand. I waited until Wolf growled and I drew back. The surprised Saxon was but ten paces away when my arrow smashed into the front of his skull and emerged with half his brain at the back. He fell silently to his death. "Good boy!"

79

He growled again and I released but there were three of them. I notched a second arrow, even as the first fell dead and the second died, noisily, screaming his pain. I dropped my bow but Wolf leapt at the hand of the third warrior and I had time to draw Saxon Slayer. His head joined his dead companions. I turned and ran to the river. I had delayed them all I could.

My companions had formed a defensive circle around Anya. Their relief at seeing me was palpable. "I have bought us a little time."

Myrddyn pointed downstream. "Their ship is there."

We were trapped. "Then let us sell our lives dearly. Anya you can always try to swim to the other shore."

She held up Pol's old seax. "I can still kill my lord."

I thought then that if all of the Romano-Britons had had the same attitude then the Saxons would have left this land empty handed. I had but eight arrows left. I stuck Saxon Slayer into the ground. The Saxons would, eventually, overcome us but they would remember the last stand of the Wolf Warrior and his brethren.

The dead bodies had made them wary but their leader had his wits about him. Despite the deep undergrowth he had his men move forward in a solid line of shields. He was driving his prey much as a hunter uses dogs to drive a stag into the waiting spears. I used my eight arrows wisely. So long as a warrior peered over the edge of his shield to see where we were he was a dead man and eight Saxons died with my eight flights. I dropped my bow and picked up Saxon Slayer whilst drawing my dagger. Ridwyn was to my right and Pol to his right. Myrddyn was to my left and, one armed, Bhru guarded the left. "I am proud to have my last moments with such brave warriors as you."

As the Saxons charged forwards I heard Myrddyn shout, "We are not dead yet, my lord."

The first warrior lost his life as I stabbed forwards when he was expecting a sweep. Ridwyn could fight Saxons all day and not lose but my other three companions were not warriors. I heard Pol yelp as a Saxon smashed his sword in two. I shouted, "Wolf, kill!" but before the dog could strike the barb of an arrow appeared between his eyes. Suddenly the shield wall crumbled as arrow after arrow struck them. Renewed with hope we hewed and hacked furiously at all before us. The hidden enemy behind them was too much for the Saxon warband and they fled but the arrows continued to fell them and then there was a silence as we looked at each other. We had been dead and now we lived.

80

*Wyrd*! "Drive them before us! They weaken!" We charged after the fleeing Saxons and struck unprotected backs.

Then a voice halted us, "I think, big brother, that we had best not ride our luck. We have won now let us go home."

Raibeart dismounted and I embraced him. "And I am glad to see you little brother. I thought that this was the end of the Wolf Warrior."

"Come we will talk while we ride but Pol and the girl will have to ride double. I did not know you would be picking up passengers."

As we mounted I said, "She was the reason we were able to succeed."

Raibeart stopped. "He is dead? You succeeded?"

"Aye; it was two nights ago and he is dead."

Raibeart's brow furrowed in a frown. "Do they know that it was you?"

"I do not think so for the ones who saw me are dead."

I then told him of Myrddyn's magic and he laughed aloud making his men all stare at him. "I do like Myrddyn and his imagination. I wonder what tales they will tell of that."

"Did you have any problems getting over here?"

"No. We used the back trails and avoided the strong points but I suspect that they will have patrols out seeking you now."

"They lost one of their ships to us."

"You sank a Saxon ship? With the little boat you were in?"

"It sank itself. We ran it towards the sunken ships from the raid on the Dunum."

"I can see there are more tales to tell but let us save them until we are safe within Castle Perilous."

He had brought twenty men with him. They were all mounted archers from his castle. Our little group was surrounded by them and I could tell that they were proud to be escorting the Warlord of Rheged. I felt completely safe. Raibeart was cautious and careful and we would get home. He pushed us hard and took us well to the north of the Roman Bridge. I did not need to ask where he was taking us; we would be crossing just upstream from the waterfall where the water was shallow and few men lived. It would add an hour or so to our journey but would ensure that we avoided contact. The problem would then be crossing the Roman Road. I asked him about that after we had paddled through the upper Dunum.

"They have a fort of sorts fifteen miles from your castle. We will join the road a mile after that and make quick time. It will be after dark and we should avoid them but by then it will matter not. So long as they do not have men in the forests and tracks we will avoid detection. I left four scouts close to their camp to watch for any movement along the road."

It was towards dusk when a figure on a pony ghosted out of the trees next to the track we were following. "The Saxons are safe inside their camp my lord. You can join the road here. It is safe."

Soon we were clip clopping along the cobbles of the sturdy Roman Road. The Saxons might hear the sound and know what it meant but they could do little about it. When I saw the castle's lights ahead I halted the column. "Raibeart I swore my party to secrecy. How will we explain this to those in the castle?" Myrddyn coughed. I smiled in the half light. "Go ahead magician. Tell me what you have concocted in that fertile mind of yours."

He did not seem upset by my tone and continued cheerfully, "Ridwyn and his brother had a falling out. Ridwyn now has a young bride."

"What!"

Myrddyn spread his hands, "My lord you are a great warrior but you know little about humans. Look at them." The two of them were looking at me and nodding. I waved at him to continue. "We say that we were on patrol with Raibeart's men and we found them and Bhru and rescued them from the Saxons. It is a half truth."

I saw Raibeart nod. "Then that is what we will say."

Raibeart raised his voice. "And that is what we will say eh? Oathsworn!"

They all chorused, "Aye my lord," and we headed towards Castle Perilous with the half truth which I hoped would save lives.

# Chapter 8

No-one thought anything out of the ordinary had occurred when we rode in my castle entrance. It was with some relief that I realised the deception I had practised, of regularly visiting my brothers, had paid off. We had only been away for a few days and we received a warm welcome. Raibeart took his men away and I settled into the comfortable life of the castle. Ridwyn took Anya and Bhru back to Banna. Riderch would be glad to have his brother back from such danger.

Pol seemed to have grown on the trip for he had more confidence and an air about him which told me he was ready to be a warrior. I took him, Myrddyn and Garth to one side a week or so after we had returned. "Pol. I think it is time for you to become a warrior. Garth here also feels that you are ready. How do you feel about that?"

His face lit up. "Thank you my lord."

"Of course it means that you can no longer be my squire."

His face fell. "Then I will decline your offer my lord for I would not give up the honourable role of squire."

I exchanged a look of amazement with Garth. We both knew how much the young man yearned to be a warrior. He had trained his body and built it up steadily. He practised with his peers and yet he was willing to give up his dream to be a servant to me.

Myrddyn, inevitably, came up with a solution. "If you recall, my lord, when I was training to be a warrior, I also studied with Brother Oswald. It seems to me that the training to be a warrior will not compromise his duties as a squire. He can still keep your weapons sharp and your armour ready for he will be doing that for himself."

"What about when we fight? He will be in the shield wall."

"Excellent, for that means that you will not and we will all feel happier about that," he added, "my lord."

I saw both Garth and Pol nod and knew that I had been outwitted. Not that I minded, as I enjoyed Pol's company and there was no sharper mind in the land than Myrddyn's. So it was that Pol started his training to be a warrior.

A week later I was summoned to Civitas Carvetiorum. I took just Myrddyn and Pol. Pol now had his own mount; a present from Raibeart and I saw how tall he had grown when he seemed right on the bigger mount. He had also begun to fill out and he would soon be the same size as me. Myrddyn too had grown taller as he had reached maturity but he had not filled out as his exercise was with his mind and not his body. As he had shown with the cudgel, he could defend himself well but that was not his main strength.

The sentries at Civitas all gave me a curious look as we entered but, curiously, they all made the sign to ward off evil when they saw Myrddyn. He just smiled but I could see that his interest was aroused. I left Pol to stable our mounts while Myrddyn sought Brother Osric.

The captain of the guard took me straight to the audience chamber of King Ywain. Dowager Queen Niamh was seated next to him; Ywain's wife, the present queen, preferred to be a mother rather than a politician. Queen Niamh rose and embraced me. "Good to see you again Wolf Warrior." As she sat down, she too, gave me a curious look.

"Sit, Lann." Ywain gestured at a seat next to the Queen. "Have you heard, King Morcant Bulc is dead?"

They both looked at me closely. I hated the lie but it was necessary to protect Rheged, even if that meant keeping its king in the dark. "I had heard a rumour."

They looked at each other. The Queen said, "That is remarkable for they say it was you and your wizard who killed the king and his guards."

"Really?"

Ywain nodded. "It seems that no-one entered the castle and yet they were all slain while seated. They did not even draw their weapons to fight their enemies and then the guards reported a spirit leaving through a door which was locked and from the description it sounded like Myrddyn. And a wolf's skull was left next to the body with a bloodied blade in its mouth."

"And of course, Myrddyn never left my side."

"Quite." He paused and waited for me to continue but I just smiled. "They scoured the country but found nothing save the tracks of some saddled horses which they recaptured."

"Ah." I saw the Queen smile and nod at me. I knew then that she approved of my action but would say nothing. Ywain also knew but could not fathom how we had managed it. I was secretly pleased that Myrddyn's apparent magic had worked. If the Bernicians and their masters, the Saxons, believed we had magic on our side then it would be an extra weapon we could use.

"The story goes that Myrddyn used dark magic to spirit himself and your wolf spirit into the castle and killed the king."

"That is hard to believe, your majesty." I could see he did not believe me but he could find no rational explanation for the murder.

I sought permission to speak with Brother Osric and the Dowager Queen embraced me, she whispered in my ear, "Well done Lord Lann. I know not how you did it but my husband sleeps easier tonight."

When I entered Brother Osric's inner sanctum I saw a knowing look on his face. "The enigmatic Lord Lann; it seems you managed to extract revenge without attracting attention. I am impressed."

I spread my arms in assumed innocence. "I do not know what you mean."

"I do not believe for one moment the story which is circulating. That Myrddyn manifested himself in the chamber of King Morcant Bulc and killed the king and his bodyguards before they could defend themselves. And this nonsense of the spirit of the wolf! Please, I may be an old man but I am not a stupid man."

"That is the story the king believes."

"And we both know it is the story which the world believes but I deserve more." I looked at Myrddyn. "I will keep whatever you tell me as though in the confessional."

I knew that, for the Christians this was the most sacred of oaths and I nodded at Myrddyn. I could see that he was delighted for the opportunity to recount the tale and he went through every detail. Brother Osric remained transfixed and totally silent as Myrddyn told him of our mission.

When he had finished then Brother Osric leaned back and said, "Satisfying. You have successfully scotched the snake and yet you have made it seem as though you had no hand in this. I am impressed with both of you. I could not have engineered a more successful outcome but you are quite right Lord Lann. This must remain in these walls. Rheged will fall soon enough but this will delay that fall."

I suddenly felt quite depressed. "We will fall?"

"You are a great leader, Lord Lann, but you are not a king. Only a king with either your skills or King Urien's could save us now." His old rheumy eyes peered deep into mine. "You must begin to make plans for escape."

I was shocked. This was the steward of Rheged speaking. "Surely we can defend against the Saxons."

"Bernicia has fallen. Even if Rheged can hold on then Strathclyde too will fall and then we are an island on an island. We will fall. There are too many Saxons and they want Rheged and all it stands for destroyed."

"But where would we go?"

He glanced at Myrddyn. "I think your magician knows... Wales."

I wondered if there had been collusion but I knew that Myrddyn always thought of me first and himself second. "But my oath?"

Myrddyn looked at me, "When the time comes then your oath will not matter for you swore an oath to protect Rheged, not just King Ywain."

Brother Osric took out a huge number of vellum sheets. "This Myrddyn, Lord Lann, is a record of Rheged and what we have done. When I die then I want your oath that the two of you will protect this record and add to it so that posterity may know what we have done. Brother Oswald can continue my work."

I think that Myrddyn was as shocked as I was. "Dying!"

"I am old, Lord Lann, and I know my body as well as any man. I will not see the fall of Rheged but I know it will come. Promise and swear!"

"I so swear."

"As do I."

"Good." The old priest looked relived as though a weight had been taken from his shoulders. "Then take it now." The look he gave us both was ominous but Myrddyn took the vellum and I felt as though I had a weight upon my shoulders which I could not bear.

As we rode home, with Pol, diplomatically some way ahead, I spoke with Myrddyn about our predicament. "I had thought that Rheged would fall long after I was dead. The Saxons have never defeated us."

"But there are so many now, Lord Lann, that I can see what Brother Osric meant. We can hold them for a while but once Castle Perilous, or Banna, or Wide Water falls then what will stop the hordes? They gather on the borders like carrion around a corpse. We are that corpse."

"Then begin to make plans."

"We need the land scouting out."

"That would be you and some horsemen. Tuanthal?"

"He is a sound warrior. Perhaps ten men might do it. It will take some weeks."

"I believe we are safe until next year."

He looked at me, "Know this, Lord Lann, you will not be able to take all of your people for some will not wish to leave the land of their birth and those people will either die or be enslaved."

I had hidden that thought in the deep recesses of my mind but I knew what he said was true. I steeled myself. "Then that will be their choice. I will save what I can of Rheged and I will have done my duty as warlord. But I still cannot see what Brother Osric foretold."

"Brother Osric is more of a wizard than I am, my lord. I believe he can see into the future."

When we returned home I summoned Brother Oswald, Garth and Tuanthal along with Myrddyn. I could not tell them all that I had been told but they needed a vision. "I am sending Tuanthal with Myrddyn to Wales to find us a new home should Rheged fall." I saw their shocked looks and held up my hand. "I do not think it will fall but a good leader plans for the future." I spread my hands, "I hope to become a good leader. Brother Oswald, Brother Osric has sent you his papers he wishes you to continue to document Rheged's life and to guard this valuable document." He took it eagerly. "Garth, we need to gather as many draught animals and horses as we can. Do it, with Brother Oswald's aid, surreptitiously and gather them out of plain sight; down close to my brothers. When we do move, if we have to move, it will be quickly and quietly. All three men looked to Myrddyn who nodded, seriously. "Keep my words to yourselves. We live in dangerous times."

My next problem was Aideen; should I tell her or not? She had a short time to go before she gave birth and I decided that, as we had a possible year of grace, I could keep silent and avoid her wrath. I would need to see my brothers and Riderch sooner rather than later. Using the excuse that the king had asked me to tour the kingdom I left with Pol and six trusted warriors. I headed first for Banna. Ridwyn now had a happily married Anya at his side when he greeted me and she rushed to my arms and embraced me. I think my warriors were taken aback but we had seen much together and I allowed her the moment. When I was alone with the brothers I explained that I was making plans should Rheged fall. Ridwyn was shocked but Riderch looked as though he had expected it. "When Bernicia fell I knew that all things must change. I will follow you, Lord Lann, wherever you lead for you have never failed me yet."

Recovered from the shock Ridwyn added, "Aye and me."

"We are gathering horses for we will need to move swiftly when we do." I hesitated. "When the Saxons come it will either be here or at

Castle Perilous. Do not feel that you have to defend to the last man. If the Saxons come here first, then delay them, and then flee with your people to, either Civitas, or Castle Perilous."

"We will my lord."

Raibeart looked distraught when I told him Brother Osric's words. He had fled Elmet to the safety of Rheged and now that sanctuary was being taken from him. "Are you sure we cannot hold?"

"I believe we can but you know Myrddyn and Brother Osric. They know more than we so all that I ask is that you make plans. They may come to naught in which case all we have lost is some thoughts and plans."

"You have always made the right decisions and I trust you now. I will do as you suggest."

"It if it is any consolation then I believe that it will be my castle which is attacked first and you and Aelle will be their prey when they have conquered the rest."

"That is small consolation brother."

Aelle had already thought of the problem. "I fear my people will wish to stay here. It is idyllic and I love it. I do not think there would be anywhere else I could be as happy."

I nodded for I knew what he meant. "But if you were ruled by a Saxon then would you be as happy? I only give you a warning brother. You use the information as you will. I have Myrddyn scouting a new home and, hopefully, it will as be perfect as here but the eventual decision will be yours. Brother Osric said that if Rheged fell then my oath, and I assume yours, would not be binding, either."

I felt that I had done my duty and my promise to our father to watch over my brothers had been kept. I could not force them to flee but I knew that, if I had no oath to uphold, and if Rheged fell then I would flee to save my family and those who trusted me. There was no point in dying for a piece of soil.

As summer drifted into autumn Garth and Brother Oswald assiduously gathered horses and had carts made. They used the excuse that we intended to move more rocks and iron for future buildings. No one seemed interested as there were other matters to worry about. The Bernicians had risen, under their boy king and his mother, to try to wrest the kingdom from the subjugation of the Saxons. It ended bloodily and Bulc's family fled north to the land of the Caledonii. It ensured that the Saxons had to spend the wet autumn sopping up the last remnants of resistance. Those true warriors of Bernicia joined Riderch at Banna for all knew what a staunch warrior he was as well as a keen opponent and enemy of the Saxons.

We heard that Brother Osric had become ill and had taken to his bed, nursed by the redoubtable Niamh who ministered to the man who had been as close to her husband as she. It spurred Oswald to add to Brother Osric's writings. I think he wanted to show the old man that his life work would not end when his life did. He took his vellum to Civitas. When he returned he told me that Osric had criticised his spelling and his penmanship, which, in itself, told me that Osric was not yet ready to meet his maker.

I was becoming worried when, after almost four weeks, there was no sign of Myrddyn and my men. Aideen too was worried. She had given birth to another daughter, Monca and now wanted Myrddyn's wisdom about the child. Aideen still clung to the old ways, as I did and Myrddyn was a priest of those ways. His youth did not matter for he was, in our eyes, a shaman and as such held in high regard.

When they trotted back into the castle grounds I counted two empty saddles and noticed that the men were road worn and weary. Having returned from long patrols myself I allowed them to wash, put on clean clothes and drink before I summoned them. I had a jug of heated wine laced with honey and they both drank appreciatively. Tuanthal nodded at Myrddyn who began to speak. "Firstly, my lord, we lost two men. One, Boru, slipped from his horse when we climbed a high col in the Welsh mountains the other fell into a river and drowned before we could get to him. We met no enemies who caused us harm. We avoided roads and kept to the secret ways known only to Myrddyn." He grinned. "We are all adept at swimming rivers now!"

Myrddyn was reading my mind. I had worried that the men had died as a result of action. I did not know if the men who lived in the Welsh hills and mountains would oppose us. "Beyond the foothills there are fertile valleys protected by mountains but the most attractive land is in Mona; my homeland. That is protected by the sea. However it is my home. Let Tuanthal give you his opinion."

"The wizard is correct my lord. The valleys would give us protection but there is danger reaching them. That is where we lost our men and they were both fit warriors and not women and children. The island is my first choice. There is a stronghold in the south. There is an island separated from the larger island and it is very rocky. We could build a smaller version of Din Guardi there. The danger would not come from the Saxons; we met none either going there or returning, nor did we meet the Hibernians. However they just raid for slaves and we could do what Myrddyn's people did not and build each settlement a stronghold."

I pondered their words as they drank. "This is why I wanted two men's opinions. I value them both. Please keep your counsel to yourselves. I will deliberate your words and, when the time is right, then I will make a decision." I looked at Myrddyn. "And Myrddyn, if I were you I would visit Brother Osric, he is not well." We both knew that my words meant he had not long for this world.

When Myrddyn returned after a week at Civitas, it was with sad, and for Rheged, bad news. The old priest had died. He had spoken with Myrddyn, indeed Myrddyn believed that the old man had hung on until the young healer arrived. He had spoken with him at length and then he had died. He died as he had lived, quietly and without fuss. I think I was as upset over his death as that of the king and my own father. I took Myrddyn and Brother Oswald for the burial.

It was just after the funeral that the Dowager Queen collapsed. We had just opened and drunk Brother Osric's last bottle of his favourite Lusitanian wine and she collapsed. Had we all not drunk from the same bottle then I would have thought it was poison but Myrddyn said it was something in her head. Her eyes were open and she was conscious but she could not speak. Ywain and I cradled her between us. Some drool came from the edge of her lips and I dabbed it with a napkin. She tried to smile at me and to say something but she could not. I saw her try to move her arm but she appeared to have no control over that either. Finally her eyes fixed on me and she tried to talk with her eyes. I know that it is hard to believe but she smiled at me with her eyes and then they closed and Queen Niamh of Rheged died. I am not ashamed to say that I wept. I had no time to weep for my parents and I was too angry at the time to weep for King Urien but Queen Niamh was a truly great queen and we will never see her like again. We buried her alongside her husband and there was a void in the kingdom of Rheged. That was the day when darkness seemed to descend upon the kingdom.

The winter was not as cold as others we had had but it was wet and miserable even with constant fires no-one ever felt dry. The garrison complained about the constant oiling of their armour and there were many minor infractions of rules and petty fights. After a week in which it had teemed with rain and two men had suffered minor wounds as a result of fighting I decided to take half of the warriors out for a hunt. We needed fresh meat and it would allow me to teach Hogan how to hunt. Aideen was happy to have her noisy and sometimes naughty son away from the castle for a week. I had decided to take my warband to the country around Aelle's domain. He had told me that the wolves there had been attacking his sheep and it seemed we could kill two birds with one stone. There were would be fewer men left to be fractious and Garth could manage those easily. Aideen laughed as we left under a stormy sky. "I am glad that you will take our son to learn how to hunt but I am glad that I will be in this warm and comfortable castle."

Myrddyn took the opportunity to visit Aelle too as there were herbs and roots there which he needed for his remedies. As we headed south, despite the rain, we were in good spirits. The rain does not seem as bad if you are hunting or fishing; just when you are standing on a stone rampart peering through the gloom for hours on end. I would let Garth take the other half of the garrison when we returned.

My brother's warrior hall was empty and warm and we enjoyed our hunting. Hogan got to join in a wolf hunt although he did not manage to kill one. Pol was alike a big brother to him, watching his every move. His dedication cost him the chance to get his own wolf skin. We also managed to kill some deer so that when we returned, after seven days, we all felt like new men. Even the rain stopped for the last two days so that we rode in the dry with the chill but refreshing wind of autumn in our faces. The same men who has squabbled and fought now bantered and joked. Pol had a new admirer in Hogan who plied him with questions he could not ask his father and Myrddyn buzzed like a summer bee with the excitement of the plants he had collected. That day I truly saw the precocious nature of *wyrd*.

I had a premonition of the disaster I was about to encounter as I approached the main gate. There were but two men on duty and they had a deathly pallor about them. Inside there were but two or three sorry looking warriors on the walls. I had left half a garrison but there was only a handful left. Had the castle been attacked in our absence?

As we clattered over the bridge Brother Oswald, looking like a ghost raced up to Myrddyn. "Thank God you have come, Myrddyn. It is the plague! " As he turned he glance up at me and said, "I am sorry, my lord." I thought it was typical of the man to apologise for something which was not his fault.

Myrddyn leapt from his horse and ran with him. The plague had struck many towns but we had been mercifully spared. The condition of the men at the gate was now explained. "Tuanthal, find Garth and send him to me. Pol see to the horses and, Hogan, let us find your mother."

When I reached the chambers, I was struck by the silence. Normally the baby would be crying or the children would be squealing but there was just silence. I opened the door to my bedchamber nervously. I wondered what I would see. Nothing could have prepared me for the sight of my wife and my bairns laid out in their shrouds. The plague had taken my family and now there was just Hogan left. As I held her dead hand for the last time I recalled that I had just left the castle as I normally did. I had not told her how much I loved her and she meant to me. Neither could I tell my dead children of my hopes for their future. I took it for granted that I would return and see them again and I had been punished, I had paid for the murder of King Morcant Bulc.

# Chapter 9

When Garth found me he too looked ill. He was tearful as he explained. "It was three days ago. A few of the men became sick and took to their beds. The next day almost all the women and half the men had the illness and Brother Oswald tried every remedy. Your wife and your children became ill last night and they were dead by the morning" He looked at me in terror. "It was so sudden and Brother Oswald..."

I patted his arm. I knew that they would have done all that they could. "I know you will have done your best. Now we will have to see what Myrddyn can do." I took a breath before I asked the inevitable question. "How many dead?"

"Sixty-three. Forty of them warriors. There are another twenty-six who are ill." He hesitated and then said, solemnly, "Scean died yesterday."

That news probably hit me as hard as the news of Aideen's death. Scean had been with me longer than any other warrior, my brothers excepted, and he had been invincible in battle. He had been laid low and taken by an illness and I had never said goodbye. I would have to wait to see him with the other fallen friends. We had lost more men in a couple of days to an illness than we had in some battles.

Hogan looked up at me with tears in his eyes. I put my arm around his shoulders as he sobbed into my chest. There were no words that I could say. Even though there was sadness in my heart I would mourn quietly and in my own way. I was Warlord and I had to be strong for the people of Rheged.

Myrddyn worked tirelessly and no more of my people died but, exhausted as he and the others were, he came to me. "My lord we must burn the bodies or the pestilence may return." The shock on my face must have shown despite my attempts to be stoic. "It is the only way."

I relented but we had two pyres; one for the garrison and one for my family. Brother Oswald said words over the dead of the garrison some of whom were Christian. I saw him looking at my family's pyre as it burned but I would have no words other than my own invocation to the gods to welcome my family in the Otherworld until I came to them. Hogan's sobs had ceased and Pol stood behind us with his arm on my son's shoulder; that made me feel better; we were unified even in tragedy. The rains returned as the fires smouldered and seemed appropriate that the skies were shedding their own tears. We collected the ashes when they were cool and placed them in a pot. The pot we buried.

After Hogan had gone to bed I sat in the solar with Myrddyn, Garth and Brother Oswald. "I have brought this curse upon my family and my people. I was a murderer and this is their punishment."

"No, my lord. If anyone is to be blamed then it is me for all the ones who were sick and have been treated by me have recovered. Had I not been in the south then I could have saved them." I looked at Myrddyn wondering if this were true. I could not blame him for he had not known the pestilence would strike us. Then he continued. "However, as I saved the people with the herbs and roots I gathered in the south, if I had been here with them then perhaps I would be dead too along with those I have saved." His eyes bored into mine and I saw Brother Oswald nod at the logic of the statement. *Wyrd!*

I am not as quick a thinker as those two and it took a moment for the import of the words to sink in. "This would have happened no matter what we did?"

"I am afraid so."

My heart went cold and I looked at the skies filled with precocious gods who played with us mortals as though we were toys. I changed a little then and pity left me for a while.

Over the next week messengers arrived telling of the same pestilence in the capital and in the cities to the north. When Raibeart and Aelle arrived I dreaded the worst but they brought good news. They had not been affected by the disease. I knew they meant well with their sympathy but that did not bring my family back. We held a feast of mourning to celebrate the lives of those who had died. We told tales of the bravery of those such as Scean and recalled those things about Aideen and the women which brought a smile to our faces.

Raibeart looked at Hogan who was sat between the two of us. "And what of my nephew, brother, what would you have with him? My wife or Freja would care for him if you wished."

Before I could speak an angry Hogan burst out. "I am not a child. Do not talk about me as though I am not here! I will be a warrior!"

All the warriors smiled at the words and it was true, if he were not my son, then he would have joined the slingers already. I looked at Garth. "Well Captain of my remaining warriors. Could we train my son to be a warrior?"

"My lord, I have a suggestion."

I looked over at Pol who had been quiet all evening. "Why not have your son as your squire. I could train him while training to be a warrior."

I saw Hogan's face erupt into a grin for the first time since we had hunted. "Would that suit you son? Before you answer, know that Pol has had to suffer my cantankerous temper and tongue." Pol nodded.

"I know and I would deem it an honour."

"Then that will be so."

Myrddyn coughed. "If I might make a suggestion, Lord Lann." I sighed and spread my hands in acceptance. "Since we have lost so many warriors and Scean has also died might Pol not become your Standard Bearer. He stood next to Scean in battle more than any other warrior and I know no-one who would be more loyal."

Garth too smiled, "I think he would be a wise choice and it would mean he could still watch over Hogan."

"Pol? It means you will not fight in the shield wall."

"That matters not my lord for I envied my friend Scean each time he raised the banner."

"Then it is decided but I must warn all of you that the losses mean that if the Saxons do come then we will struggle to defend this castle. We will need more warriors training and training quickly." I gestured towards my brothers. "Our warriors, those who you command, will have a greater burden now than they would have had."

Aelle smiled, "We know and it is a burden we accept. If any Saxons come they will not come from the south that we can both promise."

That evening saved my sanity for Pol took over Hogan's education and training. I suspect that Myrddyn had more than a little to do with it but it allowed me to concentrate on preparing Rheged for the onslaught which would come in the spring. Tuanthal and I rode every inch of Rheged checking on the incursions of the Saxons. The fact that we saw none did not reassure us.

At the festival of Yule, we all stayed in our own castles and strongholds. My brothers and their families invited Hogan and me down to theirs but we were quite happy to stay in the male world of Castle Perilous. Civitas Carvetiorum was no longer an option since the deaths of Brother Osric and Queen Niamh. The fact that King Ywain did not seem interested in our welfare also had something to do with it. His younger brother Pasgen had visited, as had Riderch. Both had suffered some losses due to the plague but not as many as we had. King Ywain was noticeable by his absence. When they had gone I wondered if this was part of the gods' plan to replace us with the Saxons. I knew that we were fewer in number than the last time we had fought.

When spring came and the land began to dry we prepared for the invasion from the east. We rode as far as the Saxon camps on the road, which had been strengthened over the winter, but there was no sign of movement. Their sentries just stared at our patrols impotent to do anything about us. The numbers of warriors who we trained began to rise slowly but it is hard to make an archer or a warrior for the shield wall overnight and I knew that the next time we fought there would be many untried and untested men. I hoped that they would not break.

Summer had already begun when we discovered why we had not seen the Saxons; they had invaded Strathclyde and defeated Rhydderch Hael in battle. He had died along with many of his men. I was sad for they were doughty warriors and had saved us from defeat before now. His sons were busily fighting off the invaders but they had few strongholds and I knew that it would be merely a matter of time before they turned their attention to us. I visited Banna and spoke with Riderch and his brother.

"They will come south and you will need to hold them until I can reach you with my men and the rest of Rheged."

I could see that Riderch had improved his defences. He had the advantage that the old Roman wall protected the north and would slow the enemy down. "We will hold them." He looked serious and asked quietly, "Do we know what King Ywain will do?"

I looked at him curiously. "What have you heard?"

"He has stopped patrolling and left that to Lord Gildas and Prince Pasgen. It is said he never leaves Civitas Carvetiorum."

"I will visit him but remember this, I am Warlord; I raise the army." My words sounded confident but I had Brother Osric's words ringing in my ears; perhaps the king would not wish to fight.

I travelled with just Pol and Hogan as my escorts. Until the Saxons crossed or neared the wall then we were safe. I was pleased that the guards at Rheged's main city still looked as alert as ever and the defences had been maintained. This was our Din Guardi and, so long as it stood, we would survive. It felt strange not to seek Brother Osric or Queen Niamh but I went directly to the king's chambers. He looked much older than the last time I had seen him. His hair was thinning and turning grey.

He had put weight on again and his eyes looked red as though he had been indulging himself too much.

I had not seen him since the death of my family but he ignored that and began, "Have you heard? The Saxons are in Strathclyde. What should we do?"

"I have visited Riderch and I will visit Prince Pasgen and Lord Gildas. The river and the Roman Wall will give us some protection and I will prepare the army to defend the wall when they do come. We will have a larger number of men available because they have attacked Strathclyde first and will have suffered casualties. How many men will be available from Civitas Carvetiorum?"

He looked terrified. "I am not sure I can let you have any. We need all the men we have to defend the walls."

I was taken aback by what I took to be craven cowardice. His father would not have behaved in this manner. "We can leave a healthy garrison but your horsemen and your warriors will serve better with the army." He shook his head. "I am Warlord."

He half stood, "And I am king."

We stared at each other. "When the Saxons come then it will be war and I will order your men into battle, King Ywain. I was appointed warlord by your father. Would you remove me from that office?" Before he could answer, I added, "Would you lead the army into battle?"

I saw the terror in his eyes. "No! No! You may continue to be Warlord but do not take the men until you need them!"

When I left I had a bad taste in my mouth and both Hogan and Pol kept their distance and did not try to talk to me. I rode directly to Prince Pasgen. His stronghold was not far from the city and close to the coast. His reception was much warmer. I spoke with him alone and told him my fears. His face told me that he knew what the problem was. "You are still Warlord, Lord Lann and you will have the support of every lord in the land."

"But if I have not the support of the king then what is the point?"

"We will use the men from the capital, even if I have to ride there and order them myself." I felt reassured. "Gildas and I keep constant patrols along the wall and we have fortified some of the towers. They will not find it easy to invade our land. I will send daily despatch riders to you. If a day goes by without one then hasten north for I shall need you!"

When I left the prince I felt more confident but I took Pol, Hogan and the inevitable Wolf, north to the wall to see the fruits of their labours. At this, western end, the wall was mainly turf. If a stone wall had ever been built then the stones had been taken. Prince Pasgen had erected a wooden wall which would slow up an enemy but could never stop a determined force. I had fought the Hibernians close to here and knew that archers could cause serious damage when warriors were emerging from the water but, as I peered west, I saw that if the Saxons brought their ships they could land their men behind the wall. Prince Pasgen would need a fort building there to deter them. We rode along the wall to Banna and I saw that every few miles was a wooden tower with sentries. They were not there to defend but to warn and I saw the beacons they had made. When I passed through Banna I would tell Riderch to do the same.

It was dark when we reached home. I would not be suffering the sharp edge of Aideen's tongue, much as I might wish it. Instead I saw the three reproachful faces of Garth, Brother Oswald and Myrddyn. The accusatory looks did not make me feel in the least embarrassed or guilty. I was Warlord; let them worry. Pol and Hogan saw to the armour, horses and weapons while I went to my hall for food. They had all eaten but left plenty for me. As I wolfed down the food with a hungry dog next to me with his dinner, I told them of my discoveries and what I had learned.

"I always worried what would happen when Brother Osric's hand was no longer on the helm. Now we can see why he pushed for your appointment as Warlord."

"Yes Myrddyn, "I mumbled through a mouthful of stew, "but the king can take that away from me in an instant. I think that the only reason he did not was because he feared he might have to lead the army. At least Prince Pasgen has got a pair of balls between his legs."

"Why did he change so much, my lord? He was always a brave warrior in his youth."

"He married, Garth, and she changed him. Some men, like my brother Aelle, become better for marriage. But others, like King Ywain become lesser men. *Wyrd.*"

"Well then Lord Lann, what are we to do?"

"Whatever we have to, Myrddyn. I want the farmers and men of the domain arming and training. We will leave the older warriors and those with wounds to guard the castle although with so many dead it does not seem as important. We will then move northwards to Banna. I will build a camp between Prince Pasgen and Riderch."

"Suppose they attack the wall further east?"

"I intend to use Tuanthal and any horsemen I can prise from King Ywain's grasp to watch there but that part of our land is more difficult to traverse. Here they just have a river and they are men of the sea. It will not pose a problem."

"And Lord Gildas?"

"I will have Lord Gildas build a fort to protect the coast in case they try to attack there." I leaned back, satisfied. My squire and standard bearer had entered and were busily filling their faces as young men do. There would be a clean cauldron when they had finished. I stared at the three men on whom I relied so much. They deserved the truth. "I do not think we will stop them this time. If I was Aethelric I would attack from the east whilst attacking from the north. We would not have enough men to defend both fronts but, even if he does not do that, we do not have enough men to defend against him and I now doubt the king's will. We will be leaving some of the best warriors guarding Civitas Carvetiorum, instead of defeating the enemy on the field."

We sat in silence. Wolf happily washed himself, oblivious to the impending disaster. Myrddyn looked at each of us in turn. "Wales then?"

I nodded, "Wales but we would retreat from here to my brothers' castles first. There are many places to slow up a large army and we would need time to evacuate all who wanted to leave." I shrugged. "There may be some who will wish to stay."

Brother Oswald shook his head. "I think all the Christians would wish to leave and, from what I have heard from the others the non-Christians would not wish to live under a Saxon yoke."

"I want you to go to Raibeart and Aelle. Tell them both what I have planned. They will make the necessary arrangements." I paused, picturing the bird like Brother Osric, "and you had better ensure that Brother Osric's works are taken there first. We may have to leave here in a hurry."

The army we took, a week later, was a shadow of its former self. We had but eighty warriors, thirty horsemen, twenty archers and twenty slingers. The farmers gave us another hundred men. They were all armed; some with sword or axe or spear and some with bow. All had a shield and most had some armour, courtesy of dead Saxons. They were brave and they were well trained but they were not killers and the Saxons were. I would not throw their lives away lightly. They would be needed later.

Riderch and Ridwyn had worked tirelessly and now we had a line of beacons stretching along the length of the wall in Rheged. Tuanthal and his thirty men were already well to the east scouting and I sent a despatch rider to Civitas to ask King Ywain for his horsemen. I left Garth to build our camp and I took Pol, Hogan and Wolf to Lord Gildas. He had a stronghold on the coast at Alavna. It was well fortified but was intended to stop Hibernian slavers and not Saxon invaders.

I had not seen him in some time and he had grown. He and Prince Ywain had been my constant companions in our youthful campaigns and, unlike the king; Lord Gildas had kept up his skills. He too was worried about the king but was diplomatic enough not to criticise." I have a hundred warriors, ten archers and forty horsemen."

"How many do you need to defend Alavna?"

"If I leave ten then the old warriors and the men of the town will suffice." He cocked his head to one side. "What do you plan?"

"We are vulnerable to an attack south of the wall if they use their ships. I want a fort building along the coast, five miles south of the wall. Alavna will be a back-up but if you are based there then you can reinforce us on the wall."

"How many men can we field?"

Myrddyn had spent many hours calculating the maximum number of men we could use. "We have no more than four hundred warriors, unless we use Raibeart's and Aelle's men and they guard the east. Archers? Less than a hundred and that includes the half-trained men. We have forty or fifty slingers and two hundred horsemen. If King Ywain releases men from the capital then we could have another two hundred warriors and a hundred archers." I paused, "but so far he is reluctant."

For the first time he looked upset. "But the Saxons have thousands."

"I know. This time it is just Rheged who will be fighting."

He clasped my arm. "I will not let you down Warlord. My men will be there."

When I reached my camp, it looked defensible and there was a message from King Ywain. He was sending just fifty of his horsemen and fifty of his warriors. Myrddyn was close by when I received the missive and he saw my face. He came over and said quietly. "The fifty horsemen will double our patrols in the east so that is good and fifty extra warriors is more than you asked for. Look on this as half full and not half empty. Civitas Carvetiorum is not far from here. When the Saxons come they will be able to reach us."

I nodded and smiled. Myrddyn was my touchstone. So long as he was close by then I had a chance. "Can you think of anything to slow them down?"

"Yes. I will take some men after dark and we will dig a ditch ten paces from the river. I will divert the river and make that land impassable. I will get others to bury stakes in the river bottom. It is the Saxons who wish to cross south. We do not wish to go north."

I ordered Garth to send some scouts north of the river to find out where the enemy was. Since the king had died we had had no news from Strathclyde. Perhaps their warriors still fought, we did not know. Lord Gildas began work on his fort and sent carts with dried fish from Alavna to feed the army. We had hunters out, constantly, but men were better employed building defences than gathering food.

Once the camp was finished Garth began extra training with the farmers and workers. I took to sparring with Pol and Hogan. Pol still yearned to use his war axe but he still needed to learn how to fight with a normal sword and a shield. It was handy having the two of them for it enabled me to improve both of them at the same time. Hogan used Pol's old seax; a fine weapon for close in work. I showed both of them how to use the shield as an offensive weapon.

"On the day you fight put ten more nails into your shields but do not hammer them in. Let them protrude a little. Then when you use your shield as a weapon you might be lucky and rip out an eye or damage a nose."

Hogan looked shocked. "But that is not honourable!"

Pol cuffed him on the back of the head. "Listen to your father and remember war and battle are not honourable. You use anything you can to win. You see a leg before you then stab at it. If you see an unprotected man's back then stab him. We are not here for glory, we are here to win."

It was only then that I realised how well I had brought Pol on and I left the two of them to it knowing that Hogan would be ready when the time came for him to stand behind me in the battle line.

The scouts returned the following day. I was pleased to see that they were unscathed but we had trained our men well and they were skilful. Garth saw me as soon as they had made their report. "The Saxons are moving south."

"Their whole army?"

"The scouts just said there were thousands of Saxons so we can assume it is a large part anyway. They will be here in three days at the most."

I was relieved. We could now add to our defences. "Send a rider to Prince Pasgen and Lord Gildas and tell them to bring their men in two days' time. I will visit the king." I left Pol and Hogan training and rode with Myrddyn to Civitas.

"Is there a reason you are bringing me along, my lord?"

"I am hoping that, as you have an intellect as Brother Osric did, you can persuade the king to be more belligerent. I have obviously failed."

"I do not think it was your words, my lord. I just think he does not want to fight. He is Brother Osric's tortoise. Perhaps he thinks he can do as Bulc did and hide in his castle."

"Then he is wrong."

The king was reluctant to see us but, as Warlord, I had the right to an audience and he eventually had to see me. "Your majesty, the Saxons will be here in three days. I need your troops now."

He shook his head, violently from side to side. Had it not been so serious I would have laughed for he looked like a dog trying to dry himself. "No, Lord Lann. I need all of my troops here to defend the city. Bring the army here and hide them in the walls."

Myrddyn tried. "Your majesty the castle cannot feed and shelter the army and besides that would mean the people who were outside would be enslaved or killed. We have to stop them at the river and the wall."

"It is a punishment sent by God because this man murdered King Morcant Bulc." He pointed a wavering finger at me. The guards just stood stony faced.

I was angry and I had no time for this. "This man is not the Warlord of Rheged and I command the army not you. I am sorry that it has come to this but you have changed and I was charged by your father with defending Rheged and I will fulfil that promise!"

I stormed out and I heard his plaintive cry. "Do not leave me to be slaughtered by our enemies I beg of you."

I sought Aidan, the captain of the bodyguard. He was in the guard chamber and someone must have told him of the words we had exchanged. He looked solemn. "Yes Warlord."

"The Saxons are within three days of us and I need every man mobilising. Send out the men to bring the army to the wall."

He hesitated. "And the king?"

"The king will stay here. Leave sufficient guards to protect the city but bring the rest." He still hadn't said yes and I was beginning to lose my temper. "Captain Aidan. I am Warlord of Rheged and I command the army. Do you understand what I have ordered you to do?"

To be fair to him he tried to stand up to me. "Yes, Warlord and I will bring the army to you but…"

"Yes?"

"Not the bodyguard of the king. They protect him and are commanded by him alone."

The one hundred and twenty horsemen of the bodyguard, the men who rode behind the dragon banner were the elite warriors of Rheged. Under King Urien they had saved the day on many occasions but Aidan had a point. "Then leave the bodyguard with the king but bring the rest and I want you there in two days."

He almost smiled as he said, "Yes my lord."

Riding back to the camp Myrddyn posed some difficult questions. "This cannot end well; you know that? The King of Rheged and the Warlord of Rheged should agree. I do not think that King Urien expected this. Do you?"

"No but what else can I do?"

"You could become king."

I turned on him. "And break my oath? Never mention the idea again."

"Then I will not but we must be ready to flee for I foresee that we will lose now."

I had no doubt that he was right. He was too good a seer to be wrong and I knew how few men we had. If we had had the horse of King Ywain there might have been a slim chance but now there was none.

# Chapter 10

Prince Pasgen and Lord Gildas rode in with their men the next day. Both approved of my defences and both seemed in good spirits. After their men had been taken by Garth to their allotted area I told the two men of the King's intransigence. "So my brother keeps four hundred men to defend a castle that only needs fifty." He vaulted back on his horse. "I will be back!"

I wondered what he could achieve that I could not but I remembered my brothers. We too had a different relationship to each other and perhaps he would succeed. Gildas and I strolled down the lines of our defences. "I have left the fishermen their boats rather than having them fight."

I smiled, "You have a good reason for that of course."

"Of course. They watch the mouth of the estuary. If the Saxons come by boat and try to outflank our lines then they will be the first to know."

"Good. That is wise."

Garth joined us. "The men have been placed along the wall. We are thinly spread but their captains know the signals which will bring them close together."

"Good. Now you had better send a rider to bring in Tuanthal. We will need those horsemen more than ever now."

We were eating when we heard the drumming of hooves and then the distinctive wail of the dragon standard. Prince Pasgen rode in at the head of fifty of the king's bodyguard. He jumped down and grabbed the standard. "The obstinate fool would not budge so I appealed to the men. These fifty chose you, my lord."

"And the banner?"

"It should be with warriors who fight for Rheged." He shrugged. "It is the banner of Rheged and not the king's bodyguard."

I laughed and felt a little happier. It was only fifty men but they were the best in the land and the dragon banner might just make the difference. I called a council of war as soon as Tuanthal reached us the next day. They had seen no signs of the Saxons and I assumed that they would be attacking from the north. If they were doing anything else then we could do nothing about it. The warriors had been arriving in dribs and drabs but the numbers were greater than I had hoped. Myrddyn had calculated the forces we had to face the Saxons when they came.

"We have almost six hundred ordinary warriors. Many have a shield and all have a weapon. We have four hundred and thirty who can stand in the shield wall. We have almost one hundred and fifty archers and slingers and just over two hundred horsemen."

Gildas was naïve and honest. "But what of the king's men?"

"We have but a hundred of those and only fifty of his warriors. None of his archers are here. But let us not worry about what we do not have and concentrate on what we do."

Just then there was an almighty cheer from the camp. It was too jubilant to be the enemy. I waved an irritated hand to Pol to find out what the disturbance was. I could ill afford any distractions. When he returned he was grinning from ear to ear. "It is another contingent from Civitas my lord, fifty warriors and fifty archers."

I smiled, "It is about time some of our luck became good. Thanks to Prince Pasgen and Captain Riderch we now have a wall to defend. We will use the less well armed men to defend that along with the archers and slingers. The shield wall and the horse we will place over on the bank." The old river bank and flood defences formed a ridge about a hundred paces beyond the river. "I will be on the wall and Garth will command the knoll." There was a roar of protest. I slammed Saxon Slayer on the table. "This is not open for debate! I am Warlord!" I softened my tone, "And I do not intend to die on a five-hundred-year-old wall. We need to hit them as they try to cross the river. The men on the wall can do that and my presence will encourage them as will my Wolf Standard." I saw Pol swell with pride. "I want them to pay for the crossing. I suspect there will be thousands but in truth we just do not know. Tonight and tomorrow I want traps and pits digging in a huge semi-circle around the knoll. When we retreat, on my command, our men will run around the sides as though fleeing the field. But we will reform behind the hill like two horns on a bull. The Saxons will charge the shield wall. They will not see the horsemen who will be hidden from view, dismounted behind the knoll and the horns of the bull. I want them to break themselves on our shield wall. We will use three lines with a reserve of fifty to enable us to rotate and we will fight as we did at Dunelm. Even if they expect it they can do little about it. The two wings are there to protect the shield wall from an outflanking move and on my command the horse will mount and charge their flanks. Had we more horse then I would be certain of victory. As it is I can only hope."

I looked around at the sea of faces. I had fought with all of these men, Miach, Riderch, Pasgen and Gildas and I knew them as well as Raibeart and Aelle. "Any questions or suggestions?"

"Smoke."

"Smoke Myrddyn?"

"Yes if we have some pyres built then just before you give the order to retreat we could light damp fires and the smoke would make it hard for them to see. It would make the traps more effective and the men could escape easier."

I nodded my agreement. "Any more?" They shook their heads but I was pleased to see more confidence amongst them. "Then tonight we dig pits for two hours. Use the men who will have to avoid them to dig them eh? We don't want our own men falling into them and then one man in four to watch tonight. I want no surprises."

After we had eaten we all went around the men. They needed to know us and many of the ordinary soldiers had never seen us all. They knew my standard and Pol happily carried it around with Hogan and Wolf in close attendance. Many just wanted to touch it as though it was a holy relic. I gave the order to stop work so that the men could rest and I stood on the walls with Prince Pasgen, Gildas and Garth.

"What if they do not come tomorrow, Lann?"

"Then, Prince Pasgen, we will have more time to build defences."

"And if they do come, can we beat them?"

"Each time we have fought them we have been outnumbered and we have always won but this time I fear that the odds are just too great."

"Did you not summon your brothers?"

"They have few horsemen and I did not want them strung out on the road. This way we can retreat to Castle Perilous if this goes wrong and we will have two strongholds to hold out against them. I am not risking all on one throw of the dice. We need a back-up plan."

Just then, Tuanthal, who had been riding the wall galloped in. "There are men in the water my lord." He pointed upstream. "Many of them.

"Stand to."

It was dark and we could see little but we could hear the men. Was it a Saxon trick? Then we heard a voice. "We seek Lord Lann. We are the men of Strathclyde."

"Watch them but help them. This may be a subterfuge."

As soon as the first warrior was helped out of the water we knew that they spoke the truth. It was Calum who had fought with me under his leader Angus. His head bandaged, he gave a bow and, offering me his sword said, "We are here to serve you my Lord Lann. Strathclyde is no more."

Myrddyn organised food and medical aid for the men of Strathclyde. There were a hundred and fifty of them and they were the survivors of the last battle. It was obvious that there would still be pockets of warriors hiding and fleeing elsewhere but organised resistance was over.

"They are five miles to the north of you. There are at least four thousand of them. We killed many of them in our last great stand but the numbers were just too great."

I put my arm around his shoulders. I could hear the emotion in his voice. "You are safe with us now." I turned to the warriors of Rheged who were watching the pitiful remnants of a great army drag their wet, weary and wounded bodies from the river. "Feed these men. They are all heroes."

Calum nodded, "Thank you Warlord. And when we are rested we will fight alongside you for we would have revenge." He suddenly smiled. "And we know the Saxons have never bested the Wolf Warrior."

As he went away I felt that accolade like a millstone around my neck. Although it was true each time we fought against the overwhelming odds we did then the chances of defeat increased and one defeat would end Rheged. The good news was that I now had another one hundred and fifty veterans to place on the knoll. We now had a third more warriors than we had. We had more good news in the night when another one hundred and fifty men left their fields and walked north through Rheged to fight with the Wolf Warrior. Myrddyn's foresight in bringing extra weapons and armour paid dividends and, once again, I rued the passivity of King Ywain. He could be consigning Rheged to history and the glory days of King Urien Rheged could become the stuff of legend.

We managed to feed all the men early. The sound of weapons being sharpened and the banter of warriors warmed my heart on that cold morning. Hogan brought my gleaming blade, polished and sharpened and donned his own helmet. Pol proudly held the furled standard in one hand and his war axe in the other. I had worried about his ability to defend himself and the standard until he showed me the metal spike he had put on the bottom of the standard. He could plant the standard and then defend it. He would wield the axe with two hands and any Saxon who approached him would need to be a brave man.

We took our place on the walls with the other soldiers, archers and slingers. Garth led the heavily armed veterans to the hill and Tuanthal withdrew behind them. When the Saxons came they would not see a mighty army arrayed before them they would see farmers, fisher folk and workers on the walls. They would be confident that Rheged was ripe for plucking and they would charge recklessly. That was our hope. Myrddyn stood with us; partly as healer and partly as advisor. There were three slingers mounted on ponies beneath me in case we needed to change our plans.

We heard the drums of the Saxons in mid-morning. At first that was the only indication of their presence but soon we saw sunlight glinting from helmets and spears. Aethelric brought them on a wide front. He had scouted well and must have known that he faced only a turf wall at this end of the frontier. I suspect the recently erected wooden wall would have come as a surprise but the Saxons knew that their axes would make short work of wood. They halted across the river and I wondered how they would cross. I half hoped that he would be foolish enough to swim his men across but he was too wise for that. I saw his men dragging something to the river and soon saw that it was the first of a number of large rafts.

I turned to one of the despatch riders. "Aedh, ride to Captain Miach and tell him to kill any targets which show themselves."

I did not want arrows wasting. Miach would use his best archers to kill those who tried to bring the rafts across. A wall of shields appeared at the river's edge with a gap large enough for the first raft. The men at the back began to push it into the water. I saw that it was large enough to hold many men. When Miach's men saw their chance they loosed their arrows. The Saxons did not try to pole the raft across; instead I saw them driving stakes into the ground to moor it. Their actions exposed them. Miach's men killed twenty warriors before the raft was secured. A line of shields appeared and I could see, behind, the second raft being carried by a hundred men.

"They are building a bridge." Myrddyn voice my own fears.

Miach too saw the danger and his men began to loose arrows at the unprotected legs of the warriors with the shields. Many fell but there were always more behind. When the shields reached the end of the first raft it was dropped on the top and they all walked backwards. Although the fragile bridge sank a little below the river, the top was above the water and I saw men at the rear pushing the second raft over the first. It was slow work but they must have greased the bottom of the second raft for it slowly edged forwards. Miach killed more men but, once it was halfway across the first raft more warriors with shields came to protect the pushers and the weight of the second raft took it across. We watched as ten or twenty warriors dived into the water and swam to secure the two ends of the raft. Miach targeted them and killed some but the water took away the power and they had a bridge which almost reached across the river.

"The last one will do it."

"True, Myrddyn but we know where they will attack. Ride and bring the men who guard the walls to the east and west. Just leave a hundred paces of wall with men. Send the archers to the walls and the rest to the knoll."

"Are you sure my lord? That will leave precious few men."

"It will leave two hundred men and a hundred and forty archers and slingers. They can only bring ten men abreast. They will get across but it will cost them dear. When you have done that, get to your fires." The wind was from the west and Myrddyn would light the fires from that end of our line. I glanced down at Hogan. This was his first battle. "Are you afraid son?"

I saw the fear in his eyes but his voice said, "No for I am with the Wolf Warrior."

"Well the Wolf Warrior is scared and that is natural but once I draw Saxon Slayer and begin to kill my enemies, then all fear will go. As it will with you my son."

The third raft would not be secured, I could see that, but it would rest on our bank. Of course they did not know that the bank was now a muddy morass and was the second of our traps. I turned to Aedh who had returned. "Ask Captain Miach to fire the rafts." I hoped that, it they had greased the wood then they might burn a little easier.

The slingers were now able to affect the battle and many of the warriors bringing over the last raft fell to accurate lead balls but Aethelric seemed oblivious to the losses he was taking. I suspect the warriors he was using were not his best and were expendable. I smiled ruefully to myself, it was what I was doing. I turned to Pol, "Unfurl the banner; let them see where we are."

I pulled down my face mask and drew my sword. As I raised it in the air my warriors roared, "Saxon Slayer!" and banged their shields. As the end of the raft dropped on to the bank with a sloppy plop the men who had built it fled. None reached the far shore. They had paid for the bridge with their lives. Miach began to loose fire arrows at the raft and, although some fizzled out, others began to burn. I could see movement on the far side and I was pleased. My action was going to make Aethelric change his plans and attack quickly. Any time you could make an opponent change his mind was a good thing. His shield wall came across too quickly. The raft tipped and rolled and some of the warriors at the sides fell to their deaths in the river. The archers and slingers had many targets. With another one hundred archers we could have cleared the bridge all day but we were limited. They were brave Saxons but six out of every ten died before they reached our side.

Once they reached the southern bank any thought they would just roll us up faded as they fell into the pits and bogs with which we had lined our defences. The javelins we had issued to our men slaughtered those who were helplessly trapped. And still they poured across and still they died. However sheer weight of numbers and the dead at the foot of our wall meant that, at last, some of them were able to scale the turf wall and begin to fight. Even then my men gave a good account of themselves. They had gained confidence when they saw that it was Saxons who were dying.

"Pol, give the signal." The standards was raised and lowered. Myrddyn would begin the fire. I was delighted that the middle raft was burning down one side which slowed up the attack but now they had a foothold on our side and I saw my men dying. Suddenly the first cloud of smoke drifted over and soon it grew thicker. I turned to Hogan who held the buccina, the Roman horn, in his hands. "Now son, give the signal!"

He put the horn to his lips and blew as hard as he could. The effect was instantaneous. The Saxons paused, wondering what it meant whilst my men leapt from their posts and raced as fast as they could back to the safety of the shield wall. Miach's men loosed three more flights and then they ran. Then there was just the three of us. I turned to the other two. "Mount your horses, I will join you." There was a slight hesitation. "Obey the Warlord!" They left and I was alone. It was not bravado; I wanted them to fear me even more. I stood at the edge and roared, "I am Lann the Warlord of Rheged, the slayer of kings and champions; the ghost who kills in the night. You will all die!" There were four warriors clambering over the edge of the wall and they made the mistake of listening to me rather than killing me. In two blows I chopped off their heads and then leapt on to the back of my horse. I hoped the effect was that I had disappeared. The three of us galloped back to the knoll.

As we approached the shield wall I heard the banging of the shields and the roar and cheers of my men. It was as though we had had a victory already; a small victory but we had killed many and lost few. That would soon change.

Pol took the horses to Tuanthal as spares and I took my place at the crest of the knoll. The smoke did its job well, too well, for we could see little of the turf wall. We knew that the Saxons would have two hundred paces to cover once they had scaled the walls and they would not see the traps. The traps on the other side of the wall were still working for we could hear the screams and curses as men tripped or fell.

Myrddyn arrived; he looked elated. "The middle raft is almost burned through. They will have to either repair it or risk not having enough men to fight us. And," he added cheerfully, "the raft fire is adding to our smoke."

That was something we had not expected and gave us a little more time to echelon the wings and position our archers. Prince Pasgen had brought with him many spare arrows from the armoury at Civitas. We would not run out of those. He commanded the left horse reserve while Gildas and Tuanthal had the right. We were as ready as we ever would be.

The smoke started to thin and we could see movement. We could also hear the coughing as the warriors fought through the smoke. Their sight would be affected after they had crossed through our screen. We watched them form up. There was no doubt that these were veterans and, even at more than a hundred paces, we could see the battle amulets and bracelets.

"Pol, unfurl the banner!"

A cheer went up from my men as the wolf banner fluttered above us. The Saxons began to walk forwards, banging their shields with their swords as they did so. Suddenly there were screams as four men fell into a spike filled trap. Soon there were others in different traps. They began to slow their approach as they watched the ground. "Miach! Now!"

The Saxons were paying too much attention to the ground and many of the arrows found unprotected skin. Soon they had to raise their shields and the slingers scored hit after hit. The Saxon line had to halt to allow the gaps to be filled and that caused more casualties. It could not last for, soon, they would be too close for the archers and we would be locked in battle. When they were fifty paces away they stopped and formed a huge wedge. The point was aimed at my standard, as I had expected. That suited me for it meant the weaker soldiers on our flanks would not bear the brunt of the lethal assault. The knoll helped us as the spears of the third rank could stab down on the necks of their front rank. They would need to knock us off the knoll before their numbers could be brought into play.

They ran at us and I wished I had Angus and his war hammers with us for they would have punched holes in the solid wedge. Garth and my oathsworn did their job; they absorbed the first shock. Their superior shields withstood the blows from the Saxon swords and axes and the spears from the third rank caused mayhem as the Saxons found that they were fighting two warriors at once. Miach, with his archers and his slingers was aiming at the ranks behind the tip of the wedge and it was becoming weaker and lacking cohesion. It was then that I saw Aethelric. He was dressed in shining mail with a helmet like mine. The difference was he had a raven emblem on the top. That told me a number of things but the most important was that their king would not be fighting for the helmet he wore was too impractical; it looked good but a blow to the raven would rip it from his head. That decided me. At the tipping point of the battle I would join the front rank and lead my men.

Aethelric was forming two wedges on either side of his main attack. I could see that they would charge my flanks. "Pol signal Tuanthal. I want the horse ready to attack the Saxon wedges."

We had already worked out a number of signals. Scean had started it and Myrddyn had worked and refined it. I did not need to look. I knew that my three leaders of horse, Tuanthal, Prince Pasgen and Lord Gildas would be putting their two hundred and ten horsemen into position. I knew I could trust their judgement about when to charge. I had placed Riderch on the left and Ridwyn on the right and given them command of the ordinary warriors. They too would use their judgement but, more importantly they were two champions and could deal with whoever the Saxons sent against them. I had no doubt that Aethelric's elite warriors were coming for me.

The traps along the sides were not as numerous and many more of the Saxons were able to charge. Although my two Bernicians fought well the soldiers were forced back. I heard the cheer from the Saxons as they thought they had broken us and the ones in the centre took heart. Now was the time, "Rotate!" In one seamless move the front rank punched with their shields as the third rank jabbed and then the front ranks exchanged places with the third rank. The spears were passed back and the fresh warriors faced the tiring Saxons. The effect was instantaneous. The Saxon wedge was pushed back to its starting point. Riderch and Ridwyn had allowed themselves to be pushed all the way around so that we were an island surrounded by Saxons. The Saxons outnumbered us but we were all together and my archers could now loose all the way around the circle.

I had seen the cavalry detach itself, unseen, from the rear and they were now in position. I watched as my warriors hacked and slashed at the Saxons who were tiring. I turned to Hogan. "We are going into battle son. Use your seax well. Stay behind me and stab at anything which is foreign. Pol, leave the standard here, you will need both hands." I grinned, "Besides no man will retreat beyond the wolf!" I raised Saxon Slayer to head height. I could see the warrior who would be the first to die. "Rotate!"

The rotation had come quicker than the Saxons had expected and they were taken by surprise. As Ragnar stepped back two spears struck the two warriors ahead and Saxon Slayer went through the skull of the lead warrior in the wedge. I thrust so hard that the blade entered the eye of the man behind. I was in danger of losing my blade and I twisted and withdrew it. I heard bone crunch as it emerged with blood and grey matter. As the two men fell dead I punched the next man as Pol's axe hacked down on another warrior's skull. Behind me I heard the roar as my men shouted, "Wolf Warrior!" over and over. They had the blood lust upon them and we were moving forwards at a steady walking pace. We were stabbing, slashing and hacking with impunity. We had the weight of the army behind us and they had no cohesion. When I heard the wail of the dragon standard then I knew that the charge of horse had begun and I renewed my efforts. One warrior had been lying on the ground, feigning death and as I stepped over him he tried to stab me with the broken haft of a spear. Hogan's seax ripped across his throat. I grinned at him and nodded. As I punched with my shield I drew Saxon Slayer across my body and gave the Saxon line a sweep of its steel sharp edge. I know not how many it took for Pol chose that moment to swing his axe in the same direction but there was suddenly a gap before us. "Pol, the standard! Charge!"

It was a risky order as I could not see beyond the men around me but, as I saw that we were close to the traps and I could see the wall I knew that we had advanced further than we had hoped. We could drive them back to the wall. It was we who had now lost cohesion but the Saxons turned their backs and an unprotected back is an easy target. As my men spread out the Saxons just ran and headed for the wall. I could no longer see the raven helmet of Aethelric and that meant his men could not either but they could see the wolf banner being waved behind the Wolf Warrior and any Saxon heroes were long dead. Had they halted at the wall they could have defeated us for they still outnumbered us but they had had enough and they ran across the disintegrating bridge which still burned in places. A large number had crossed when it finally fell apart and the last few hundreds threw themselves at the timbers or tried to swim the river. We were too tired to do anything but watch. The Saxons had been driven back. They had conquered Strathclyde but Rheged, despite the inactivity of its king, remained free.

# Chapter 11

For the first time since I had fought alongside my brothers my first reaction was to check that Hogan was intact. He was covered in blood but none of it was his. He looked at me and threw his arms around me. "I was always proud of you but today…" and he burst into tears. I felt like crying myself but I just held him. I was proud of him. He had faced an enemy who must have seemed as numerous as ants and he had not flinched. He was my son.

The worst part of any battle is the aftermath. It matters not if you win or lose you still have to see who paid the price and that day was expensive. The heaviest losses had been amongst the horse although it was they who had caused the rout of the Saxons. Lord Gildas lay dead and Prince Pasgen had a bad wound. Over a hundred had been slain and many others were wounded. We had only just over three hundred warriors who could stand in a shield wall again. Calum had died as had the faithful Riderch. Both would be welcomed in the Otherworld but I would miss Riderch most of all for he chose to change his country and that was a choice made because of me. Our archers and slingers were largely intact and we had only lost two hundred other warriors. It could have been worse. Even though the Saxons had lost many we could see, from their camp fires which burned across the river that they still outnumbered us.

We sent Prince Pasgen and the rest of the wounded back to Civitas. Before he left the prince gave Tuanthal the dragon standard. "I watched you today, Captain Tuanthal, and you deserve to carry this into battle. I will never need it again and my brother deserves it not."

Tuanthal was touched by the gesture and was about to refuse the honour when I said, "That is the symbol of Rheged and so long as you carry it in my retinue then Rheged will be free." I thought that Prince Pasgen would fight again but, as he had lost some of the fingers on his left hand as well as being hamstrung, I did not think he would be leading his warriors. His was a serious loss.

We buried our dead but kept apart Lord Gildas, Riderch and Calum for they were the leaders of their people and they were buried with their arms in honour of their prowess. After we had stripped the Saxons of anything worth taking we burnt their bodies as their comrades watched.

When it became obvious that the Saxons would not attack again for a while I sent the soldiers back home, keeping just the horse, slingers, archers and shield wall. Garth gave me a worried look. "They might be waiting for us to do as we have done and then they will flood across."

"No Garth, Myrddyn and I agree." I pointed across the river. "See there are fewer tents than there were. They are moving. We will give another day and then we will retire to Civitas and Tuanthal can watch them. We have merely won the battle. Not the war."

We waited for a few more days and then the Saxons were suddenly gone. Myrddyn had managed to save many men and the wait had not caused problems but I now worried where they had gone. I sent Tuanthal east to see if he could find them and I led my army back to Civitas. My men, and especially Pol and Hogan, were in an exceptionally good mood. I had noticed Hogan looking at me in a different way. I suppose he had seen me before as the father who played with him and his sister- an affectionate and doting father- but now he had seen me as a warrior.

"Will they make a great celebration at the castle father?"

"I do not know. We did not defeat the Saxons."

Hogan looked shocked. "But they ran away!"

"They ran away and still have most of their men. Warriors call that a retreat. We did well, you and Pol did very well but it is only the start."

"I want a longer sword."

I shook my head. "Pol used that one, very successfully for many years. You need the weapon to be a part of you."

"The Warlord is right Hogan. Keep it sharp and it will save you." Hogan took out the seax and looked at it as though he had never seen it before.

Hogan was disappointed with the reception we received at Civitas Carvetiorum because there was no reception. It was as though we were just visiting. The sentries looked at the ground, shamefaced as we rode in and the king did not bother to see us at all. I went to the infirmary with Myrddyn to see Pasgen and the other wounded warriors.

Prince Pasgen was furious with his brother. "I cannot understand Ywain. He was annoyed because we did not kill the whole Saxon army." He shook his head. "I tried to explain that we were heavily outnumbered and it was a miracle that we did what we did." He paused. "Lord Lann, your plan was perfection and your attack a masterstroke. My father would have been proud of you, as would Brother Osric."

116

"Thank you, Prince Pasgen, your words more than make up for the cool reception." Myrddyn had been examining Pasgen's wounds and he nodded. "Myrddyn thinks that you can get up tomorrow. I would like to meet with the king, you, Myrddyn, Garth, Riderch and Miach."

"Gladly, but you had better be careful. Ywain is becoming secretive. He might think that we are ganging up on him."

"I care not what he thinks. It is time he began behaving like a king."

When we arrived at the king's chamber the two guards looked embarrassed. "You may not enter, Warlord."

Garth's hand went to his sword but I restrained him. "Why not?"

"The king wishes to see no one."

"You have done your duty. Do not be ashamed. Tell the king that his counsel will be meeting in the main hall to decide what to do next. We will inform him of our decision. Come gentlemen. Let us go to the hall."

Pasgen was incandescent with rage. "That jumped up... how can you take these insults, after what you have done?"

"I serve Rheged. I promised your father that I would do so. We will talk and then the king will join us."

We sat around the table and Myrddyn unfolded the map which Brother Osric had begun and he now added to each time we travelled. He had just identified all the places on the map when the door burst open and King Ywain came in flanked by two armed guards. "So this is where the conspirators meet. I should have you all put in chains."

"Your majesty; it is good of you to join us."

Prince Pasgen stared at me. "Warlord. Did you not hear what he said? He is accusing us of conspiracy!"

"As the king has not left the castle I assume that he has been misinformed." I stared at the two guards. "Lying and spreading false rumour in time of war is a very serious offence. Who had told you this your majesty? Is it these two?"

The two men stared at Saxon Slayer lying across the map and they paled. Seargh, the older one dropped to his knees and said, "No Warlord. We were ordered here by his majesty."

King Ywain looked puzzled. I stared at him. "Then if you would sit at the head of the table we can explain what we think ought to be done about the Saxons and you can give us your opinion."

He sat down but pointedly left his two bodyguards in the room behind his chair. I pointed to Myrddyn, "Continue with your analysis."

"The Saxons have left Rheged which leaves them with two main options and many minor ones. They could use their ships and land from the seaward side of Rheged or they could come from the east. Although, as we have seen, Aethelric is cunning and clever and may use a combination of both."

Prince Pasgen asked, "Why not the south?"

"There are two strongholds barring his route, Aelle's and Raibeart's. We would have ample warning and he would lose many men."

"So your majesty what do you think we should do?"

"I thought that you were invincible and that you would have killed them all. We do not have enough men to fight them. It is hopeless. And my poor wife has lost her father."

"Brother we lost our father but he was murdered!" Pasgen's fury made his face white.

"We can make it hard for them. Lord Gildas had built another fort on the coast. With Ridwyn at Banna and me at Castle Perilous then we can halt the enemy and you could bring the horses and the army to wherever they are."

I could see the nods from the others but the king just shook his head. "We must protect the castle. We need every man we can." He sank back into his chair. "Protect your castles but I wait here." He stood and left with head hung down.

"My lord, the warriors who fought with us did well. We could train them to become warriors."

"A good idea, Myrddyn; if the Saxons give us time."

"I am afraid, Warlord, that we will have to buy that time."

We argued back and forth but Myrddyn's solution was the only one anyone could come up with. We all left the next morning. Each of us took our own men to protect our castles while all the horsemen we could muster were assigned to Tuanthal. Pasgen took it on himself to ride around the kingdom, despite his wounds and gather volunteers who would be trained at Castle Perilous by Garth and me.

Aedh had proved himself to be adept and I gave him command of the slingers. With Hogan as my squire every boy for twenty miles around wanted to join. Pasgen managed to find some riders but our horsemen would never be the force they had once been. Every man and boy who could be found was brought to my warrior hall and training started at first light and ended at dusk.

Brother Oswald became more of a quartermaster than a priest but he was a resourceful man and a clever organiser. His work in procuring wagons and horses meant that we were able to gather supplies quickly. "We will still be heading for Wales, my lord?" He was also astute.

"I would imagine so. I cannot see that King Ywain will relent and although we can hold out for a while we will fall and then we will go to Wales."

Raibeart and Aelle came north with their bodyguards and we held a counsel along with Garth and Myrddyn. "We will keep our horsemen ready to join you at a moment's notice and then we can bring our other forces north."

"Do not throw your men away on a lost cause. My hope is that King Ywain comes to his senses and then you warriors will be needed."

Myrddyn cast doubts on that idea. "In this room I will say that our only hope is for Prince Pasgen to become king."

"That cannot be, Myrddyn, for that would be civil war and we would be doing the Saxon's job for them."

"I did not say it was a good solution but it would give us hope."

The day after my brothers left the Saxons came. We heard later that they arrived at Banna at the same time. There were a thousand in each warband but they seemed content merely to build a camp across the two Roman roads. It was a repeat of the previous year's tactics. This time, however, we were in no position to shift them. When Tuanthal's patrol returned it was with the news that there was a further warband to the south and it was threatening Raibeart's domain. They were closing for the kill. I sent my despatch riders to the others to keep them informed. Prince Pasgen sent every available warrior, not to Civitas Carvetiorum, but to either Ridwyn or me. Soon Castle Perilous was full.

They timed their attack for the start of the harvest. It was a clever move. The men from the camp closest to us were reinforced by another thousand warriors and they began their attack. Ominously they did not attack the castle but the bridge over the river. They intended to bypass us if they could and take King Ywain's castle. All of our hard work building the defences paid off for no matter how hard they tried they could not break through Myrddyn's cunning defences. Our archers and slingers were able to kill those advancing with impunity and our losses in return were negligible. I had begun to think that we might be able to hold them when I received a despatch rider from Ridwyn; the Saxons had spread south of the wall and bypassed Banna; they were heading for Civitas Carvetiorum. They were going for the king.

I had to hope that he would be able to hold out for the only forces I had available were the horsemen of Tuanthal. I sent despatch riders to Raibeart and Aelle asking them to send a force to relieve us. Then we would be able to relieve the king. Gradually more and more of my people fled to the safety of my castle and we put them in the camp we had built beyond the castle. Brother Oswald had gathered in much food but, with the harvest uncollected there would be a lean winter ahead. The Saxon attacks slowly petered out as they seemed willing to wait for the results of their attack on Civitas. None of my despatch riders had managed to breach the ring they had thrown around the stronghold. I did not fear that they would breach its solid walls but their presence had ground Rheged to a halt and starvation would be the enemy.

As I had expected Raibeart and Aelle had set off with their men as soon as they had received my message. They approached my castle from the west and beyond the prying eyes of the Saxons. I rode out with Tuanthal and we met them five miles from the castle. "You did not leave your own lands undefended, did you?"

"No brother. Our walls are defended but we brought our best."

I looked at the warriors and I saw that they had spoken true. Many looked as I did, scarred and grey but it bespoke skill. I recognised men from Elmet who were still keen to avenge the death of their king and kingdom. All told they added two hundred warriors for the shield wall, a hundred archers and eighty slingers. The forty horsemen they brought, doubled my force and gave me the chance to relieve the siege. I quickly outlined my plan and we set it into motion. I led the eighty equites and twenty mounted archers whilst Raibeart and Aelle joined my garrison. The walls would be bristling with armour and steel. Tuanthal took the Dragon standard and I left two disgruntled retainers in the castle with my standard. Hogan and Pol felt put out, despite the fact that I told them that neither was good enough on a horse. I had to be blunt. This was not the time for honeyed tongues. I eased the disappointment by telling them that they could raise my banner from the ramparts when they heard the buccina.

We left in the small hours of the night and rode first south and then east. We arrived a mile east of the Saxon camp just before dawn. Their camp was secure on all four sides but the land to the north and south was open and rolling. They had not put ditches across them. They were confident that they could defeat us. Their normal practice was to line their warriors up to intimidate us. They had learned to stay out of bow shot but they jeered and catcalled as they knew we could not sortie. There was a small hill about two hundred paces from the camp and I sent my archers there under Raibeart's captain, Gwallog. Raibeart had spoken highly of him as a sound and reliable warrior. The archers had bellied up to just below the crest and there, they would rain arrows into the camp. When dawn broke we saw, from the shelter of some trees, movement in the camp. As soon as they had eaten they marched out. Their chief had placed them in a single line to give the impression that they had more men than they actually did but we had counted them carefully and knew that we faced one thousand eight hundred and fifty warriors. We now had almost seven hundred to face them and those odds favoured the Wolf Warrior and his men. As they lined up, we emerged from the woods. We all had two javelins and a spear and each of us was mailed from head to foot. My horse, Raven, also had a metal headpiece which afforded him a little more protection.

I could not see my castle as the enemy were in the line of sight but I heard the buccina. That was our signal to charge. We did so in a single line. The wailing of the Dragon Standard seemed to come from the skies or the ground; those who heard it were never certain. One thing was certain, it terrified our enemies. Gwallog and his men loosed arrow after arrow into the camp. I could tell from the shouts and the screams that they were being effective. Although I could not see what was happening I knew that Garth was leading a wedge of my best warriors up the road to the Saxon camp. Their warriors on their left began to run, disordered, towards the wedge. They did not see us. Their shields faced my wedge and when they did hear us we were forty paces from them. I had spread the line quite thinly for I knew how good my men were with javelins. Over one hundred men fell to the javelins we threw and then we waded in with our spears, stabbing at unprotected backs. The warriors to the south, over five hundred of them were isolated and Raibeart led more warriors, mainly archers protected by a shield wall to rain death upon them.

My horsemen reined in and we dressed our lines. The wedge was now close to the camp and surrounded by Saxons. I could see that Gwallog still dealt death with his deadly arrows and we charged again. This time we had no javelins to throw but our spears were just as

121

effective. We stabbed and withdrew as we reached their lines. Raven raised his hooves to smash into the helmet and skull of one warrior while I speared another. The third warrior managed to get two hands on the spear as it struck him and he ripped it from my hand as he died. I drew Saxon Slayer and leaned forwards to stab the next man. Having cleared some space I laid about me with the wicked blade. The Saxons were caught between my equites, my shield wall and, now that the camp was cleared, by Gwallog and his archers. It was too much and they fled the field. Leaving Garth and the wedge to kill the beleaguered war chief and his oathsworn, we set off to chase the survivors. There would be no mercy. We would not allow any to escape. I needed the land close to my castle to be free from threat and then I could aid my king.

It was late afternoon when we stopped. Our horses could go no further and I do not think any had escaped. When we reached, what had been the camp, we saw that Myrddyn and Garth had destroyed the walls and used them to make a pyre on which the bodies of the Saxons burned. The pall of smoke would have been visible at the coast.

As I rode through my gate the army all cheered and I saw Pol and Hogan proudly clinging to the standard watched over by their uncles. It was a great victory; but it was probably the last victory. Our losses had been light and our booty was great. Even Brother Oswald was delighted as he had gained much food as well as arms and armour.

Even as we were celebrating I sent a despatch rider to the capital to gauge the numbers we would have to fight. The feast was a joyful occasion with my son, brothers and close friends all gathered around the same table. Everyone spoke of their part in the battle and it gave all of us the full picture. Raibeart and Miach had totally destroyed five hundred Saxons in their warband while Garth and his wedge had barely been troubled by the Saxons.

"I do not think they were ready for battle. They had watched us and thought we would not attack. It was a master stroke to turn the tables."

Myrddyn held up a warning finger. "The problem is that only works once. Had they used ditches or three deep lines then it would not have been as easy. Is that not true, my lord?"

"The wizard speaks aright. A single line of men is no obstacle to horsemen and a man with his back to cavalry is walking dead. Keep clear heads for tomorrow we rescue the king."

There was an optimistic mood that night. If we could repeat what we had done then there was hope that we could defeat the Saxons. The troubled dreams I had that night should have warned me that *wyrd* could still play cruel tricks with men and their hopes. When I rose the next day I kept my dreams to myself but Myrddyn came to me. "Your mother came to me again last night."

I knew that it meant trouble. "And it was an ill omen."

"Now you are getting the second sight."

"No my friend but I too had troubled dreams. And what was her warning?"

"That the Saxon tide is rising and you would need all your wits to avoid drowning."

I said, almost to myself, "The water dream again. As much as I appreciate the warning it is vague, is it not? Besides we do fear the Saxons. I would have been more worried if she had warned me of danger closer to home."

We both remembered when there had been a spy in my castle, placed there by the perfidious King Morcant Bulc. "If you do not mind, my lord, I will stay close to you for a while."

I looked at him askance. "I have warriors you know."

"It may need intelligence and not brute strength."

"Well we need not worry for a while. We will take the army to Civitas as soon as the scouts return."

We had had few injuries and wounds and the army was ready to march. Those with wounds and the old were left to guard the castle whilst the rest prepared to march west. Before we could do so the despatch rider rode in whooping his joy. "My lord, the Saxons have fled!"

His high pitched, piping voice carried to the waiting army and they cheered and roared their approval. As we waited for him to close with us Garth said, "They must have heard that we had defeated this warband."

Neither Myrddyn nor I were convinced. "They had good intelligence then but let us wait until the excitable young Corin has reported.

The young rider leapt from his pony and bowed. "My lord as I approached the castle I saw the Saxons fleeing north to towards the river and the sea. They let me in the castle and I told them of our victory. The king sent riders to follow the Saxons and they took ship and headed out to sea. He sent me to bring you and Myrddyn. He wishes a conference with you two and Prince Pasgen."

I ruffled his hair, "Well done but next time a little less shouting eh? The news should come to me first."

He looked crestfallen, "Sorry my lord."

"I am not angry but you need to learn."

Raibeart and Aelle looked relieved. "Should we come with you?"

"No Raibeart. The king would have asked for you. I suspect he is becoming a little paranoid so let us obey his wishes while he appears to be in a more belligerent and approachable humour. Take your armies home for I fear the Saxons may try to take advantage of your absence."

"Very well but just send a messenger or light a beacon if you need us."

As they prepared their troops I turned to Brother Oswald and Garth. "Have Tuanthal patrol to the west and then repair the damage to the ditches and the walls. Let us keep the people here for a while longer in case the departure is a trick of some kind."

Pol and Hogan wished to join us but I refused. "I do not want the king to think we are ganging up on him. I will go as Warlord and you two will continue to train. You did well the last time you fought but that was not the last battle. There will be more."

Myrddyn was still ill at ease as we rode, the next morning, along the familiar road to Civitas Carvetiorum. I could not divine if this was a result of the dream or if there was some other reason. "Do you not think it strange that the Saxons withdrew so quickly?"

I think it something of a miracle that they realised that their attack on Castle Perilous failed but other than that..."

"Aethelric has armies to the north. He could have gone to the wall and sent for reinforcements. King Ywain would never have attacked him and none other has sufficient forces. Why did he take ship?"

That had worried me too. "I do not know and, like you I am worried but no matter how many different ways I look at this I can only see that it is good for us. The Saxons have left Rheged. They had conquered, or controlled half of it, at least, and now it is all in our hands and the land is littered with their dead. And yet..."

"And yet I, too, am uneasy my lord. It is too easy. Aethelric is not the man to give up when he loses a few men. There is more to this than meets the eye but, like you I cannot make it a threat; no matter how much I try."

"Perhaps Prince Pasgen can throw more light on the matter. We know that he was raising an army. Perhaps he raised one and the Saxons thought it was a better army than it is."

"That could be the answer and I will be pleased when I see Prince Pasgen for he alone, remained free whilst we were all besieged."

We could see the effect of the Saxon siege as we neared Civitas Carvetiorum; there were discarded pieces of cart and piles of rotting food. Flies and midges buzzed angrily around. "The siege works look a little, well a little inadequate to me."

"And to me, Myrddyn. Where are the ditches? The walls look free from damage. Was there any fighting here at all?"

"I would say that the Saxons were not good at sieges but those who fought us seemed to know their business."

"I think that Aethelric, or whoever commanded here, knew the king as well as we and decided that he did not need to risk his warriors for the king would soon acquiesce to their demands."

Myrddyn nodded. "That would seem the most likely explanation."

The sentries again looked shamefaced. When this was all over I would need to find time to work with these warriors; they were good warriors but their confidence had been sapped by the indolence of their leader. This unexpected and unlooked for victory had given us a breathing space which I would not waste. Aidan strode over to me. He was another with whom I would need to build bridges. He was a good warrior. I had fought alongside him but it must have hurt when the rest of the army fought off the Saxons and he and his fellows hid in the castle. "The king asked to see you as soon as you arrived, Lord Lann."

As we walked towards the king's chambers we made small talk. "Were there many casualties from the siege? I saw no pyres outside."

He looked at Myrddyn and then me. "No. They seemed content to make sure we could not leave." He half opened his mouth and then shut it then he said, "We saw the smoke from your castle and wondered... I am glad that you have survived."

It seemed a strange thing to say but I smiled and clapped him about the shoulders. "I think I am one of life's survivors. So far the Saxons have not got even close to me but, I thank you for your kind words."

I do not know what I expected when I entered the chamber but I did not expect what I saw. The king and his queen were on a raised dais. There were twenty of his bodyguards around the room. In front of the

125

king was a table with a map but there was no sign of Prince Pasgen. Two guards stood behind the chairs and King Ywain smiled as he waved his hand. "It was good of you to come so swiftly. Pray take a seat we have much to talk about."

As we began to sit the two guards each pulled a sword and held it to our throats. Aidan and another two men disarmed us; as Aidan took my sword he said quietly, "Sorry Warlord."

I was bereft of words. "What is the meaning of this? And where is Prince Pasgen?"

A strangely insane look came over the king's face. "Oh you will see him soon enough. I know of the plot to replace me with my brother. Do not think that I do not know what you have been planning with your brothers, behind my back. Luckily King Aethelric, although he might be a Saxon, watches over me with better care than you did."

I felt the bottom dropping out of my world and I saw Myrddyn's eyes suddenly light with understanding. "You have spoken with King Aethelric? Was that before he fled?"

Ywain laughed and the queen smiled too. "He did not flee. He left for home but he will be back. You see he has promised me that, when I hand you and the wizard over to him, then I can continue to rule Rheged under his protection. There will be peace in Rheged," his face change to a scowl, "but not for you traitor, not for the Wolf Warrior who betrayed his king. You will be the guest of the Saxon king and I do not think that it will a peaceful time for you. Take them away and put them with my brother. Leave the sword there for I think King Aethelric would like to destroy that himself."

As we were taken away I felt a sudden despair. We had won the battle and lost the war. Hogan, my brothers and all my people would be the slaves of the Saxons; all because of one king's paranoia. *Wyrd*!

# Chapter 12

The guards were obviously uncomfortable as they escorted us away from the hall but they did their jobs and, as oathsworn of the king, I expected nothing less. I had gone to the meeting without armour and only carrying Saxon Slayer. It would have been suicide to attempt anything with the six armed warriors who escorted us. I was comforted by the fact that Myrddyn was with me and if anyone had a mind creative enough to escape then it was my wizard. They took us to the old Praetorium, the room that had formerly been Brother Osric's office. I felt angry at this sacrilege until I saw the smirk on Myrddyn's face. It was obvious why they had chosen that room, there was no way out save the one door which was easily guarded. It also had no natural light so that an escape by the window was not feasible either. The guards were gentle with us and one even said, "Sorry, Warlord, as he opened the door to let me in.

When my eyes became accustomed to the dim light I saw Pasgen lying on the floor. He had been assaulted. "Myrddyn see to the Prince."

Even though it was useless, I began to look for a means of escape while Myrddyn saw to the wounds of the king's brother. The room was much as Osric had left it. The three chairs, the table, the map and parchment rack. It was but twelve paces by twelve but it had always been a neat, welcoming room before but now it seemed smaller and felt like the prison cell it had become. "I am sorry they got you as well, Lann. That brother of mine is a snake. He lured me here with a plan to rid the land of the Saxons. I came alone."

"Do no worry Prince Pasgen, we were just as gullible but perhaps we are all gullible for if your brother believes that Aethelric will let him keep this land then he is an even bigger fool that I take him for."

Pasgen snorted, "And when Aethelric returns we will all die. We are caught like rats in a trap."

"We won't die. We will be out of here tonight."

We both looked at Myrddyn. "How…"

He held up his hands. "Let the magician have his moment. We need to wait until midnight when the guards change. I want a big audience. What I need you two to do is move swiftly when I say so and do exactly as I say."

I stared at the four walls. "There is no way out!"

Myrddyn looked at me, calmly, and shook his head. "Who lived in the room for most of his life?"

"Brother Osric of course."

"And do you think he would have stayed here without knowing every inch of the place and having a way to get out?"

Pasgen and I went to each wall and touched, stroked, banged and cursed every wall. "Come on Myrddyn, give us a clue."

"No, my lord, for it will spoil the surprise. Let us just say that this was part of the first building erected by the Romans and they always built to a plan." He tapped his head. "And the plan is here."

Exasperated I slumped to the ground next to Pasgen. "Let us assume the wizard does get us out. What then?"

"My brother thought I would not take the kingdom from him. Now I shall. I will raise an army and return to wrest this land from him. Will you aid me?"

I had dreaded the question. I could feel Myrddyn's eyes boring into me. I shook my head. "This breaks all oaths and now I have a responsibility to my people."

"Your people?"

"Yes Prince Pasgen, my family, the people who farm my land, and the ones who came to join me, the men of Elmet, the Bernicians and the men of Strathclyde. They have been loyal to me. I will not see them die to protect a land whose king has abandoned them. When we escape," I smiled at Myrddyn, "and I believe that he will manage to get us out, then we will go south to the mountain stronghold of Wales. We will settle there for the Saxons know not of it and we will have the chance to create a haven for those who do not wish to live as a Saxon."

Myrddyn looked pleased but Prince Pasgen slumped even lower. "Then we have lost if the Wolf Warrior leaves us."

"Come with us Prince Pasgen."

"No, Warlord. I will try to save the kingdom . If that fails, and I live, then I will join you but first we escape." He looked pointedly at Myrddyn.

"Tell us. We can be of little use if we do not know what we are about."

He sighed. "Come with me then, behind his desk." We moved and sat with our backs to the parchment rack. Myrddyn lowered the candle and pointed to the floor. "This room was the office of the legion that was based here. Every legionary fort had a room which was a strong room in which the soldiers could keep their money. This is a legionary fortress and the room is beneath our feet."

I looked but I could see nothing. "Where?"

"Give me your hand my lord. "He took my fingers and ran them along a groove in the ground.

"But the room is a strong room. It goes nowhere."

"True Prince Pasgen and if it were just the two of you in here then you would not escape but they believe me to be a wizard; a wizard who could fly across the country and walk through the walls of Din Guardi. When we disappear, it will be with a spell and with the guards watching. When the candle goes out, that is your job Prince Pasgen, then I will lift the trapdoor and we will all descend. They will light the candle and see that we have gone. They will bring more guards and more light and search but we will have gone. Then they will leave the cell and search the castle. We will emerge and then we can make our escape at leisure for they will not search again, the place from which the birds already have flown."

I smiled and clapped him on the back. "That will work. But are you sure you can lift it?"

"Brother Osric was old and he liked to keep his wine in the strong room for it was both cool and safe. He wanted to be sure he could open it easily and he had constructed a little piece of wood which when touched opens the door and it closes with a rope. I have been down here before and it takes less than a heartbeat to open, enter and close the door but you must be fast."

Prince Pasgen was caught up in the moment too. "What a trick this will be and how scared will my brother be that we have been spirited away." He looked suddenly serious. "We could kill him tonight."

"I think that once we are found to have flown he will surround himself with guards. No, our priority is to get my sword, our horses and escape."

"Your sword?"

"Yes Myrddyn, as you know that is part of me, part of the dream. If we are to succeed then I need the blade."

Myrddyn nodded, "You are right, Warlord, and we will get it."

"No my friend, I will get it!"

We heard the guards as they approached and Myrddyn nodded to us. He began to incant while dropping something in the candle. It made the candle flame with different colours and the room brightened. Although there was no window in the door there was a large enough gap that the guards would see the strange lights and investigate. At first I had been incredulous that he would want more guards when we escaped but I now saw that it was to add authenticity to the act. "Oh Great God of the earth help us now to free these earthly bonds and to fly away from this cell. Make our enemies die as they try to catch us. Come now and take us! Come now and take us! Come now and take us!" On the third shout Myrddyn threw something which made the room so bright it blinded us and then we snuffed out the candle as Myrddyn opened the door and pushed Pasgen and me down the stairs. As we hit the bottom we saw all light extinguished and we were in the dark.

At first there was silence and then we heard someone shout. "Block the door and get a light."

A few moments' later we saw the faint light around the edge of the trap. We heard Aidan's voice. "What foolery is this? Where are the prisoners? If you have let them escape then your deaths will be painful!"

"We swear! All of us heard the wizard cast the spell. There were bright coloured lights in the room and then a light so bright that it was as though the sun burned and when we entered they were gone. We had two men standing in the doorway. No-one could have got by us. They were spirited away."

"Fools, search it. Take out the desk and the parchment rack. I want the room empty."

That was the most dangerous time and the most frightening as they scraped and scratched the furniture from the room. Then we heard, "Bring in more lights. They are here somewhere. Tap the walls. Find another entrance."

The banging and tapping continued until even Aidan was satisfied. Then we heard the voice of King Ywain. "Where are they?" The panic in his voice was palpable; even underground and hidden from view.

"We have searched majesty but they have been spirited away."

"Idiot! This is a trick of that wizard. Search the castle. I want them found." There was the noise of the men leaving and then all we heard was the heavy breathing of someone waiting. Ywain was still there; he remained for what seemed like an age. Finally all became silent and we were alone.

Myrddyn cautiously opened the trapdoor and peered out. He suddenly leapt up and then we heard him whisper. "It is clear."

Pasgen struggled out and I followed, closing the trapdoor behind me. Myrddyn looked out and then returned. "They are racing around like headless chickens."

I nodded. "You two get the horses and I will get the sword." They both looked as though they would argue. "Just do it. I will not leave without the sword, if I do so then we are all lost." They scurried around the corner. We had assumed that the stables would have been the first place they would have looked and should be a safe place for them to wait. I still had my wolf cloak about me and I put the hood over my head. It would disguise my features and, I hoped, would add to the supernatural element we had fostered. I walked boldly across the courtyard, deliberately not hurrying: to do so would draw attention to me. There were no guards on any of the doors. They were all looking in the recesses and dark places of the castle, not the brightly lit main rooms. As I approached the king's chambers I glimpsed a guard. I had no weapons save my mailed gauntlets I still wore. I moved quietly along the dimly lit corridor. When I was but ten paces from him he turned. I did not know him, he was a young warrior; probably a recruit. The look of terror on his face told me that he saw not an enemy but a wolf spirit, and he hesitated. I raced towards him and punched him on the chin. He fell like a sack of wheat. I removed his sword and entered the chamber. It was empty. I retrieved my sword and felt the rush of power as I slipped it into its scabbard. There were two spears on the wall and I took them both down and plunged them into the back of the king's throne. I wanted him under no illusion; we were now enemies. As I passed the unconscious guard I took his helmet. I slipped down the stairs and out into the courtyard, feeling much more confident now that I was armed. I saw no-one as I approached the stables but I could hear the furore as the garrison searched in vain for the ghosts who had vanished from within a locked and guarded cell.

As I entered the stable a blade slid towards my throat. I glanced at the wielder, "Myrddyn, this is no time to kill your lord."

He laughed. "We have saddled Raven and two others, now how do we get out of here?"

"Leave that to me. Mount your horses and lead mine. Watch from the stable door. When you see the gate open, then ride like the hounds of hell are upon you."

I could see the guards at the gate. They guarded the heavy bar which prevented entry. There was another gate ten paces further on but that one did not have a bar on except in time of war. I gambled that only one would have a bar on it. I lowered my hood and put on the helmet I had taken from the guard. Keeping my face down, I walked over to the two guards. One I recognised. I had fought with him but the other was an unknown surly looking fellow. They both looked at me with an unspoken question on their lips. I watched as they expected me to slow but I did not. I strode up to the surly one and hit him so hard he also dropped to the ground. Saxon Slayer was out in an instant. "Tadgh. We have fought together and you are a comrade but be under no illusions unless you do exactly as I say then you will die. You know I am Warlord and do not use lies."

He bowed and dropped his sword. "I am sorry it has come to this. My lord..."

"This is not the end, Tadgh, things will change. Help me to unbar the gate." We lifted the bar and dropped it to the side. As I swung open the gate I said, "Now open the other," I waved at Myrddyn. The galloping hooves drew the attention of the searchers. Seeing the gate open I said, "Thank you Tadgh," and then struck him on the chin. I mounted Raven. Pasgen and Myrddyn were with me in a heartbeat and we sped off across the drawbridge. I felt the arrows as they ghosted over me but it was dark and they were hurried shots. Had it been Miach then I would have been dead but King Ywain did not value archers as I did.

We rode hard until we were clear of the castle and then I took us south into the wooded land there. We halted. "Prince Pasgen, You are more than welcome to join me and my brothers."

"No, Lord Lann. I will always be your friend and, if I fail, then I will join you, if I am still alive. But I owe it to the memory of my father to try to save Rheged. I will ride to Alavna and raise an army of loyal warriors. "

We clasped arms. "Then take care."

We retraced our path and left the wood. We had gone barely half a mile when we heard the hooves and shout of the pursuit. I grinned in the early dawn half-light. "It seems the king is keen to get us Myrddyn?"

"Then let us lead him a merry dance my lord."

We gave our horses their head. They rode freely but not hard. Both were fine mounts and grain fed; both had been well exercised. I suspected that the garrison horses had not been out of the stables for some time. The road to Castle Perilous had one steep section and then it levelled off. I deliberately slowed at the steep section. We were highlighted against the eastern sky and the riders thought they had us. They kicked hard up the slope, weakening their horses. Once we reached the flat section we kicked on. Our horses were fresh but I knew that the ones behind would be labouring soon. The closest they came was two hundred paces and we could almost see their faces but one look at the frothing mounts told me that they had nothing left to give. They gave up the chase some four miles from my home. We had escaped.

The guards at the gates were surprised to see us so early in the morning. They were even more surprised when I ordered the whole castle to stand to. While Myrddyn went to fetch Brother Oswald, I roused my officers and led them to the main courtyard. "I want every warrior here before me while I address you." I could see the confused looks on their faces. Lord Lann did not go in for public speeches; what was afoot?

When they were gathered I looked at Myrddyn and nodded, he left. I began. "Myrddyn and I have just been held captive by King Ywain. He has surrendered to the Saxons." There was an uproar, which I expected. I saw the look of horror on Pol and Hogan's faces as well as the shock on Garth's face as the enormity of it all sank in. I allowed them a few moments to voice their feelings and then I raised my arms. There was silence. "I am telling you this because some of you may feel more loyalty to King Ywain than to me. If that is so then Myrddyn has opened the gates. You are free to leave, with no hard feelings and to join the king. I suspect he and his Saxon allies will be along soon." No-one moved. "If you stay then know that, once we have secured our survival we will be leaving Rheged to find a new home. I say again either stay or go."

In answer Garth began chanting, "Wolf Warrior!" Soon it was taken up by all. When it was obvious that no one would be leaving I nodded to Myrddyn who closed the gates once more.

"I intend to give our people the same chance of leaving as you and when I leave here that is what I will do. To buy us time we will have to defend the castle against our enemies so that our wives and family can escape. For those who have no families then you will be fighting for our family." I spread my arms. "This family." Again they cheered. "Now back to your posts and officers to me."

I led my officers, Brother Oswald and my family to the main hall. I quickly told them what had befallen us and Prince Pasgen. "It is Wales for us. Tuanthal, I want you to ride to Ridwyn and explain what we are about. He can join us if he wishes. Tell him that we will be leaving within the next few days. It may be that the king does nothing but I suspect that Aethelric will want me dead. Oswald, get the carts ready. We will send the people to my brother. Myrddyn, ride to Raibeart and explain. He will know what to do. My plan is simple, defend the castle until the people are with Raibeart and then fight our way out." There were a couple of dubious looks and I smiled, "Do not worry. Myrddyn and I have a plan to secure our flight. We will need all our warriors if we are to create our own country." I looked them all in the eye and I saw no doubts. "You are my brothers. Let us do this."

I took Brother Oswald with me to speak with my people. I told them the same but not the country. "I know you are leaving your homes and you can stay here with my blessing but your masters will be the Saxons. If you wish to join me then go to your homes and bring what you need. Be back here by sunset and then we will escort you to safety." I could see heated debate and many tears. I knew from my own parents how hard it must be to leave your home and all that you had built up to leave for the unknown. My brothers and I had no choice, but as we trudge up the hill I realised that their choice was equally stark.

When we walked back to the castle I could see that Brother Oswald was worried. "We may not have enough carts and wagons my lord. I have done my best to acquire horses and ..."

"Do not worry. The people can walk. It is but fifteen miles to Raibeart's domain. Tuanthal and his men will act as escorts and Raibeart will bring his army. We just need them away by dark." I put my arm on his shoulder. "Bring all your papers Oswald. We need Osric's account to be there for my great grandchildren."

We all had a busy day for even I needed to collect together the things I would be taking. Although I would not be leaving until there was no time left, I sent all that was precious to Hogan and me with the carts. By the time sunset had arrived I felt quite touched by the loyalty of my people. All of them had opted to leave with us and when Ridwyn came it was with all of his Bernicians and the men of Strathclyde. Ridwyn summed up the attitude of the warriors. "We know that wherever you are my lord, the Saxons will get their arses kicked and we like kicking Saxon arses after what they have done to our people. Count us in."

We had no time to waste and Brother Oswald quickly organised the carts and the villagers. With Tuanthal's horsemen as guards, they set off. The priest was right, there were not enough wagons but when Myrddyn returned it was with Raibeart's horsemen and the carts Raibeart could spare. Soon the only people left in the castle were warriors.

Leaving only a skeleton force to guard the walls I sent all the men to their beds. The next few days would need minds and bodies that were alert and I was sure that the Saxons could not reach us until then. I suspected that Aethelric had merely gone north of the estuary and would have returned to Civitas when King Ywain had told him of his loss. We would have the walls filled the next day and would prepare our surprises then.

As soon as we awoke I set the men to gathering as much material that would burn as possible. As soon as we had enough I began to get the men to pack the stables, the buildings, and the drawbridge with every piece of it. Every piece of wood, old wool, bark and chippings we could get hold of, we used. By noon we had just finished and not before time. The Saxons arrived from the poorly defended western side, the side protected by the king. It mattered not, we were going to give the Saxons a painful and deadly surprise.

They tore through the walls of the enclosure which had protected the villagers and roared towards the walls of the castle. Every archer and slinger was on that wall and they loosed and released with impunity. The Saxons died in their hundreds as they relentlessly advanced towards the wall. Once they reached the ditch, where they protected themselves with their shields, I withdrew the archers and the slingers and replaced them with my shield wall warriors. The archers and slinger left the castle by the southern gate and Miach led them south to the ambush point on the road to Raibeart's castle. The Saxons had learned about siege work and they began to dig under the foundations of the wall. I was more than happy for that event as we were able to kill even more by dropping rocks and boiling water upon them. Our javelins killed the reinforcements they sent and soon they were weakening. As I had expected the wall began to crumble and I withdrew all the men from the walls.

Myrddyn stood by me and he led half of the warriors, along with a reluctant and complaining Pol and Hogan out of the castle by the southern gate. Garth, Ridwyn and I now had but one hundred and fifty warriors to face the onslaught from thousands of Saxons. It seemed an impossible task. I sent the five despatch riders we had retained to fire the traps we had laid on the northern and western walls as well as the drawbridge. As they came back and the flames began to rise, I felt sad for I had built the castle to what it was from a shell and now I was making it a shell again so that the Saxons would not enjoy the fruits of my labour.

As the boys ran to join Myrddyn I formed my shield wall. We had no wolf banner but they knew whom they faced. It was a cornered Wolf

Warrior and they sensed victory. They made our job easier. As they poured over the walls and through the collapsed wall they had no order and ran at a wall of shield and steel with made them a bloody sea of bodies. They were brave and they were reckless. Still they came on and we gave way, steadily. That encouraged them and made them think that they were winning. We withdrew towards the stables and the warrior hall. The other three walls and the rest of the buildings were now burning furiously which slowed their advance and killed many.

"Ridwyn! Now!"

Ridwyn roared, "Bernicia and Strathclyde, to me!"

The warriors he commanded suddenly left the flanks of the shield wall and ran into the stables. It confused their opponents. My Rheged men spread out and stepped back. There were now but eighty of us but our flanks were secured by burning buildings. We edged slowly back, Saxon Slayer killing all who came within its deadly arc. Garth was once more by my side and he hewed men as a man might hew trees. The Saxons had not formed a shield wall and their best warriors were not together; mine were. When I felt the stables behind me I shouted, "Aedh! Now!" The young despatch rider was waiting inside the stables for just such a command.

I turned to Garth and grinned. "Let us put the shits up these Saxons eh? Charge!"

We ran at the Saxons. My eighty men punched and stabbed like maniacs until a barrier of bodies lay before us. Garth shouted, "Back! Now!" And then there was just Garth and me.

I stepped forwards." The Wolf Warrior will disappear but one day he will return and all of you will die." Aedh had timed it well and, as I stepped into the stables, the whole building erupted into flames. I quickly headed for the secret passage we had built all those years before. The light from the fire aided me but the smoke was thicker than I had expected and I found it difficult to see and breathe. I kept my hand on the wall to my left so that I knew where I was and soon I smelled the fresher air of the outside. Willing hands pulled me clear and then my men began to throw wood into the tunnel and that too was fired. We hurried down the track towards safety before the Saxons realised what had occurred.

The afternoon was almost gone; the sun was beginning to settle in the west although the day was so grey it was hard to tell if it was day or night. We were tired but we were also elated. We had taken few casualties and killed many Saxons but more importantly we had destroyed the castle and confounded them. They would wonder where the army had gone. Of course, as soon as they tracked us the next day they would find our trail but that mattered not, we had planned for their pursuit. Even now Raibeart was building serious defences to deter the Saxons and Miach had laid traps and an ambush for when we passed.

It was dark when we heard Miach say, "Now if you were Saxons you would be dead!"

He came from the woods and clasped my arm. "I am glad that you escaped my lord."

"Me too. Remember Miach, no heroics. Slow them down and make sure that you and your men all escape. We will need you and your archers where we are going."

"Do not worry my lord it will be Saxons who will die and not my boys."

Raibeart and Freja were waiting for me when we reached their sanctuary. Hogan threw his arms around me and said nothing. "We sent your people down to Wide Water and Aelle."

"Good. And your people?"

Raibeart looked at Freja, "We are not certain, and neither is Aelle. We will see."

I nodded. I could not make my brothers leave and why should they? This was a beautiful and verdant land which provided a good living for all of them. We were all leaders now of our own tribes and clans. I could no longer make those decisions for my brothers as I had all those years ago "Miach will warn us when they come. Hopefully we will break them."

My men marched behind me as we entered the first of three wooden walls to the place Raibeart had made for us. There was food and there was ale and we all ate and drank gratefully. We had survived all that the Saxons had thrown at us and we had escaped Aethelric's trap. That in itself was a victory.

# Chapter 13

When I awoke the next morning I was stiff. I had fought for three hours the previous day and walked fifteen miles. I was no longer a youth and my age was showing. War was a young man's game. Miach rode in with his archers at midmorning. He slid from his horse, looking tired. "They came at full tilt this morning and my lads made them pay. We only stopped because we had empty quivers." He pointed behind him. "They are two miles up the road."

"Good. Take your archers and get some sleep." I pointed to Raibeart's archers. We have others who are keen to emulate your exploits."

The ditches Raibeart had dug were lined with stakes. The wooden walls would merely slow them up but we intended to retreat slowly until we reached the real defences eight hundred paces down the road. By then we hoped to have thinned their warriors out with arrows. Once they reached the last defence it would be the shield wall that would do its worst. Pol and Hogan made sure that they were by me but this day I would not be in the shield wall; that honour would go to Raibeart's men. My warriors were already forming up before the last defence with Garth and my best warriors at their centre. I was the bait to draw them on. Raibeart had chosen well for the site of his defences. There was a long lake protecting our right flank and steep slopes to our left. The huge mountain, Halvelyn, which towered over us to our left would stop any warrior from outflanking us. They had but one choice. Attack us frontally or go home. Both choices suited me and my small army; we would hold them in the gap. Osric had told me of some ancient Greeks who had done the same when three hundred held up thousands. I was not sure I believed him but he had never lied to me. Today I would find out the truth.

Aethelric, or whoever led these warriors had learned their lesson and it was a mailed wedge which came up the road. Our arrows were less effective but they had managed to slow down the Saxons, weighing down their shields and dealing a fatal lesson to any who did not hold his shield high enough. They took many casualties as they hacked through the wooden wall and as soon as they were through Garth's wedge struck them and hurled them backwards into the body filled ditch. We then retreated behind the next wall. The results were the same. The Saxons broke through but at a high cost and then there was just one wooden wall before the real fortification. As they stepped over their dead to face the combined forces of Raibeart and me they must have thought that victory was within their evil grasp. They dressed their lines and they put their best, most magnificently armed men in the front rank. I saw Aethelric at the rear on a horse. It was a white horse and looked remarkably like King Ywain's. That image made me both sad and angry at the same time.

A huge warrior dressed in mail from head to toe with a helmet like mine stepped to the fore. He had a Frankish axe, which could be used in one hand. His shield had the emblem of a raven upon it. He roared in Saxon. "I challenge the Wolf Warrior to face me, Bjorn the champion of King Aethelric. I will send him to join King Urien and the other Rheged cowards."

My men became angry at the insult to their king and their officers had to restrain them.

He repeated his challenge and added, "If he does not come forwards then he is a coward who hides in burning buildings and pretends he has magical power! He is a nithing!"

I began to step forwards and Raibeart grabbed my arm. "Are you a fool, brother? Our plan has almost succeeded. You do not need to fight him."

I smiled at Raibeart, "If I kill him then I rip the heart from our enemy and our plan will succeed even more."

"But you might die!"

"I could die in battle it is true but not today and not against him." I turned and pointed to the rear. "If this was meant to go badly then Myrddyn would be here stopping me. Remember, he sees the future." I drew Saxon Slayer and shouted, "All Saxons speak loudly and in my experience they die loudly; squealing like stuck pigs. Prepare to die, Bjorn the Blowhard." I could not see his expression because of his mask but I knew I had angered him. I turned to my men and surreptitiously drew my dagger and gripped it in my left hand, behind my shield. "Saxon Slayer will claim another Saxon Champion!" The roar that went up was so loud that I saw Aethelric's horse rear.

I stepped forwards. This was not going to be an exhibition. This was a fight to the death and I intended it to be his death. He was slightly taller than me and I am a big man. He would have the height advantage but I would have the speed. He was counting on his axe to destroy my defence but my shield was covered in metal. Hogan had hammered five new nails in that morning; they stood proud of the shield. He had never struck a shield like mine and it gave me an advantage. I did not wait for him to attack, I wanted him angry and I feinted with my sword and, as he raised his shield, I punched him in the mouth with mine. I heard a crunch as I broke some of his teeth and saw him spitting teeth and blood out as he stepped backwards with the blow. Some of the nails had cut into his chin below his mask. That made him angry. He swung his axe overhand at my shield. It was a powerful blow and made my arm numb when it struck but it did not penetrate the shield. Instead it held it there as he struggled to pull it free. He held his shield to protect himself and I stabbed Saxon Slayer down into his foot. He roared in agony and I saw the blood spurt. It would not slow him down but it would anger him. As he stepped back on to his good foot I spun around and stabbed my dagger into the small of his back. It pierced the rings and came out red. Before he could react, I was facing him again.

"You are not a warrior, you are Loge the trickster and I will kill you for I am a true warrior and champion." A real warrior does not talk when fighting and I stabbed forwards with Saxon Slayer. I had a helmet the same as he had but I had a mail coif beneath it. He did not. The tip entered his throat and came out at the rear. Even behind his mask I could see his eyes widen in shock and then, as I withdrew the blade life left them and he died. I quickly stepped back to our lines.

There was a shocked silence and then the Saxons hurled themselves forwards. At the same time Ridwyn launched the attack of the Bernicians and the men of Strathclyde. They had been waiting in a dell, hidden by bushes. The horsemen of Tuanthal followed them. The last reserves I had streamed down the slope into the unprotected flank of the Saxons. They were caught between two bands of angry warriors and the lake. The battle was bloody but brief. The Saxons outnumbered us but they could not bring all their men into action. Inevitably they broke. When I saw Aethelric flee on his white horse I knew we had won. Tuanthal and the horsemen pursued the Saxons all the way back to Castle Perilous. It was said that the carrion crows, foxes and wolves were bigger that year than anyone had ever seen. Saxon meat suited them.

Myrddyn and the other healers worked for the rest of the day. Our warriors were more valuable than gold and we needed all of them. I took the opportunity of taking off my armour and taking a bath in the cold lake. I knew that I would no longer be able to enjoy the hot baths of Civitas Carvetiorum but that was a small price to pay for freedom. I felt much better as Hogan and Pol helped to dress me and strap on a freshly sharpened Saxon Slayer. Raibeart and Aelle awaited us in their hall.

The smell of hot food wafted towards me as I entered the warrior hall which still looked new. My captains were there although Tuanthal was busy chasing Saxons still. I sat next to Raibeart and Aelle. I could tell from the worried looks on their faces that they were wary of speaking their minds.

"Whatever decision you two have arrived at will be fine with me."

Aelle spoke, "We feel that we are being disloyal but we wish to stay here in the land of the lakes. Raibeart and his people have been displaced once already. They feel secure and happy here."

I chewed on some late lamb and then spoke, "I understand but I fear that the Saxons will still come for you and that will be my fault. I am the one who angered them and they will want revenge."

Raibeart spread his arms towards the lake outside. "The lake and the mountain of Halvelyn will protect us. I do not doubt it will be a hard fight to defend the land but it is a land worth fighting for."

"Then I wish you well. Know that when we reach Wales and settle I will send a message so that you could join me when the time is right." I gestured for Myrddyn and Brother Oswald to join us. They had both been eating at a discreet distance and they hurried over. "My brothers will remain here. Go to my people and begin to load them on the carts and wagons. When Tuanthal; returns we will head south. It will probably be tomorrow."

"So soon?" I could see that neither of them expected me to leave so quickly.

"Firstly we are a drain on your supplies and hospitality and secondly the Saxons will return and I want a head start. It is a long way to Wales."

Myrddyn nodded. "By my estimate it is over one hundred and twenty miles."

Aelle gave him a bemused look. "I know you walked from Wales when you arrived but did you measure it?"

"No, my lord. The Romans kept excellent records and they noted the distance between places. Brother Osric and I worked it out when this was first mentioned."

Aelle nodded, "I miss the old priest."

"As do we all and Rheged would not be in this state had he lived."

"I estimate, my lord, that it will take us between eight and nine days to cover the distance."

Again Aelle looked impressed. "Explain the accuracy of that statement."

"The Roman soldiers marched between fifteen and twenty miles a day. We have wagons and will be using a road. I estimate a minimum of fifteen miles a day but the length of the journey means that we will do fewer miles each day. Eight days is the minimum but nine is what I expect. Even if it is ten days that will not be a problem as we have sufficient supplies for twelve day's."

"You have been planning this for some time then."

"Since Brother Osric first suggested it."

Tuanthal reached us before dark. He had only lost two warriors and one of those returned after dark having become lost. "We chased them all the way back to Civitas. There they entered freely. I fear you are right, Lord Lann, and Civitas Carvetiorum is now a Saxon hall despite the fact that the king still lives."

"Aye well we did all we could. Get your men fed and rest your horses. Tomorrow we begin our journey south."

Although my army went to Wide Water immediately I stayed with my brothers as I was reluctant to part. I did not know when I would ever see them again. Thus it came about that I saw King Ywain again. He was at the head of a small army. He rode to within three hundred paces of our lines. He had too much respect for our bowmen to close any closer but he would have been safe. None of us would kill the King of Rheged. He had with him his mounted bodyguards and I recognised Tadgh. The king looked angry even at that distance. He did not address me or my brothers even though we stood on top of the walls instead he spoke to our men.

"Men of Rheged! You have been led astray by evil men and you have rebelled against your king. I forgive you and ask you to take up arms and kill the brothers called the Wolf Brethren for they are traitors. Do so and Rheged will have peace once more!"

There was a brief moment of silence and then two things happened, Ridwyn, Garth and my officers burst out laughing and the warriors began jeering and catcalling the king. I saw one archer notch an arrow and I yelled. "Silence! Hold that arrow!"

The men all fell silent. The king spoke again and sounded like a petulant child. "Do not listen to him. He is a traitor."

142

A wag from Raibeart's army yelled out. "We heard you thought he was a ghost who spirited himself out of your castle!"

The laughter erupted from my men. I waited until it had subsided and then answered. "King Ywain you do not know our men and I believe you do not know your own. You have sided with Rheged's enemies. You have sided with your father's enemies. If we wished you dead then you would be." I nodded at Raibeart who had an arrow notched. The arrow landed between his horse's forelegs. The horse reared in shock and Ywain struggled to control it. "If we were traitors and wished to take your land then your head would be on a spear and your men, at least, know it." His men were shifting uncomfortably on their horses. I was Warlord and I had led them for years. They knew my words were true but they had sworn an oath to King Ywain of Rheged and they were men of their word.

The red faced king pointed at us. "When Aethelric comes for you I will enjoy watching you being roasted on a fire. Traitors!" He turned and galloped away.

Aelle shook his head sadly. "I knew he had fallen far but until I saw and heard him I could not believe how far. You are right to do as you do."

I nodded sadly. As I was leaving these warriors I said, "Farewell men of Rheged. It has been my privilege to lead you into battle. I will see you all in the Otherworld!"

Their cheers rang in my ears as I led Pol and Hogan up the slopes of Halvelyn towards Wide Water. We could have travelled down the valley and then up the lake but I had a notion to look on the whole of Rheged one last time from the top of the highest mountain in the land. The trail was clear and zig zagged up the sides. Our horses were sure footed and Wolf ran ahead showing us the way. When we reached the top and looked north we could see all the way to Strathclyde. I nodded to my two companions. "Look on Rheged. It was the last kingdom to stand against the Saxons and now it is gone. I shall never look on it again." We stood next to our horses, each lost in our thoughts. I was no longer a young man and I had spent most of my adult life fighting for Rheged against the Saxons. I had lost my parents and my family save for Hogan. I had lost dear friends like Brother Osric, Riderch, Gildas and Angus but that part of my life was over and, as I mounted Raven and turned my back on Rheged, I looked forward to my new life.

We rode in silence down the mountain, through the forests to the two pretty lakes surrounded my small hamlets and settlements; clear evidence of the prosperity of this land. As we turned on to the road to Wide Water I wondered how long it would last.

# Part Two

# The road to Wales

## Chapter 14

Thanks to Raibeart and Aelle we had enough carts and wagons to carry the women and children as well as our supplies. Tuanthal and his horsemen rode ahead of us while Miach and his mounted archers watched our flanks. The warriors marched closely in a protective circle around the whole caravan. Almost as soon as we left Wide Water and the land of the lakes we found the land to be gentle and undulating; drifting away south westwards towards the sea. It was wide open country with few hills of any note and the Roman Road ploughed a straight furrow south. Although few people had used it for a hundred years or more it was a well made road and we managed twenty one miles that first day. Myrddyn was full of himself as he showed us the milestones which enabled him to accurately measure our progress. At the end of that first day we could still see the hills and mountains of Aelle's domain but it was like looking at a foreign land now.

My warriors did not suffer at all having marched across the country before but the farmers had problems with their feet. While my men threw up a defensive wall and rough ditch Myrddyn and Brother Oswald doled out the salve they had made for the sore and blistered feet. As we had many women with us we ate well and they busied themselves organising each other and their children to create the meal. It was almost celebratory as we tucked into that most rare of luxuries whilst campaigning, a hot meal. Tuanthal's scouts had seen little human occupation in the land we would cover in the next part of the journey and that boded well. We did not want to have to fight our way south, especially as the Saxons could pursue us at any time.

"If it continues like this my lord it will be like Yule, without the snow!"

145

We laughed at Garth but Myrddyn warned, "So far it has been dry and it has been warm; when the weather changes then we shall see. We have food and we are well fed at the moment but if we run out then that may change things and we do not know of the people who lie ahead. When I came north all those years ago I did not use this road as I was trying to avoid attention. Let us not count any chickens just yet."

"This pessimism is not like you Myrddyn."

"Rather than pessimism, call it caution. I believe we will get to Wales and that we will not suffer too much but we both know that *wyrd* has a way of trickling us or perhaps it is Loge."

"Perhaps you are right but I will sleep easier tonight than I thought I would."

For the next four days all went well and we travelled through the flattest land I have ever seen. Thin tendrils of smoke in the distance bespoke human habitation but we did not come close to any signs of people close by. The scouts reported a river some fifteen miles ahead with a bridge and an encampment or settlement of some description nearby. When Myrddyn had done his reconnaissance all those years before, he had avoided the roads and taken the direct route to his island. I regretted that now. We could have planned better had we had a detailed map of the land through which we travelled.

"There are two large rivers my lord and they are quite close together. The second is the last obstacle before we reach Wales. I would suspect that this will be where we may find opposition for there is an old Roman fortress called Deva and it guards the second river crossing. We must go carefully." Myrddyn knew the general geography of the land while the writings of Osric told him what the Romans had built.

I pondered the problem. I did not think that we would find superior numbers but I wanted to lose no-more men. If I could negotiate a peaceful solution, then that would save lives and I wanted no more deaths. "Garth, I will leave you in charge tomorrow. Take your time heading south. I will go with Myrddyn, Tuanthal and ten of his men to meet with the people of the bridge and see if we can negotiate a passage."

They nodded and then a wee small voice piped up, "And Pol and I as well father?"

My officers fell about laughing as I replied. "Of course, for you are my squire are you not?"

The road to the bridge was a blessing for the land to the sides was boggy and marshy. I could see why it had been shunned by the tribes of the area. Tuanthal pointed to the smoke emanating from the low-lying ground ahead. "They have a wooden stockade and, perhaps ten huts."

"Is there a warrior hall?"

"We did not see one but we did not wish to give ourselves away. Sorry, my lord."

I smiled, "Not to worry. You did the right thing. This is better. Of course what we do not know is are they Saxons or are they related to us? We shall find out soon enough." I turned to Pol and Hogan. "You two keep quiet and watch. Use your ears. These are strangers and they may be friendly or they may not be. We shall need all of our wits about us this day."

The settlement was on the northern side of the Roman Bridge. They kept a watch and as soon as we were seen the gates were slammed shut.

"Well that means they are unfriendly."

"Not necessarily Tuanthal. We are armed men and we do look dangerous. I know we are used to our martial appearance but these folk may not be. Let us keep an open mind."

I had toyed with the idea of discarding the mail but it was too much of a risk. As we rode towards the wooden walls my mind was already assessing how we would take it should the need arise. I could capture it with five archers and twelve warriors. It was no obstacle but something in the back of my mind made me more cautious. We halted fifty paces from the walls. It was within bowshot but we all carried a shield, Myrddyn included. At the first sign of aggression we would raise our shields.

I waited patiently for there was no-one in sight. Suddenly a disembodied voice spoke and I relaxed a little. It was not Saxon. Nor was it my own language. It was related to it and I understood many of the words but not all. Myrddyn saw my frown and said, "I understand him, my lord. He asks what we want for they are poor and have nothing worth stealing."

"Tell him we are not thieves but warriors from the north, Lord Lann and his people. All that we wish is to cross the bridge in peace."

Myrddyn shouted my words and a handful of people stood on the wood wall above the gate. When he spoke I listened carefully for I wished to answer.

"Warriors from the north this bridge and the river is our livelihood. It will cost you one copper piece for each of you."

Tuanthal murmured, "Robbing bastard. Let me and my men take them my lord and we will get through for nothing."

I held up my hand, "Peace Tuanthal. Let me negotiate." I raised my voice so that they could all hear. "We are not the whole of my people." I pointed north. "They will be arriving soon and there will be many of them. One copper piece for each person would be too expensive." I reached into my bag and drew out a King Urien silver piece. I held it between my fingers. "This is silver. I will pay you ten of these to allow all of us to cross and my people will buy any spare supplies you have."

My words caused a debate and I could see much gesticulation and raised voices although I could not hear the words clearly. "Come closer Lord Lann but come alone."

"I will bring my counsellor for he speaks your words. I want no misunderstandings." I rode forwards followed by Myrddyn. I was not stupid enough to put myself in harm's way. As I passed Tuanthal I said quietly, "Watch for treachery but I can see no weapons yet."

By the time we reached the gates it had opened and half a dozen villagers were standing there armed with the most rudimentary of weapons. There was one sword, three axes and a couple of spears. Not one of the weapons could harm any of us. Their attire was more basic than that of my people. The homespun wool was of poor quality and shabbily made. Two of the men wore crude leather jerkins. This was not a rich community.

"I am Gareth, the headman of this place, it is called Witherspool." I was now close enough to the river to see why it had been named; there was a small eddy of water which spiralled below the bridge. The bridge, I was pleased to see, was Roman built. "Let me see the coin."

I threw it to him and he examined it closely, tasting it, biting it, and then he passed it to the others. They seemed impressed. "You said twenty of these?"

"I said ten."

"Twenty would be better."

"True but you will only get ten."

He pouted a little. "Then you will not pass."

"Ah," I smiled the smile my men called the wolf smile and the one which terrified my enemies. I could never understand why. I reached

148

around and brought out my helmet which I donned. "If I had a mind, Gareth of Witherspool, I could ride through your village alone and slay every man woman and child within. That is not my intention but I will not be robbed."

He vainly held up his sword. "We will stop you Lord Lann!"

In one sudden and swift movement I drew Saxon Slayer and sliced though his blade. The effect was instantaneous. The others dropped their weapons and started to run back. "Stop! I have not finished." I slid my sword back into its scabbard and removed my helmet. "You are a brave man Gareth. That could have been your head." I counted out ten coins. "Keep that first coin I gave to you for your courage. Here are the ten I promised. When my people have crossed the bridge then they will buy any spare supplies you wish to sell. Is that fair?"

A faint smile appeared on his relieved face as he took the coins. "It is fair, Lord Lann." He hesitated and then pointed at my cloak. "Would I be correct in saying that you are the Wolf Warrior. The one the legends say kills Saxon kings and can fly with his wizard."

I saw Myrddyn's hand cover his smile. "I am the Wolf Warrior and I have killed many Saxons."

"Then thank you my lord for sparing this fool's life." They opened the gates fully and I waved Tuanthal and the others forwards.

Myrddyn chuckled, "That story is growing. Soon you will be a dragon slayer."

We rode through the small hamlet and it was pitifully poor. The pigs and goats wandered around their own filth inside and the children that we saw looked thin and emaciated. It was such a contrast to my people who would be coming through later. We rode through and crossed the bridge. Tuanthal and his men began to lay out the camp. I left the horses with Pol and Hogan and walked back to speak with Gareth; I took Myrddyn with me. The headman walked eagerly towards us. He had almost died and now was the richest man in the town. I suspected that most of the silver would find its way into his hands eventually.

"Is there anything else I can do for Lord Lann?"

"We are heading for Deva and then Wales."

His face fell. "My lord, the Welsh tribes are a wild and violent people. They eat babies!"

Myrddyn snorted and I smiled. "It does not matter we will go there. Now there may be more people following us. You will know they are with me for they will wear the wolf skin. They are to be allowed across without charge." I saw the indignation on his face and I held up my hand. "I will pay ten silver pieces for the crossing. You have my word." Gareth nodded; satisfied that he would be rewarded. "I will reward you and your settlement for good service. I will provide better arms… when you earn them. Now tell me about Deva."

"There is a violent warband there my lord. They are Hibernians and we all know what mad bastards they are." I nodded my agreement. "They do not charge to cross their bridge. They kill any who come." He suddenly looked apologetic. "If you travelled upstream you could have crossed this river at a ford."

I had already worked that out. The whirlpool and the narrowness of the river suggested that it was not the Tinea or the Dunum. "I do not mind. It is worth the ten pieces of silver to have a friend. "I looked at him. "You are my friend, aren't you?"

He dropped to his knees and kissed my hand. "Oh yes my lord. Had I known it was you I would not have been so foolish!"

I lifted him up. "How many Hibernians are there?"

"Many my lord, many more than your ten men and two boys!"

I almost laughed. He had no concept of my army yet. When they arrived he would understand. "Good. I am pleased."

Just then Aedh galloped up to me. "My lord, Captain Garth is half a mile up the road."

"Good, tell him to cross the bridge and we camp on the other side of the river."

I amused myself by standing next to the headman as first the horsemen, then the archers followed by the wagons and carts and finally the warriors crossed through the hamlet and over the bridge. Gareth looked over at me with a wry smile on his face. "You could have slaughtered us all and not even noticed it. Why did you pay?"

"Because my land was stolen from me by violent Saxons; I will fight for my people but I will not take from someone who has so little."

He knelt again. "I know it means little to you my lord, but I pledge allegiance for my people. We will be your oathsworn."

I raised him up. "Good and I will send men, when we are settled to make your town secure and better protected for you are important to me."

As we walked across the bridge Myrddyn said, "That was well done my lord. That was worthy of King Urien."

"That, Myrddyn, is the most complimentary thing you have ever said to me."

After we had eaten I gathered the counsel around me. I had gradually collected them as we rode south. There was Myrddyn, of course and brother Oswald, as well as my officers but there was also a Bernician a warrior of Strathclyde and two men from the villagers. I wanted them all to have a say in what we did.

"We will wait here and rest for two days. This is a safe place and it is easily defended. Some of our people need recovery time and we can hunt and fish for supplies. Gareth and his people will sell us surplus supplies although I fear that they will be poor quality. Brother Oswald, find a good Saxon sword and a shield and helm and give them to him. They have sworn allegiance. We will leave twenty men here and take the rest to Deva. The Hibernians are there and they will be slightly more belligerent." Even Brother Oswald laughed at that. "The gods have been kind to us." Brother Oswald's face turned sour at that but we cannot expect it to last. Harder times will come. Autumn will be upon us soon and we will have no crops to reap. The Saxons will be reaping our work in Rheged. We will have to tighten our belts but we can do this. We are but a few days away from our new home. Now is not the time to weaken." Their cheers told me that they were in good spirits and I went to sleep happier than I had been for some time.

I took all of my men, apart from the twenty guards, as I hoped to avoid conflict. A show of strength might make the Irish capitulate but Garth was not hopeful. "The Irish are all mad buggers my lord and will as soon fight to the death as talk."

Myrddyn was more positive. "They are also very superstitious. Let us see if we can bewitch them eh?" The old Roman fort was built right next to the river and controlled the bridge. I suspected there might be a crossing upstream and I sent my scouts to find it. We unfurled my Wolf Standard and the Dragon Standard to impress these warriors, whom Myrddyn had assured us, were superstitious.

The ditch around the walls had rubbish in it and the sides had begun to crumble. It had ed. So far as we could see there were no traps in the bottom. The walls were manned before we reached the gate but there did not appear to be an overwhelming number of men. Tuanthal and his men rode the perimeter and estimated that there were less than two hundred of them. We outnumbered them but tackling a Roman Fort, no matter how much it had decayed and fallen into disrepair, was no easy matter.

As with Witherspool we approached to two hundred paces. My archers and warriors spread out behind me, their arms gleaming in the sunlight. Myrddyn spoke Hibernian if we needed it and he was standing next to me. I did not wait for them to speak first, instead I took the initiative.

"I am Lord Lann, Warlord of Rheged, and I ask permission to cross this bridge over the Dee."

My answer came from two warriors who put their rears over the wall and shat in the ditch. "Miach!"

"With pleasure my lord." Four arrows flew and each arrow punctured each one of the four buttocks on show. The men dropped back within the walls and the rest ducked below the parapets.

"As you can see, we are able to be quite persuasive."

A tall red headed warrior appeared on the gatehouse and shouted, "Kiss my fucking arse. You want to get across the bridge then fight for it."

"I suspect this may be a bit bloody my lord!"

"Surround the fort and begin to dig a ditch. They may have bows so keep it more than two hundred paces from their walls." The problem the Hibernians had was that they could not man every part of the wall. We could. I summoned Miach. "As soon as it is dark then begin to loose fire arrows into the fort. It won't hurt them but it will annoy them. "I gestured Ridwyn over, "Get your Strathclyde boys to make a few hammers. I don't think they will have met them and it will worry them more than the fire. Garth, Take fifty men and begin to dig beneath their walls at the corner."

Myrddyn said, "I will join Miach. I have a few surprises for them."

We soon had a better ditch than they did protecting us and we had tents erected. The arrows of Miach and Myrddyn surprised even me. They flamed in blues, reds and yellows as they soared over the walls. They looked magical although I knew it was a wizard's trick. The hammers of the men from the north soon hammered at the gates of the fort. The wood was old and fist sized holes began to appear. I wondered at the panic within as they took the punishment, unable to fight back. Garth and his men were hidden in the shadows and worked silently; removing earth from the base. Apart from the archers and Garth's fifty

152

men who were digging, the rest of the army slept comfortably. The Hibernians did not.

When dawn broke we could see fires burning in the fort and the gate looked to have been weakened. Garth and his men had returned before dawn satisfied that the corner closest to us had been weakened sufficiently to succumb to an attack. I rode to the gates again. "Do you allow us crossing?" I saw the archer and raised my shield so that it took the missile. The Hibernian archer plunged over the side with four arrows in him. The rest disappeared from view.

I turned to Garth. "They want to do it the hard way. Attack!"

The slingers moved forwards followed by the shield wall and then the ranks of archers. Tuanthal took his horsemen to the far end of the fort and I knew that there would be indecision amongst the Hibernian leaders. Where would we attack? Which was the feint? The slingers cleared the walls and then retreated behind the archers. The warriors reached the wall without losing a single man. The archers picked off every face they saw. Garth and his men began to tear rocks from the bottom of the wall with the picks that they carried. The work of the previous night was being rewarded. The Hibernians realised what they were doing but were powerless to intervene. The archers and slinger slaughtered any who showed themselves on the walls. Suddenly, with a crack, the corner collapsed and we could see inside the fort. If the Irish expected my men to make a suicidal charge they were wrong. My archers loosed volley after volley to clear the ground just inside the corner. When Garth was satisfied I heard him yell, "Charge!" and two hundred mailed warriors rushed over the debris and into the fort. I led the rest of the warriors towards the gate and, by the time we had reached it, it was open and my men were slaughtering the brave but badly led Hibernians who died to a man. We now had our own stronghold. We controlled the road into Wales.

Garth brought me the tally of dead and it was remarkably light. None of the defenders had survived. We could tell from the poor quality of their weapons that they had not been particularly successful as brigands. They had been fortunate to happen upon a deserted Roman fort and a bridge. I left Myrddyn healing the wounded and Garth stripping and clearing the dead. My people could now camp within sight of the fort. I took Pol and Hogan back to the rest of my people.

Gareth was obviously in awe of the Hibernians and when just three of us returned he assumed that the rest had died. "I am sorry you have lost your army my lord."

I laughed, "I can see that you know little of war my friend. The Hibernians are no more and I will have men in the fort from now on. Should you need aid then send there to the captain." He nodded with a look of amazement which was comical. "Brother Oswald, start our people to the fort. Pol will lead you."

"Yes my lord."

"Tell me Gareth do you have any dealings with the Saxons?"

"No, my lord. They are rumoured to be to the east but so far we have not had any dealings with them."

"If you hear of them then send a message to Deva and you will be rewarded."

The headman looked at me, almost shyly, "My lord, are you rich?"

I shook my head. "No Gareth but I use what gold I have for my people. What is a leader without his people eh?" I leaned forwards. "Perhaps you should think on that headman." The caravan was slowly winding down the road towards Deva and I took my leave. "Thank you for your hospitality and pray that the Saxons do not come for they are a cruel people."

We reached the fort just after dark. There was hot food ready as the Irish had not lacked supplies and we had a comfortable night when the rains lashed down. We had found our fort at just the right time. The next morning I gathered my counsel around me. "I have a mind to keep a garrison here. What do you think?"

One of the villagers ventured. "There are two families who are tiring of the journey and I think they would like to settle here."

"Good. Garth, are any warriors feeling the same?"

Mungo, the new leader of the men from Strathclyde stood. "We serve you my lord and I believe we would like to stay together. This would be a good place to live. "He grinned. "Besides I think they want to start families sooner rather than later and some of the men have formed attachments to the single girls."

Micah snorted, "More like going at it like bunnies if you ask me."

Mungo flashed an irritated look and I waved my hand at Miach to be silent. "I would be more than happy about that for you are doughty men. I know that you will repair the fort and protect it and the road. I would appreciate it if you kept an eye on Witherspool. That bridge is almost as valuable as this one."

"I will my lord."

"Good. We will send supplies here when we have reached journey's end."

"And how far is that my lord?"

"Good question Mungo. Myrddyn?"

"Almost a hundred miles and there is the sea to cross."

I could see that the farmers on the counsel looked dismayed. "The island will afford protection from the Saxons and with Mungo here and his men prospering we will be even safer but if any want to settle on the way they are welcome but remember this." I pointed at the mountain in the distance; Myrddyn had said it was holy and called Wyddfa. "There may be tribes around here who are hostile. There may be a king of this land who would object to incomers. I can only protect those who settle on the island. This may be a good place to settle but it will be the first to feel the wrath of the Saxons. Mungo knows that do you not?"

"Aye my lord."

"So speak with your people and we leave in the morning. Across that bridge is Wales. That is the start of our new life."

# Chapter 15

There was a low range of hills to the south of us but the Roman Road was unerringly straight as it crossed them. The estuary of the river was to our right as we headed westwards. I could see how the Irish had happened upon Deva. They could have sailed their ship right up the estuary. I suspect they came as pirates and slavers but found the pickings around Deva easier than the rigours of the sea. There were more homes and farms along the valley sides but we saw no people. It was not surprising that we encountered none for we were a mighty host. Gareth's perception of a large army was probably like the people here. We did not bother any although if they had come to speak with us they would have seen that we meant no harm.

The Roman Road enabled us to make good time. Tuanthal and his scouts were excited as they reported the sea some fifteen miles ahead. We found a sheltered campsite overlooking the estuary and my warriors dug a ditch. The people had seemed harmless but there were forests which seemed to creep towards Wyddfa and who knew what they contained.

Although many of the women and some of the men complained about the length of the journey, to the children it was just an adventure. With the tireless energy of the young, they ran and raced each other between the carts as we trudged along the road. I noticed, as we set up camp, that there were few single girls or women left. The only ones were little more than children. The war widows soon found men to look after them and the girls had their choice of lusty young warriors. Of course once they were all coupled then I would have warriors who wanted women and that was a problem I would have to deal with at some point. Myrddyn's skills meant that no-one had succumbed to either sickness or wounds. He had saved all those who fell ill. It was strange; the closer we came to his home the more skills he seemed to show. His power was growing. He attributed it to Wyddfa where he had spent time with his grandfather. Certainly it was the highest mountain I had ever seen and would have dwarfed Halvelyn. I had never before seen snow on a mountain top at this time of the year.

The next day we crossed the ridge into the valley and saw the sea. I knew that this was the same sea we had seen from Rheged but it seemed somehow, more exotic. Tuanthal suddenly galloped in. "My lord there is a large settlement in the next valley. There are thirty buildings and some of them are large enough to be warrior halls."

"Garth, take charge of the column and keep moving but be alert. Tuanthal bring all of your riders. Myrddyn, you had better come with us."

We were no longer following the road although, as we rode, Tuanthal told me that the road passed close by the houses. When we crested the rise above the buildings I could see no defensive wall. I was puzzled. "We will ride down but be careful it looks innocent but like the rose, it may have hidden thorns."

We were halfway down the slope when Myrddyn said, "I know what it is. It is a monastery. Brother Osric told me about them."

I had heard the word but I was unfamiliar with its function. "A monastery?"

"Yes priests like Brother Osric live together to pray to God."

"And?"

"And that is all."

"How peculiar."

I headed for the largest building. The men who lived there appeared to wear just a plain woollen shift and they did not appear to be bothered by such a large number of mailed warriors riding into their home. An older man came out of a small building attached to the main hall and walked boldly up to me. He peered at the Wolf Standard held aloft by Pol.

He smiled. "You must be Lord Lann, the Warlord of Rheged. Please dismount and we will take refreshments. Your men and horses will be cared for." He glanced at Myrddyn, "Bring your wizard too."

Although I was dumbstruck I had never before seen Myrddyn stuck for words but he was. As I dismounted I turned to Tuanthal. "Just keep a sharp eye eh?"

The old man took us into a plainly furnished room. The table and chairs had obviously been made locally. There were pots of honey and bread on the table and some ale. "You were seen when you crested the rise and we prepared this for you."

"I am sorry but you are?"

"I am Asaph the bishop of the monastery of St. Kentigern. It was rude of me not to introduce myself."

"And how do you know me?"

157

"Why Brother Osric wrote of you of course; did you not know? He knew St. Kentigern and he wrote to me of you and your exploits." He pointed a piece of honey smothered bread at Myrddyn. "He was particularly impressed by this young man. Even though he is a pagan, as are you, Lord Lann."

I shook my head. It was typical of Osric to have kept this information from us. We would have bombarded him with questions and he liked his secrets.

"As his letters stopped I assume that the dear man is dead?"

He said it so calmly that I almost shuddered. "Yes he fell ill. It was a black day for Rheged when he died."

"We all die, Warlord. It is how we live that people remember and they will think well of Osric. Did he finish his book?"

I shook my head, "My priest Brother Oswald toils at it still."

"Then tell your priest we would happily continue the work of the good brother."

"We have much to record about Rheged first but when it is complete then Brother Oswald will return it here for you to make a copy."

He suddenly laughed, "You may be a pagan but I can see Brother Osric's influence. You, too, value the written word. Excellent! Have you had an eventful journey so far?"

Whilst eating we filled the old Bishop in on the exodus of the last free men of Rheged. He was particularly interested in Deva. "I am pleased that you have rid us of that nest of vipers. They preyed on the innocent. They even tried to raid us once."

I looked around, "I am surprised you survived. There are no defences."

"The people who live close by are very protective of us and they drove them away."

"We had seen none."

"No they are a careful people and your arms and weapons would have intimidated them. I take it you are not staying close by."

I smiled, "Would that worry you Bishop Asaph?"

"No, Osric spoke highly of you despite your pagan beliefs. He said you were a good man and you had a Christian heart."

"I am not sure about that. No, we will be heading for Mona."

"Ah the centre of the Druidic cult." He gestured towards Myrddyn. "Where your wizard's power will increase eh?" Myrddyn blushed. I wondered then at the monk's words. "You will need to beware of the people at the edge of the mainland. They are a violent clan. When they are not slaving they are fighting amongst themselves."

"And Mona?"

"We hear little." He shrugged. "If there are any peoples living there then they are few in number. The Irish use it to gather slaves."

"Well when we reach it that practice will stop."

Asaph looked searchingly into my eyes. "Osric was right. You do have a Christian soul. You have just to find it."

"What of the king of this land?"

"King Beli ap Rhun. He lives south of the mountain. He largely ignores this part of his land as it is not very productive." He smiled "St. Kentigern and the other priests spread the word of Christ and King Beli is only a recent convert."

"Will he object to our settlement?"

"That I do not know but your motives are honourable and he is, by all accounts, a reasonable man."

I stood. "We must leave and rejoin our people."

"If you head towards the sea then you will meet them. The road passes the end of this valley. May God be with you Wolf Warrior."

Myrddyn kept looking over his shoulder as we headed for the column. "You think that you know someone and then something like this happens and you see how little you really know."

"I am just pleased that we have friends here. They may not be an army but they are reassuring." I waved at the men toiling in the fields. "They are brave men, foolish but brave. They defend themselves with nothing more than their beliefs."

"As you do, my lord."

I clapped my hand on my sword. "Aye but I have a little help from this eh? I think it is better than relying on a God who wishes you to turn the other cheek."

The closer we came to the coast then the closer the mountains came to the sea and we were forced to travel along the road with no room for the flanking archers. Garth was not happy. "This is not good my lord. If we were ambushed here then we would not be able to defend ourselves."

Myrddyn cocked his head towards the slopes. "Unless the enemies are mountain goats I think we are safe."

"Wizard, stick to your healing! Look at the slopes they are littered with rocks. All it needs is one boy to start them rolling and we will all be swept into the sea."

I held up my hands. "Peace! You are both right. Garth, send the despatch riders ahead on their ponies. They can watch ahead for any movement. Myrddyn let us slow down the column so that there are bigger gaps between the carts."

"But that means it will take us longer to reach Mona!"

"And is this a race? We now have three places to delay pursuit, Raibeart, Aelle and now Mungo. Do you think they could get by those three in a short time?"

Myrddyn was an honest fellow and he knew he was wrong. He beamed a smile at me. "Sorry Lord Lann. I know you are right it is just that we are so close now that we can almost touch it." He pointed to the headland which jutted out to sea. "When we pass that headland then we will see it. That is how close we are."

"And we will continue to do as we have done hitherto. We will be measured and cautious and we will reach this promised land of yours safely with no losses."

That day was a hard one. The road actually twisted a little when the Romans had encountered the rocky peninsula jutting into the sea. We covered but twelve miles and the campsite was a bare rocky platform without ditch and without a hot meal. It was our most miserable night as a storm blew in from the sea and we all had a salty soaking which did nothing to mend ill tempers. The warriors, in particular, became annoyed as mail showed signs of rust and the long journey stretched to a second week.

When we awoke we were all in a better humour for we could clearly see the isle of Mona. It looked close enough to touch. Myrddyn almost danced with glee and told us that we were now less than fifty miles from our final destination. The road, however, was just as narrow and the mountains were just as close as they had been before the peninsula. My military mind told me that this would be a good place to halt any invader. A shield wall of twenty warriors with archers behind could hold off an army. There was no way they could be outflanked.

After the hardest six miles we had walked in the entire journey the road finally had space on both sides. It was not a huge space but it felt less claustrophobic. It was as though you could breathe again. I could see that there were no obstacles in our way save the sea crossing and we would face that soon enough. We were less than five miles from our last camp before Mona when Tuanthal brought bad news. The clan we had been warned of lived in a place called Llanrug. Although it was further away than our crossing place we would be in plain sight and if the Bishop was to be believed then these carrion folk would fall upon us.

"Miach, go with Tuanthal and begin to build the camp at the narrows. Keep a good watch on the hillsides. I fear this may be a harder night than the one at Deva." As they rode away I summoned Garth. We rode to the side to allow the column to pass us. "We will need at least one whole day to get across the narrows, probably two. I cannot see this clan being benign enough to allow that."

Myrddyn suggested, "Talking?"

"I think I believe the Bishop. He had no reason to lie. Let us act as though we are going to be attacked. How should we defend?"

Myrddyn looked at Garth, "I think Garth may have been right. They will try to use the mountain against us and roll rocks down the hillsides."

"Then we dig ditches and fell trees to make barricades. Anything else?"

"They will probably be lightly armed and have no armour. Our archers and slingers would be more use than the shield wall. I fear that the horses may not be much use because of the slope."

"I think you are right Garth. Myrddyn, how do we cross the sea?"

"We steal a Saxon idea. We build a huge raft. If we tie two strong ropes from shore to shore then the men can pull the raft across. We should be able to fashion something to tie to the end of the raft to help us to pull it back and forth."

"Good, then the warriors first job tonight is to cut down many trees; the longer ones for the raft and the shorter ones for the barricades."

My men had worked wonders and the camp was ready when we reached it. I sent the two men with their archers and horsemen as a skirmish line a mile from the camp while Garth and Myrddyn organised the cutting down of the trees. Myrddyn's comments had made peace between them and they happily worked together again. Brother Oswald organised the food and there was a happy air about the camp as they could see their new home across the water. Most did not realise that it was the sea. It was no wider than a river at home but Myrddyn had told me it was deep and had dangerous currents.

We had to stop work for food, the warriors were exhausted but the wood was cut and the ditches partly dug. Tuanthal and Miach's men ate in shifts and then Garth's men began to build the crude barricades which would, hopefully stop the rocks. As an added precaution we placed the carts all along the landward side of the defensive wall; better to lose transport than lose a life. As night fell, I sent half the warriors to sleep and pulled back all of the skirmishers. They would need sleep and they could do nothing at night anyway. I stayed awake until after midnight and then handed over to Ridwyn. I had an uneasy night's sleep which I put down to the sound of the sea in the narrows and... I had a dream.

*My mother came to me and she looked like Aideen, but she spoke with my mother's voice. She appeared to be running, I thought it was towards me but, although she spoke to me she carried on running towards the sea. She spoke in the same way she always had, soothing and reassuring but her words were ominous. 'Beware the men from the sea. Beware the smiling Irish. Build on rock and trust not to sand. Awake my son. Danger is near.'*

I awoke and felt nervous. When I saw Myrddyn staring at me I knew he had heard the same dream. "Stand to!" In the still of the false dawn, hidden behind Wyddfa's bulk, the men awoke instantly and grabbed weapons. I heard a rumble like thunder and Myrddyn said, "Avalanche!"

"Protect yourselves, flying rocks!"

We threw ourselves beneath the carts and pushed our backs against the wood for protection. I just had time to put on my helmet and hold my shield above my head. Hogan looked anxiously at me as he, too, sheltered beneath my solid shield. The first few rocks were held by the ditches and traps. Some others, sent from higher up the slopes, bounced up and over and crashed into the cart reinforced wall. I saw one old woman panic and leave her place of safety to run towards the narrows. A rock struck her head with such force that her head disappeared in a mass of red and grey ooze. After a few moments it became silent and I saw relief on faces. I knew that it was not over. The avalanche was the prelude to the real attack. "Face the enemy. We are under attack!"

As we turned with weapons drawn we saw the screaming, half dressed savages who hurtled down the slope towards us. Their hair was stuck up with lime and their faces were painted with blues and whites as were their bodies. They all carried wicked looking curved blades with long handles which they wielded with two hands. Their technique of clearing the walls was astounding they ran to the fallen rocks and threw themselves in the air, some of them managed to land behind my men. They made prodigious leaps. I swung at one who soared above me and took his right leg off in one blow. The ones who landed safely swung their blades around. I saw one of the Bernicians lose his head before Ridwyn stabbed him. It was a terrifying ordeal. A shield wall was useless and we had to try to kill them in the air or get in as soon as they landed. They were reckless but after a fierce and bloody battle they lay dead. It had been costly for us and fifteen warriors, archers and slingers lay dead.

We threw their bodies into the sea. Their vicious and random attack deserved no honour and we disposed of them like discarded bones from a meal. As we began to see to the wounded I sent Tuanthal on a mission. "Find this Llanrug and destroy it. Kill any you find there. Miach go with him."

Brother Oswald came to me. "Warlord this is not like you. Are you wounded?"

"No Oswald, I am angry." I pointed to the headless corpse of the old woman. "She was no warrior; she was a frightened old woman. These savages will prey on no more travellers." Garth and the warriors busied themselves building the raft. Like me, they wanted to be away from this place of death.

Tuanthal and Miach returned with grim faces. "What a living shithole that was, my lord. They had skulls decorating their walls and some of them were from children. We found a few of them and they fought like cornered rats." Tuanthal pointed to Miach. "The Captain here stopped them getting close."

"Aye my lord but my lads wouldn't collect the arrows. They reckoned they were cursed." Over their heads I could see the smoke rising. "We burned it." He spat. "Good riddance. Give me the Saxons any day. It was like fighting animals and not humans."

I turned to Myrddyn who had just come from the wounded. "We owe the Bishop a great deal." I saw Hogan's frightened face and I ruffled his hair. "And now let us get this raft built eh?"

While the raft was being built I took the saddle off Raven and then my own armour. Garth looked at me curiously. "What are you doing Warlord?"

"We need ropes taking across the narrows. Raven is the best horse and I have swum rivers before. I will ask for another four volunteers."

"But you are Warlord!"

"All the more reason then. I should not ask a man to do something I will not do." There were more volunteers than we needed and the five of us each took a rope. We had had to join together some lengths. The narrows were about four hundred paces wide. We needed the rafts securing on the other which meant longer rope than carried. One end was secured to a tree on the mainland and we carried the other over our shoulders. It was comforting to think that, so long as we held on to the rope, we could be rescued, but not so our horses. I kicked Raven on and he entered the water. He was fearless. The current was strong and I turned his head against the current. Unlike the rivers I had crossed this deepened very quickly. I had no time to look for my companions; I was fighting the sea. Raven was a powerful swimmer and soon I could see that I was less than fifty paces from the shore. I turned his head slightly so that the current took us towards the beach and when I felt his feet strike the sea bottom I breathed a sigh of relief. I had paid out the rope as I crossed and, as we rode up the beach I looked for a mooring point. I saw a huge rock as high as a man and I leapt from Raven and began to tighten the rope by walking around the rock. Fortunately the action of the sea had made it smooth.

As I walked around the rock I saw three of my companions also struggling ashore but of the fourth I saw nothing. I tied my rope off and then ran to help the next man. We needed the ropes to be parallel to help the raft to sail safely. We found a second rock and, as we tightened that rope I shouted to the other two. "Take your ropes and attach them to trees there!" I pointed to two small trees at the edge of the beach. By the time we had all four secured I was exhausted but pleased. "Where is Cimri?"

"I saw him come from his horse. The horse is ashore, there it is."

"Get his horse."

I ran to the beach and saw the end of the rope carried by Cimri floating free. The crossing had already cost us a warrior. We never found his body. "Keep watch on the beach. I am going ashore to scout." As I mounted Raven and rode off I knew that my officers would have tried to dissuade me but the warriors were in awe of Warlord. They might disapprove but they would say nothing. I was pleasantly surprised as I crested the small rise. This was nothing like the mainland. It was flat and verdantly wooded. Riding along the ridgeline I could see that it would make perfect farmland. My only worry, at that point was that it

164

would not stop an invader and yet Myrddyn had assured me that it would. Perhaps there was something I was missing. I rode for a mile or so and saw no sign of human habitation and I rode back towards the beach.

It was a busy scene I saw as we dropped from the ridge to the beach. The first journey of the raft was about to take place. Miach and his mounted archers were the first. Miach showed no emotion but I saw a few fearful glances at the bubbling water. On the shore the people also watched, knowing that their turn would come. The archers themselves pulled this cargo across with my three swimmers aiding on our side. It seemed to take a long time but I knew that the next journeys would, perforce, be quicker. As soon as the raft beached the horses were quickly disembarked and the archers led them to a picket line which had been hastily assembled. Even as I watched the raft returned, quite swiftly now that it was empty and hauled by my warriors.

The second voyage held carts and women and children. The sides of the raft were lined by my warriors who hauled on the ropes as did Miach and his archers. The raft seemed to fly across the water and I heard the squeals of delight form the children. The mother's faces showed their terror. Once the women and children were ashore then the rest of the voyages were quick. Now that those on shore had seen the success of Myrddyn's raft they all wanted to board. We rotated the warriors on the raft and those ashore until just Tuanthal and his horsemen were left. This would be the trickiest crossing. Every warrior we had on the Mona side held the ropes. When they were aboard Tuanthal and Aedh slashed through the mooring ropes as we all pulled. The raft lurched with the current as it was freed from the mainland. Tuanthal and his men had to calm their frightened horses but we pulled the raft so quickly that their journey seemed but a moment. As they came ashore we all congratulated ourselves.

Hogan came up to me and asked, quietly. "Why did you destroy the raft? We can't get back."

I pointed at the raft which was being pulled to the ridge. "The raft is not destroyed but we do not want our enemies to benefit from our hard work do we?"

Understanding flooded his young face. "Now I see why you are Warlord."

"No, my son. That idea came from Miach. I am successful because I have good men that I listen to. Remember that."

We moved some three miles inland to a pleasant glade with running water and trees. Even the weather seemed to have changed for the better as the sun set over the western seas and we were a little closer to our new home. We had a pleasant fire going and I sat with Myrddyn, Oswald and my officers. "How far Myrddyn?"

"Less than twenty miles and it will all be flat. Tomorrow we see Holy Island." He swept his arm around us. "Any of this land would be perfect for the people to farm. The island is just the place I deem to be the best for a stronghold."

Oswald smiled, "Then I think we give the people the chance to choose where they will live. Some may wish to be here but we may also pass pleasant places on the way to this Holy Island; a title, Myrddyn, which intrigues me."

"There are pleasant spots which we will see tomorrow and I will tell you on the journey of the name."

"Do you all agree that we give the people the option?"

Garth nodded, "It is the reason we came here isn't it? This land is now Rheged."

"No it is not Rheged but we will just call it our land for the moment."

When they had all gone I drew Myrddyn to one side. "Last night, did my mother come to you then as she did to me?"

"Aye she said you were in danger." I told him my dream and he stroked his chin. It was a habit he had picked up from Osric. "The men from the sea will be Saxons. That is interesting. The island will be safe from them but the tricky Irish prophesy, that intrigues me too."

The next morning I sat astride Raven and addressed what had become, 'my people'. "We have travelled many leagues from our home and now we have reached the island of Mona. This is our home. I will be travelling to the western extremity of the island where I will be building my stronghold. Should any of you wish to find land as we travel west then we will try to give that land to you. Should we meet any people on that land we will buy it for you. I do not want to kill, as the Saxons did to take someone else's home. When we have built our stronghold then my men will patrol our land and defend us all from any who try to take it."

There was a brief silence and then a spontaneous cheer erupted with roar of my name and 'Rheged'. It was enough and I smiled and waved.  I headed west followed by my son and Pol.  The last free people had come home.

# Chapter 16

Many of my people took the opportunity of settling as we crossed, what appeared to be, an empty land. As we later discovered most of the people lived at the coast and there was no one to question the new owners of the land in the centre. When we reached the end of the main part of Mona there were just my warriors and eight families left. The island, Myrddyn had called Holy Island, was separated from the mainland by a narrow strip of sea. I could see why he had identified it for there were cliffs on both sides. They were not insurmountable but I could see that any attacker would struggle to climb them and it would be difficult to attack a fort there.

"We will camp here tonight and then tomorrow; Myrddyn and Brother Oswald put your minds to a bridge which we can build to cross over!"

While the two engineers began their bridge I walked down to the beach to examine this new stronghold from the viewpoint of protecting from ships. I was mindful of my mother's words in my dream and aware that we were close to the place Myrddyn had had his first encounter with my mother's spirit. There appeared to be a narrow strip of sand surrounding the cliffs which were only twenty or thirty paces high. But the rocks were sharp and they were steep. It was as though the gods had taken a rock and placed it in the sand. In Bernicia we had seen, about thirty miles south of Din Guardi, such rocks and the Saxons did not try to land there. I was aware that I could only see one side of the island and the other side might enable someone to land but I was pleased with my wizard's choice.

I clambered back up the rocks and saw that Garth and his warriors had cut down some trees and they were being prepared. There were few trees and a thought struck me. "Tuanthal, take the horsemen and take apart the raft. We have ready-made timbers there."

Eager to be away and riding free he gleefully mounted his horse. Hogan's expectant face peered at me. "Father, can I go?"

Tuanthal; grinned, "An extra pair of hands is also welcome my lord."

"Then I had better come and make sure that the hands are usefully employed." The look on Pol's face belied the nature of his words; he too wanted to be with the young and charismatic leader of horse. Had I been young then I, too, would have wished that.

We still had a few families who wished to be close to the new stronghold. There were also others who had worked in Castle Perilous and wanted to continue to do so here on Mona. I missed Aideen the most at times like this. She had a way of organising them and bringing the best out of, what she called, 'her people'. I saw that Oswald had them preparing food for the warriors who were toiling away. Aideen would have enjoyed living here on this beautiful island. I missed her. By noon the bridge was ready for the first crossing although it would need Tuanthal and his timbers for it to carry the weight of wagons.

I crossed with Myrddyn, Garth and ten of my warriors. The rest would cross later and build a fort to guard the bridge. I was keen to explore the small island. We climbed to the top of a gorse covered hill and Myrddyn pointed out the features of the island. "That is the western tip. It is but a mile and a half away." He turned slightly to the right. "Over there is a place we can land ships." He frowned as he saw the smoke. "And it appears that someone lives there."

"Then let us visit our new neighbours and introduce ourselves."

Myrddyn led us to the craggy knoll he had first identified. We paused there to drink from the water which flowed from a spring. "It was here where we lived. This is the sacred home of the old druids. It would make a good place for your stronghold." I looked back and saw that it was less than a mile from the bridge. We could build a wall so that the defenders of the bridge would have less than eight hundred paces to reach safety. All my thoughts were on defence. All my thoughts were on the Saxons and their plans for revenge.

We walked across the heather to the cliffs, which were thronging with seabirds. They would make good sentries for they rose noisily squawking as we approached. When we walked back to the spring I noticed that the ground steadily rose to a natural crown of rock. Despite his personal views Myrddyn had chosen a good spot. Now that we had less than two hundred men in my army we could accommodate them easily. Myrddyn pointed away to the east to another lower knoll about a hundred and fifty paces away. It was closer to the bridge. "We could extend a wooden wall and enclose that too. It would make a good place for stables and a warrior hall."

Once again his keen eye had seen beyond the obvious. There was turf there and a flat swathe, perfectly suited to horses. "Good and now, before we get above ourselves let us introduce ourselves to these neighbours and hope that they are friendly."

Myrddyn chuckled. "My Lord Lann, since we left Rheged have you seen anyone who is as well armed as we are?"

I had to admit that we had not. With my wolf cloak, shield, full face helmet and sword I was an intimidating sight. I considered taking off the helmet and slinging the shield at my back but I remembered the rabble from Llanrug. If these were from the same stock then I would need all the protection I could get. Besides it hid the angry scar which ran down my face and I did not want to frighten any children just yet.

We followed a man-made track down the slope towards the smoke. Myrddyn explained that collecting the sea bird eggs was a way of supplementing a winter diet. We reached the crown of the hill and looked down upon an untidy straggle of crudely made huts. They were not the wattle and daub we used but appeared to be an eclectic mix of styles and materials. The people there would be scavengers of that there was no doubt. The only partly stone building was a Christian church, recognisable from its cross. It looked to be inside a derelict fort of some description. There were half a dozen small boats drawn up on the narrow beach and I saw men mending nets. They were fisher folk. I could see the remains of what must have been a Roman Fort but it had been damaged by the sea, war and thieves although the fishermen had not touched it. We walked down into the village and the mothers grabbed their children and ran inside the crude huts. I almost laughed, had we evil intentions then the pathetically built huts would offer little protection.

I could see indecision on the faces of the twelve men and boys at the beach, fight, flee or surrender? I gestured Myrddyn forwards to speak. He had come from the island and knew their words. "We come in peace." He gestured towards me. "This is Lord Lann, the Warlord of Rheged and he has come here to Mynydd. We will be building a fort on Mynydd y Twr. It will afford you protection."

A man, older than the rest came up and dropped to his knees before me. "I am Gwynfor ap Gryffyth and the headman here; that is the church of St Cybi and this is called Caergybi. We have been expecting you. Before she died, our witch told us to watch for the wolf that would come and protect us." He pointed to my wolf cloak. "And you are he. We will serve you my lord and you will protect us. Our king has deserted us and left us to the depredations of the Hibernians."

I turned to Myrddyn who shrugged. "I told you my lord, this is a special place. We will be protected in this most holy of islands."

170

"Know this, Gwynfor ap Gryffyth, I will protect you and all of your people. When my stronghold is built, if danger threatens then come there. Understand too that we will buy any fish and other food you do not need to use." I pointed to the towering Garth besides me. "We have big appetites."

The headman laughed as did his men. "We will need to catch bigger fish to make giants such as you."

As we walked back towards our new bridge I thought about the differences in people. The men of Rheged and Bernicia were tall and powerfully built. The men of Llanrug, Witherspool, and Mynydd were all much smaller than we and even smaller than the Saxons. To them we appeared as giants. Perhaps *wyrd* had sent us here for a purpose and we had left our homes for a better life.

Brother Oswald and my men had worked hard and there was now a camp and a wall on the island side of the bridge. Once we returned we joined in and, by the time Tuanthal reached us with the timber all had crossed the bridge and were safely in the camp. The carts and horses would have to wait until the morning to be brought across. The horsemen stayed in our original camp while we spent the first night on the island Myrddyn called, Holy Island.

The bridge took less than half a day to build and we managed to finish the fort at the end of the bridge. We wanted protection above all. The new settlers brought their carts over and began to choose their own plots. Brother Oswald had told us of a story from the book of the White Christ and how a man had built a boat and brought two of each animal. We only had a few but those with animals chose the land which had the best pasture and soon there was the industrious noise of building all around the camp.

"Ridwyn. This fort is for your Bernicians. I think they would like to be together and I know that you will guard this entrance." I pointed to the settlers. "These are your people. Care for them."

"I will my lord and I like this place. It is like a clean Din Guardi!"

I laughed with him for what he said was true. He would be able to make the fort suit him and his men who were resourceful. I was just sad that his brother was no longer with us for Riderch would have loved this place too. "Our fort will be less than a mile away. I want our people protecting; all of them!"

As I led my depleted band across the headland I rode next to Tuanthal. "Tuanthal, you have been one of my most loyal warriors and I now have a favour to ask."

"A favour? You are my lord, command."

"No, I will ask and you can refuse. We need a fort at the end of the island, where we crossed and we need patrols to travel the island. That would suit horsemen. Will you be lord of the eastern half of the land? I know that the country there is horse country and you can breed more horses."

He looked delighted. "I would do that gladly my lord."

"Good then take your men when you are ready and when the fort is built send a despatch rider to me for I would tour my new land." Given the independent command Tuanthal led his horsemen away and I knew that the narrows would be secure.

My men built with a renewed vigour. Winter was rapidly approaching and we needed a comfortable home building. There was no stone for quarry although many of the boulders and rocks from the nearby beach were used for the foundations. Brother Oswald and Myrddyn had read about Roman cement and they had concocted their own version. The wizard and the priest were weaving their strange magic again. There was little local wood and Miach and his mounted archers had to forage far and wide for materials. When they returned they spoke of many small isolated farms but no one was to be seen when they approached. I remembered Myrddyn's words; we were intimidating and when I had the time we would need to assuage their fears.

The stronghold was on the high point, overlooking most of the island. We built a stone base as high as me. Half of this was buried below ground. We managed to build two stories with the ground one being used for livestock as we had at Castle Perilous. We built one warrior hall close by the stronghold so that we could escape to our final defence quickly. Quarters were built for me and Hogan, Myrddyn, Brother Oswald with a separate hut for Garth and Miach. Once that was complete we extended the walls to include the open area where we built a second warrior hall. The slingers, archers and despatch riders could use that one. The building took time but, until the Saxons came, we had plenty of that.

It was when I watched the despatch riders and slingers toiling with the archers and warriors that I realised they were growing rapidly and there were none to replace them. They had been boys not long ago and

172

now they were young men. We would have to wait for the fruits of the union between the warriors and the single women. Some families had stayed at Strathclyde whilst others were in the distant parts of my land.

When winter came it was not like Rheged; we had no snow. There was snow in the air but it disappeared before it struck the ground. Myrddyn had that smug self satisfied look on his face which implied it was because the island was so holy. I did not know the reason but I welcomed it for we finished the halls and walls before it became cold and the first frosts chilled the bones. We had few supplies and Brother Oswald was becoming worried. "The fishermen are good at their job my lord but they cannot feed us over winter we need another source of food."

The families and farmers who lived nearby were also in need of food until their crops could be gathered in. The land we had crossed had been fertile and I knew that there would be a little surplus in all the farms. I could just take it but I was determined to buy the friendship of the people. I led a strong patrol of archers with pack horses and I set off for the unexplored northern side of Mona. Myrddyn accompanied me, partly, I think, because he had had family in those parts and partly to see the island he called home.

We found a farm some five miles from the bridge. There appeared to be no-one around but I could see a few sheep and goats and smoke coming from the hut. Myrddyn dismounted. As the one who looked least like a warrior I felt he was the best chance we had for a peaceful discussion with our new neighbours. He went to the door; we knew that it would only be barred from the inside and he tapped on it speaking in the language of the island. I could not hear what he said as he spoke quietly but I knew that he would be reassuring the occupants. Eventually a youngish man came out looking fearfully first at Myrddyn and then us with our weapons. He looked like the young man who had been torn apart by wolves when I was a boy and living at Stanwyck. I smiled but it seemed to add to his fear. My scar made even my smile look fearful.

"We mean no harm. I am Lord Lann and I have built a castle on the Holy Island. We are neighbours." I saw what must have been his wife and young children peer around the edge of the door. "We would like to buy, with silver," I held out my hand showing a few coins. "Any supplies you have that you do not need."

His face changed to one of curiosity and his family edge out. "Supplies?"

"Food. Corn, milk, meat… supplies; we have travelled far and we have used our own."

"We do not use silver."

"Well we could exchange for things you might need. We make fine weapons and tools." I was glad we had brought our own blacksmith. "And we can offer you protection."

The woman came out. "We can hide from the Irish?"

Myrddyn could understand that sentiment. "If the Hibernians come you will be safe in our castle. It is on the island."

"But the sea…"

"We have built a bridge."

The looks they exchanged suggested that Myrddyn was a magician to have created a bridge. "We will return in seven days. If you have any spare supplies then we will buy it from you."

The same scene was repeated over the next seven farms. Miach said wryly, "We have a lot of promises my lord but precious little food."

"When you fish or hunt you lay down bait. Myrddyn's honeyed words are our bait."

We saw our first settlement on the northern coast. It was a fishing village. The headman was more confident than the others had been and I saw that they had a rudimentary wall of wood. It would not stop my men but it might deter pirates and slavers who would find easier pickings elsewhere. Like Gwynfor he was pleased that there was a military presence and he liked the idea of making money. He promised to bring fish by boat to Mynydd. I liked this better. If we could make Mynydd a market then we would improve the prosperity of that town and save much leg work.

By the time we reached the narrows we had made contact with most of the northern half of the island. Tuanthal had made a fine fort and he and his men had also built another raft, albeit smaller which they kept moored beneath the fort. "We thought this would enable us to get wood from the mainland. There is little on the island." He looked at me apologetically. "I am sorry I did not return when we built the fort but I wanted the raft completing."

"Do not apologise. You were thinking and planning. That is more important. Come with us now. We have visited the northern half of the island. Myrddyn you take Miach and return the way we came. Negotiate and barter; see what you can get."

As I rode with my horsemen I saw more of our people who had built homes. They were obvious, even from a distance as they built their huts in the same way and all of them had a protective ditch running around. I promised that there would soon be a market and invited all of them to the island for Yule. It would not be the cold and icy festival of the north but it would bring us together again to remember those we had left.

We found more isolated farms and I had now learned enough of the language to be able to do as Myrddyn had done. We were just five miles from the island when we came upon a strange sight. There was a hut and the animals were bleating and lowing pitifully. The place had a deserted look to it. When we dismounted there was the smell of death about the place and we drew our swords. When we opened the door the smell really hit us. There were six bodies within. A whole family had died. Turning to the horsemen I said, "Four of you get in here. The rest see to those animals. Give them water and food." The men halted in horror at the door. "Take the bodies outside and we will bury them."

Tuanthal looked at me. "It might be better to leave them in here and burn the hut."

The idea had appeal but there was a nagging thought in the back of my mind; an insistent voice which told me to look at the dead. "No, we need to be able to describe them to others and find out who they are."

There was a man and four children. They looked to be between four and eleven. As the woman was carried outside one of the men suddenly started. "My lord. The woman, she is alive!"

There was a mixture of excitement and panic; what was the cause of death. If this was the plague then we were all in great danger. I had to act urgently. We were but five miles from home. I could take her there and isolate her. "Put her on my horse. Return the bodies to the hut and fire it. Tuanthal leave me three men to drive the animals to the fort and then you return to the narrows."

"Lord Lann, is this wise?"

I laughed, "When have I ever done anything that is wise? I will be safe, believe me. This is *wyrd* again."

The woman was thin and emaciated and she was no weight. Raven bore us both easily. She might have been pretty once but whatever illness she had suffered had ravaged her looks. I rode as gently as I could whilst listening to her rasping breath as the bridge came ever closer.

I felt quite proud as the bridge and gatehouse loomed up. Having seen the whole island I could see that the only structures of any size were on my island. The gates were flung open when I was recognised. They looked in silence at the body slung across my horse's neck. I risked a little more speed as I rode the last mile to my fort. I headed for the archer's hall. It was more isolated and the men who lived there could go into the main hall. As I rode through the gate I said, "Send Brother Oswald to me. Quickly."

I dismounted and went into the hall. There were just six slingers inside. "Take your gear and go to the main hall. I need this hall now."

"Can we help my lord?"

"Aye, bring the woman from my horse inside and then take Raven to the stables." I made a bed of straw which I covered with a leather cloak I found hanging on the wall. "Bring her in, gently, and lay her down." They did so and then stood around. "You have done as I asked now go; I know not what ails her." They left and Brother Oswald entered. "Her family is dead and we thought that she was dead."

He knelt down and began to examine her. "This is where we need the healer."

Leaving him ministering I ran to the door where two of the boys were leading Raven away. "You two. Get your ponies and ride north, find Myrddyn and bring him here. Say the Warlord needs a healer." They grinned and ran with a bemused Raven in tow towards the stables. I ducked back inside the hall.

"It looks to be an infection of the chest."

"Can we catch it?"

"You could but we can cure this if we treat it early enough. I can help her but it is the healer who will have to save her. Get the fire banked up and put on some water to boil." He suddenly realised that he was talking to the Warlord. "Sorry my lord, forgive me…"

"This is no time to be precious about rank. A life is at stake here." I got the cauldron and went out to the water butt. When it was full I put it on the fire which was almost dying. I grabbed some dry wood and placed it on the embers and blew. It took me a few moments and I was sweating as though I had fought for an hour but the fire blazed away and the hall was brighter and felt more comfortable.

"My lord, open her shift and bare her chest. I need to apply this salve." He took some paste from a bottle and mixed it with a little of the water which was heating. As soon as he did so there was a pleasant smell which seemed to clear my head. I took my knife and slit the thongs holding her shift together. Her breasts were small and shrunken, clear evidence of the illness which had taken her family. Brother Oswald began to massage the paste onto her breasts. I noticed that within a few moments her breathing became less laboured. When he had finished he sat down. "That is all that I can do. I will make a broth for her. I will send one of the girls from the kitchens to sit with her."

"No Oswald. I am doing naught else for the moment. I will stay. What should I do?"

"Keep her warm my lord." He paused and put his hand on my shoulder, "Despite all your words, my lord, you a good man with a Christian heart."

Before I could berate him he had gone. I was tiring of being told I was a Christian! I took my wolf cloak and laid it on her; as much to cover her naked breasts as to keep her warm. She deserved dignity. I watched her and tried to work out her age. If her eldest child was about eleven then she would have been the same age as my mother when she had died. Perhaps that was why I was taking so much care. She looked a little like my mother, with the same hair and green eyes but I realised it felt good to be saving a life rather than just taking one.

I do not know how long I sat there but when the door opened I saw that it was dark outside and the fire was dying a little. Oswald hurried in with a pan of steaming soup. I went to the fire to bank it up as the priest took a wooden spoon and began to feed her. "Your people are terrified that it is the plague and it has killed their Warlord. You had best show yourself." I was not sure I ought to. "Go my lord, I will feed her and then you can return."

I left the hall and saw that a cold night had fallen whilst I had watched. I walked across to my warrior hall and found that the priest had spoken true. There were terrified and worried faces watching for me as I strode across.

Garth was at the gate to greet me. "When you sent for Myrddyn and then did not appear we feared the worst, Tuanthal's men told us that the woman's family were dead and we feared the plague had returned."

"No," I raised my voice as all needed to hear my words, "the woman has an illness of the chest. I live and I am well. Go back to the warm hall. I cannot minister to you all."

Hogan ran to my side and grabbed me tightly. "I feared you would be taken as mother was."

"No my son, and I am sorry that I did not tell you what I was about."

Just then there was a drumming of hooves as Myrddyn arrived. He leapt from his horse. "The lads told me there was a sick woman?"

"In the other hall, Brother Oswald is with her." Now that Myrddyn was back I could relax. I put my arm around Hogan's shoulders. "Now then let us go and eat for I am famished!"

Myrddyn entered the hall an hour later. "The worst is over and she will survive. I have given her a potion to put her into a deep slumber. Brother Oswald is watching her. It was a good thing you reached her when you did or she would have died. She is a lucky woman."

I wondered about that. If I had not chosen to take the bodies out of the hut and just burned the dead then she would have died and I would never have seen her. Her face now haunted me. Life and death were in a fine balance and a thread no bigger than a spider's web was the difference. When I was summoned, late the next morning she had awoken. She tried to struggle to her feet but Myrddyn restrained her.

"No, my dear, you need to rest. You were close to death."

"And I am told that I have you to thank; Lord Lann, Warlord of this land. I owe my life to you and I will serve you in any way I can."

"You owe me nothing save to get well...?"

"My name is Myfanwy, my lord, wife of Rhun."

"Well Myfanwy we will move you to a hut in the main compound." I swept my arm around the hall. "These are the quarters for my archers and a hut with the women will be more appropriate."

As I left with Myrddyn he asked, "What will you do with her Lord Lann?"

I was perplexed, "Do? I do not understand?"

"Your lives are now intertwined and do not tell me that she does not remind you of your mother."

"Well... she can help in the kitchens, we always need workers there."

He laughed as he went to his cell. "Do not try to persuade me she means nothing. I can read your mind my lord but I will keep my silence."

I hated the fact that he was right but I was now used to being alone with Hogan. My mind could focus on my people and keeping them safe. I needed no entanglements.

The first market at Mynydd was a small affair but I made sure that Brother Oswald spent plenty of silver and copper. The people of Mona were not used to coins but I hoped that by using it I would encourage them to continue to attend. The second was much more successful and, as it was but fourteen nights before Yule, there was quite a festive atmosphere. I stood on the walls of the old Roman fort and enjoyed watching the people of Mona who were bartering, negotiating and generally enjoying life.

Gwynfor joined me. He now dressed better and I noticed he smelled cleaner. He stood next to me and bowed, and said shyly, "I want to thank you my lord for coming to Mona. Before you came we were at the mercy of every pirate and raider who wanted to steal from us. When we heard of the armed warriors coming across Mona we feared for our lives but," he spread his arm, "this is better than any of us could have hoped."

I did not know what to say. "I just wanted to save my people from the Saxons."

He laughed, "Then you have saved two peoples and we thank you." He nodded at the people talking with each other. "Every person you can see is better off and that is not just because of your coin; you have brought peace and stability." He looked at me earnestly. "Promise me you will not desert us." He suddenly looked embarrassed. "I am sorry my lord, that was presumptuous of me."

"No Gwynfor, I am your lord and I owe you a duty as much as you owe me. I shall not leave."

# Chapter 17

Yule was joyous. Brother Oswald had fewer Christians but he seemed not to mind. There were many shared areas of belief and the edges of both pagan and Christian religions were blurred. Tuanthal and his men had been over to the mainland and hunted resulting in much fine food. He had left a skeleton garrison watching the mainland and many of our settlers came to the place we had called Caergybi. Gwynfor told me it was the name of the old Roman fort and, as the last descendants of the Romans and the Britons we thought it apposite. We feasted for twelve days which seemed significant to Brother Oswald and to us pagans the right length of time to feast and eat and drink. Hogan got drunk for the first time and it was gratifying to see Pol, now a fine young warrior, watching over him and putting him to bed. Our world was as close to perfection as one could get. I wished that my brothers were with me and hoped that their lives were as safe as ours.

Myfanwy had shown a remarkable skill with healing, all the more remarkable given the fact that her recovery was down to a spectacular healer. She began helping Brother Oswald and Myrddyn with the day to day medicine they used. She was particularly useful when it came to dealing with the women of my land. She was a gifted midwife. The fact that she had lost her own family made her even more determined to save lives and to bring new life into the world. For my part I enjoyed seeing her around the stronghold and blossoming so much.

That first Yule on Mona was a happy time. We had an almost perfect world. All that I lacked was the presence of my brothers but they had made their choice and I hoped and prayed that it had been the correct one. We continued to work on the fort during the cold months of winter. There was little else to do but Gwynfor and his boats went out for fish almost every day save when there was a westerly storm and we ate better than we had in Rheged. I could not get over the lack of snow. When it was a clear day we saw Wyddfa and the mainland shrouded in white but Mona seemed immune from the icy snow we were used to at home in Rheged. Perhaps Myrddyn was right and it was protected by the gods as a special place. It was special to me anyway.

I noticed Oswald and Myrddyn deep in discussion one day; they were just outside the fort on a flat piece of ground. They looked to have a toy they were making. Hogan was too big for such things; he was almost as tall as Pol now and so I asked them what it was. "Remember the men of Strathclyde and their war hammers? It set me to thinking about the Romans. We found some of Brother Osric's writings in which he describes this. It is called an onager or mule. It is a weapon which throws objects a long distance."

The toy looked to be a frame supported by four wheels with a leather cord and what looked like some sort of winding gear. I was curious. "How far can it throw things?"

"We are about to find out. We have made a scale model so that we can build bigger ones later." Brother Oswald turned the winding gear until it clicked into place. He put a lead ball, as used by the slingers, in a small piece of cloth and then, at a nod from Myrddyn he released the gear. The small lead ball flew threw the air and cracked into the wall of the fort. The two men whooped and cheered like children.

"That is an impressive piece of engineering but how would we use it?"

"The Romans used these in their forts and on their ships but without the wheels. If we repaired the Roman fort we could place a couple there and protect the fishing village from raiders. Remember how much fear fire caused my lord? We can send lighted balls towards any pirates or ships who try to land. If we put a couple on our walls and they threw stones then they would destroy any shield wall."

Myrddyn pointed to the warriors inside the fort; they were either practising with their swords or gambling. "We have many idle hands. With wood from the mainland we could build five or six of these. It may be we would not need to use them but..."

"You are both right. I will ride to Tuanthal and arrange for the wood. It will give me something to. Pol, Hogan, get your horses!"

Wolf had been a little bored of late and he enjoyed racing and ranging far ahead of us. There was a cold wind blowing from the east which meant we would have neither rain nor snow but it was a biting wind. Suddenly Wolf went down on his haunches. I did not think it would be an enemy but I was taking no chances. "Weapons at the ready!" I drew my bow and we rode cautiously towards the recumbent Wolf. To my relief I saw a small herd of fifteen sheep. I peered around but could see no homes nearby. They were probably strays. Myrddyn had told me of the Irish raids and these were probably the remnants of a herd which had been forgotten.

"Wolf!" I pointed at the sheep, whistled and Wolf did what he did best, he rounded them up. He lay down, tongue out, happily wagging his tail. We were six miles from the fort.

Hogan looked at me admiringly. "How did you do that?"

"I was not always a warrior. Until I was your age I was a shepherd as were your uncles with Wolf's grandfather to help us. If you like you could take them back to the fort for me." I pointed to Poll too, the two of you."

"But my lord you will be alone."

I laughed, "I think I am safe enough on my own island but if you do not wish to take our own herd back…"

"We will father, it's just that…"

"I know you do not know the commands. One whistle means stop. Two means walk on and three means catch the stray. If you ride behind the herd it will make Wolf's job easier but, in truth, he could do it alone. I will ride with you for the first mile to see how you do."

It gave me much pleasure to see my son doing what I had done all those years ago and they happily took the herd to the bridge. I wheeled Raven around and kicked hard to make up the lost time. The frosty road made for good travelling and I reached the narrows fort just afternoon. There would be just enough time to return. Tuanthal had also used beach pebbles to reinforce his foundations and the raft had been made studier with a hand rail down both sides. There was a small group of huts gathered close by and I saw families toiling away.

My captain of horse greeted me cheerfully. "This is an unexpected pleasure my lord."

"I came to request more wood."

"Would you wish the same lengths as previously?"

"Not just six paces long."

Tuanthal was intrigued and I explained about the onagers. "They sound like a good idea. When they are built I will look at one. They might prove useful here."

I gestured at the huts. "I see you are growing."

"They came from the mainland. We keep visiting Llanrug to discourage the savages but they have just moved further away, terrorising hardworking farmers. They have learned to avoid us. The settlers met us when we were gathering wood and asked for sanctuary. I saw no harm."

I could see the concern on his face and I put my arm around his broad shoulders. "On the contrary, it is what I wish. I want Mona to be a sanctuary for those fleeing the Saxons or any other predator and this is your land my friend."

"No my lord I am steward of your land."

I mounted Raven, "I have little time to stay on this visit but I will return with carts within the week and then I will stay." I peered across the open, rolling land. "When I came across the island I saw wild flocks of sheep. You might think about herding them. They will provide food and wool." I gestured at the villagers. "Some of these may well be shepherds. With more people we need more food."

My return journey was swift and Raven enjoyed the gallop. I reached the bridge just after dark and looked forwards to my hot meal. I saw that the sheep had been penned and Wolf was standing guard. He wagged his tail in recognition but never took his eyes from his charges. Myrddyn and Garth had waited for me before eating and I told them of my day. "There will be many animals which were domesticated and are now feral. Perhaps we could send out the archers to round up any strays. We could distribute them amongst the people of the island."

"And it seems we have immigrants too. Tuanthal now has a small village of refugees from the mainland."

"There will come a time Lord Lann when you need to make the mainland safe. I think it is what Bishop Asaph hoped would happen."

"We need to be secure on this island and we no longer have the huge army we once had."

Garth laughed. "So far I have seen little that would worry us my lord."

I pointed to Wyddfa, hidden in the dark but always present. "How would we dislodge men from the mountains and the passes? Our warriors are not mountain fighters. They like firm and open ground beneath their feet."

He looked crestfallen. Garth believed that his shield wall could best anyone but he was intelligent enough to understand my point. "Then I will have to train men to fight that way."

"We could use the boys who are too slight for the shield wall. If we train them with javelins and slings they could scurry from rock to rock. Early training would give them the skills." Myrddyn pointed to the bay which the locals called, Porthdafarch after a young man who had drowned trying to save his young bride. It was rocky and accessible. "They could use Porthdafarch as a practice ground."

I nodded my agreement, my mouth full of food. "When the weather improves that will be our goal."

Brother Oswald hurried towards us. "When will the wood be ready my lord?"

"I said we would take carts next week."

"We also need iron. One disadvantage of not fighting Saxons is the lack of booty."

"Ah the man of God misses war." Myrddyn could not keep the glee out of his voice.

"Until the whole world is Christian then war is a necessary evil."

I shook my head. These two would argue all night. "We need traders to visit the port. I will speak with Gwynfor." Garth looked at me curiously and I could sense he did not understand. "When he is fishing he may see ships. The ships that travel to Rheged have to pass by the channel. He could encourage them to visit here. Especially if he says we have silver."

Myrddyn leaned forwards. "We have examined Brother Osric's papers and just south of here, say sixty miles or so, there are gold mines that the Romans used."

"Perhaps that might be worth a visit. The trouble is with so few men we cannot spare many to take such a journey but we will see."

Gwynfor confirmed that many ships used the straits and he would be happy to hail them. "The trouble is my lord that the harbour is not as good as it was. The Romans used to keep it clear for the bigger ships and the quayside used to have bollards to tie up their boats."

"Leave that with me. Brother Oswald can put his fertile mind to the solution to those problems."

The priest did indeed have solutions and he also suggested building a hut where the ships crews could buy and exchange goods sheltered. "And," I added, "watched; very clever Brother Oswald. Perhaps we can replace Rheged as the port they visit."

"It would be a shorter journey and they would not be exposed to the pirates for as long."

A month later saw the onagers built and the first ships bring goods for trade. The first visitor was from Byzantium and the Roman Empire. The captain had a cargo of excellent pots and amphorae. The island did not have many potters and it was a valuable cargo.

"It was intended for Rheged, Warlord," he had recognised me, "but since the two brothers began fighting there is not as much money to be made there." He spread his arms apologetically. "When your fishermen stopped me I thought I would see if this was worthwhile." His look suggested that he was disappointed.

"I know that we are not an Alavna and certainly not a Civitas Carvetiorum but one day we shall be and," I took out a fat bag containing coins. "We do have coins so perhaps it might be worth your while visiting and spreading the word."

His greedy eyes took in the bag and he nodded. "If you would like to come aboard and examine my wares…"

I saw Brother Oswald give a slight shake of his head. "No, bring a sample of each pot and the Brother will negotiate. That means you can just bring ashore what we need." I could see the disappointment on his face. He hoped to get rid of his cargo for an outrageous profit and then leave quickly.

"Very well."

"And of course there is a hut over there for you and your crew to use. We have beer you may wish to buy and fresh meat." I nodded at the priest. "And the brother will negotiate a fair price for that too." The trade went well and we were all satisfied. We were turning Mona into a Rheged. Brother Oswald was keen to begin producing honey again and the island was perfect for bees. There was gorse as well as many crops and the mild climate meant they had a better chance of surviving the winter.

Spring came with an unexpected bounty. The animals produced many young, more than in a normal year and the fruits of the liaisons between my warriors and the young girls also produced many children. Moe ships came, some from North Africa and some from Italy. We were able to buy wine but Brother Oswald warned against profligacy. "We are not rich any more my lord. We need to buy only those things which we need and not what we want."

When I next rode around the island with Miach and his men I was greeted warmly. I told all of my people about the ships and trade and encouraged hunting and fishing for the sailors were always desperate for fresh food. I told them that they could trade whatever surplus they had for pots and amphorae. The women's eyes lit up when I mentioned those. Brother Oswald had suggested a twice weekly market and we advertised that fact. The roads were safe and the more we could communicate with each other the better.

All was going well and I was feeling proud of my achievements when we reached the narrows. There my world was shattered. As I rode through the gates I saw Mungo and the remnants of the Deva garrison and their families along with Gareth and a handful of his people. The Saxons had come and driven them off.

# Chapter 18

"The first warning we had was when their ships arrived in the estuary. They landed and surrounded the fort. Some of them went north and some east. We were well provisioned and we were not worried. Then they captured Witherspool and Gareth barely escaped with a few of his people. All the rest were slaughtered. They cleverly floated down the river and we hauled them in at the bridge. Then the Saxons built a ram. We did not have enough archers to slow them down and the gates began to break. I ordered the women and children over the bridge with Gareth's men and then we piled great quantities of flammable material under the bridge. Once they broke through the gate we attacked them and caused many casualties. When they were regrouping I fired the bridge and we fled across it. I waited with a few of my men and sent the rest south and west to find you. The heat from the fire was so intense that it made the bridge brittle. When the first Saxons tried to cross it they caused it collapse into the river. The Roman Bridge is no more. We came the same way as you and when we reached the monastery the Bishop helped us and told us where you where. He said to tell you, '*The time is ripe for the Wolf to bare his teeth.*' Whatever that means."

"I understand and you have done well." I looked at the last fifty men from the army of Strathclyde. "You have a home on the island. Your people can choose where you will."

Gareth asked, "And what of me and my few remaining people my lord?"

Smiling I said, "Of course, if you return with me to Caergybi I think you can continue to do what you did at Witherspool." He did not know what I meant but I saw a role for him dealing with the ship's captains thereby freeing up Brother Oswald.

The news that the Saxons had come with their ships was worrying. I had thought we would have had warning of their arrival through Raibeart and Aelle but they had bypassed those two and could arrive at my home at any time. We had only just made the onagers in time. As I left to return home I noticed that Tuanthal had two onagers. "Have you tried them yet?"

"Aye my lord. We managed to strike the beach over there on the mainland once. No ship can pass these waters unscathed."

I rode west in silence. What Tuanthal has said was true but we were an island and they could land anywhere they chose. I hoped I had some time but I needed to plan as though I had not. We reached the fort after dark and I held a meeting with my advisers.

"What you need, my lord is a series of beacons across the island. It is flat and there are a few highpoints. We could light the beacons when we want the people to seek refuge. They could use my stronghold or Tuanthal's."

"Now that Mungo is here we need Tuanthal to patrol the island. What we need is ships to warn us of impending danger."

"The fishing ships are too small and we have neither the skills nor the resources to build our own."

What Oswald said was true and, for the first time since coming to the island, I felt under serious threat. Gareth joined me after we had finished making our plans. "Tell us of your ordeal Gareth."

"We heard them coming and saw that there were many of them. We would not have been able to fight them off." He smiled ruefully, "you showed us how ill prepared we were, my lord. We crossed the bridge and headed for Deva. They must have thought that we had more in our poor homes than we had for they spent a long time there and then they fired it. We reached the river and my people were tired." He hung his head. "I am sorry to say we stole some boats. But I was tying to save my people."

"Do not worry Gareth, sometimes leaders have to make decisions they do not like."

"The boats were overcrowded but we headed down river; the current made life simpler. When we drew close to Deva we saw the Saxon ships on the other side of the bridge and the men with the ram trying to breach the gate. We were less than a hundred paces away when disaster struck; one of the boats capsized and took all but three to their deaths. Those three clung to our boat and we bumped alongside the bridge. We climbed as quickly as we could and your man, Mungo saved us by letting us in. We barely had time to think. We were all armed from those who had already fallen in the defence of the fort. Mungo sent us across the bridge with the women and children from the fort. The Saxons tried to hit us with arrows but Icaunus must have been watching us for they missed. When the bridge was fired I thought that our saviours would perish but they ran unscathed through the flames and told us to hurry down the road. When we reached the monastery the good monks there asked us to stay but we all wanted to reach the sanctuary that is Ynys Mon." I smiled. Because Brother Oswald and Osric had written our plan for escape we had used the Latin name, Mona. It sounded strange to hear it now named in our language. "We were terrified when we saw the narrow piece of sea. It looked so angry but your horsemen brought the raft and we cried with joy at our rescue."

"Your people are more than welcome to stay here and, if they do I have a task for you."

"We would wish to stay here my lord. I feel safe."

"Good. We have ships that have begun to arrive to trade with us and the people bring their goods to our market but we need someone to run it, to manage it." I peered into his eyes. "I need an honest man. Will you do it?" He nodded gratefully. "There is a hut there that we use for meetings and you can use that as your home." He grabbed my hand to kiss it. I felt embarrassed. "Yes, well, you will be doing me a favour so thank you."

The next month was spent preparing for the attack we assumed would reach us sooner rather than later and building up our army. It would never be the Army of Rheged but with our new weapons and the magic of the isles protecting us I was hopeful. A message reached me close to the festival of Eostre. There were Irish ships just outside the port. I took ten mounted warriors and Miach with his archers. Pol and Hogan accompanied me. I did not think that the Irish would be here for a social visit and I was prepared for war.

There were three ships and they were the same type as those used by the Saxons. They each held thirty men and although they had a sail oars were the preferred method of propulsion. Gwynfor looked worried. "Their leader is a warrior called Felan. He says he is here to trade but his eyes looked shifty."

"I think if he was here to cause mischief he would have attacked first and negotiated only if he failed." I glanced up at the newly restored walls. The onagers were in place and hidden but, as yet they were unmanned. That would need to be remedied. "Miach. Man the onagers and aim them at the ships. Do not use them yet. I will try to talk with them. Gwynfor, will you take me out to them?"

"Aye my lord."

"Miach, keep watch from here. You do not need me to tell you what to do. Hogan and Pol come with me. Wolf, stay!" Hogan grinned whilst Wolf put his head down and looked very sorry for himself.

The boats the men used were long and narrow with a small sail. I had seen them scurrying about the island and they were very nimble.

Unfortunately, they had a tendency to heel over and the water looked frighteningly close. The two boys did not seem to mind but I gripped the side for all grimly. We bumped next to the ship Gwynfor said was the boat of their leader. Willing hands helped us aboard and Gwynfor said, "I will wait just here my lord. Call me when you need me."

A huge red-haired man almost picked me up when I boarded. "You must be the Wolf Warrior I have heard so much about!"

"If you let me down I will introduce myself."

"Ah sure and don't mind me. I like a fighting man and I hear you have done more fighting than any other man alive; the king killer and the killer of champions."

I demurred and held my arm out. "This is Hogan my son and squire and Pop my standard bearer."

"So this is the famous Wolf Standard. That too is famous as is the dragon you use with your fabulous horsemen."

"I was told you wished to trade."

He put his arm around me and led me away from his men. "Aye, the thing is it is more of work I would like to do with you. I heard from a few of the captains that you pay silver and not just barter for bits of jewellery."

I wondered how he had spoken with the captains; he had probably captured them but I smiled, playing his game. "Aye we do."

"Now I cannot help but notice that you have no fighting ships and as you can see I do. I have heard that King Aethelric has put a price on your head and is coming here with his ships. So if you hire me, we will do the fighting for you eh?"

"That is generous of you but I am not sure we can afford to pay for your three ships."

He leaned in and spoke conspiratorially to me. He stank of onions and he needed a bath but I forced a smile. "The thing of it is you would be paying me. I will deal with my men. How does thirty pieces of silver for every day we sail sound?"

I disengaged myself. "It sounds a little steep to me. How about thirty pieces of silver for every month you work for me?"

"I can see that you have a shrewd mind but if we are watching for you then we aren't earning any money are we?"

"I'll tell you what I will do and we will call it a trial. I will give you ten pieces of silver and you sail to Deva. Come back and tell me if the Saxons are still there. Then I will know if it is worthwhile to hire you."

He greedily eyed the bag of silver. "Of course I could just take the money and not come back."

"True but I think you want the other twenty pieces." I shrugged. "Let us call it a gamble. I am gambling that you want more gold."

His eyes lit up when I said gold and he spat on his hand and held it out to me. "Then we have a deal Wolf Warrior."

I took his hand and gave him the bag of silver. Felan took us to the side of his ship and waved at Gwynfor. "Sure and I like you. I might just bring a Saxon ship back. Will you pay for it?"

"Twenty for every Saxon ship you bring."

"You have that much silver?"

I smiled enigmatically, "Thank you for coming to see me. Your men are welcome in the town but only if they come ashore unarmed and in small boats."

"A very kind offer but we will be away to the Dee. I can see more money coming my way."

As we tacked back to the land Pol asked, "That is good news is it not my lord? Now we have ships to aid us in our fight."

"We shall see Pol. We shall see." Once back on land I gave Miach his instructions. "Keep the onagers manned and leave thirty of your men here with a good leader." I turned to Gwynfor who had just tied up his boat. "Could we put a rope across the entrance to this port? Could it be just below the water? I have a mind to stop ships entering the harbour it we don't like the look of them."

"Aye my lord but it would stop us getting out."

"We could have men operating the rope to let in those we wish to"

He grinned. "I will put some of the young lads on that. They can lower it when we need to use it."

"Gareth, I want all of your people arming. It may not come to a fight but if it does I want you prepared."

I leapt on Raven feeling better than I had for some time. "Back to the fort. We have plans to make."

I spent some time with Garth, Myrddyn and Brother Oswald discussing what we would do if the Saxons came. Garth appeared puzzled. "But if this Hibernian can find the Saxons ships then he can destroy them."

"The problem is, Garth, that we do not know how many ships the Saxons have. This Felan has but three ships. The best that we can hope is that he finds them and warns us. Oswald how goes the beacons?"

"They are all in place and men are placed to light them."

"And the people?"

"They know to seek the safety of a fort."

I relaxed a little. "Good."

"We need to practise using the new onagers."

"There are plenty of stones on the beach. Make sure that Miach's men at Caergybi have the opportunity too."

I closed my eyes briefly. This sudden danger was new and I felt suddenly tired. Suddenly I hear Myfanwy's voice. It was sharp and angry. "You men are fools, Cannot you see that the Warlord is exhausted? Leave us!"

I opened my eyes and saw the three men scurrying out of the chamber. She stood with her hands on her hips. "And you, my lord. You must take better care of yourself. If you were to fall... well I just don't know what would happen. I don't think you have eaten today have you?" She did not wait for an answer but handed me a bowl and a spoon. "Here, game stew. Now eat it and then get some sleep. There are others here who can watch."

As she stormed out I saw Hogan peer shyly around the edge of the door. "And she is right father. You need to eat and sleep more. Too many people rely on you."

I held up my hands in surrender. "Enough. I will eat and then I will sleep."

They were both right and I woke with a much clearer head the next day. I sent a message to Tuanthal to watch out for Saxons by the mainland. It would not do to underestimate Aethelric although it could be any of the other Saxon leaders. They had the free run of my country now. We had more volunteers and they were armed and prepared but they were not trained. If they survived the summer then we could begin to turn them into a warrior but for now they made up the numbers. The blacksmith had been working flat out preparing weapons and armour. He had confided in me that he was running short of iron and I knew that we would have to find a new supply soon.

The day was an anti-climax. There were no lit beacons and neither the Saxons nor the Irish reappeared. Had I read the Saxons wrongly? Perhaps my foolish Irishman had taken them on and lost. I was assuming they would land close to me but they had the whole coastline to choose and only Tuanthal's horses would be there to see them. I was creating my own riddling doubts and I rode, with Myrddyn, Pol and Hogan to Caergybi.

Gareth was there and he proudly paraded the men of the town who he had armed. I was not sure that they would stand up to a Saxon attack but all that they needed to do was boost our numbers. "They are a credit to you Gareth." I pointed up at the onagers. "Have you seen them at work?"

"We have my lord. We watched them this morning and they are terrifying. I would bet that Gwynfor was happy to have escaped with his boats before they started. The whole of the harbour was filled with splashes."

"He left for the fishing grounds?"

"Aye, we have a market tomorrow. Folks will be coming for their fish and to bring their trade goods."

"The markets are going well then?" I did not bother with the peaceful activities of my domain and I felt sad about that.

"They are growing. It takes people time to change to new ideas but they are coming round, never fear. The last one we had forty visitors. When we have a ship in then it is even busier."

"How do you know when a ship is due?"

"You don't. Even if the captains told us it would depend on the weather and the pirates. Sometimes we get three in a week and then we might go three weeks without one." He shrugged. "I cannot see how we can be more accurate."

Myrddyn said, "All the ships have to travel from the south. It must take those boats hours to get around the headland. If we kept watch from the towers in the castle then we could signal you that a ship was due and you would have eight hours' notice."

Gareth shook his head in amazement, "They are right, you are a wizard!"

"There is a fishing boat and he is coming quickly."

"Good eyes Hogan. Stand to. He may just have a big fish but we will not take chances."

The onager crews and the archers laughed. Myrddyn added, "Begin a fire just in case it is danger."

I went down to the harbour to greet Gwynfor. He began shouting excitedly as he lowered his sail. "It is the Irishman. He has captured a Saxon ship and they are heading in."

I looked at Myrddyn and then asked, "Was there any damage to any of the ships?" His expression told me he did not understand the question. "Broken oars, damaged sails. That sort of thing."

Understanding flooded his face. "No, my lord."

"Get the boom across the harbour. Gareth; send your men to the ramparts. We may have a problem." I grabbed Hogan's arm. Ride to the fort and tell Miach to being every archer and tell Garth to stand to. There may be something up."

"But father he said they have captured a Saxon ship."

"And that may be great cause for celebration but I find it hard to believe that there is no damage to any of the ships." I raced up the steps to Miach's men. "Have the fire ready. When I give the command I want one of you to target the Saxon ship and the other the ship of Felan. Use rocks for the first three attacks to gauge the distance and when you are happy then change to fire."

"And if you give no command my lord?"

"Then we have a Saxon ship to begin our fleet."

"Sail in sight!"

I saw the three ships as they edged into sight. Gwynfor waved to show that he had the boom in place and I went down to the harbour side. The rope was well hidden and the four ships did not see it until it was almost too late. They began to rapidly back oars and Felan appeared on the prow of his ship.

"You appear to have a boom in place. Do you want to shift it so that we can bring you your prize and I can get the rest of my money?"

He had such an easy smile and seemed so genuine that I almost doubted myself. Luckily Myrddyn's eyes were shaper than mine and his mind moved quicker too. "Lord Lann, those boats are loaded with men. Look how low they are in the water. If they had a fight I would have expected them to have fewer men; especially as he would have had to crew the Saxon ship too."

"You are right." I cupped my hands. "The boom is new and we are trying to work out how to use it. I will come aboard your ship and give you the money now eh?"

There was a sharp intake of breath from Pol. "If they are with the Saxons then they will have you."

"I have no intention of stepping foot on any of their ships. Watch."

"No that's all right. We don't mind waiting until you fix it."

"If you would move your ships closer to this bank and take off our prize crew my men would like some target practice for their arrows."

"You can't do that. It is a fine boat."

"A few arrows will not sink a Saxon ship. I know I have fought them before. Just ask your crew to drop the anchor on the Saxon boat and rejoin you." I spoke with a smile on my face but Felan's face contorted in anger.

"You bastard. At them!" The three ships tried to row over the boom.

I dropped my arm and stones and arrows began to fly across the water. Myrddyn's assessment proved accurate when a wall of shields appeared on each ship. There had to be fifty men on each boat. Even with their shields the arrows struck flesh but even more devastating was the crash of the stones. Only one struck the water and the others hit the sides of the ship and the shields. Planks shattered and oars broke. Suddenly there was a whoosh as the first fireball flew at the boats. It stuck amidships and the sail of the foremost Irish boat erupted in flames. The Saxon ship was also struck and suddenly there was panic amongst the small fleet. The two ships at the rear tried to back out. The onager crews had their distances well worked out and, with the archers adding to the destruction, the two ships were ablaze from stem to stern. The shifted to the other and, before they could escape, they had been struck four or five times.

We watched as men threw themselves from their stricken ships. Gareth and his men moved down to the harbour wall where they butchered all who tried to land. I saw Felan strip off his armour and begin to swim to his last boat. By the time the two ships had settled in the water the battle was over and the sneak attack had failed.

Myrddyn turned to me and just said, "Another accurate prophesy eh my lord?"

He was right; the men form the sea and smiling Irish. We had been saved by dreams again. Gwynfor and his fishermen fished out the dead bodies. This was partly to recover any weapons and iron we might use and partly to save the waters becoming polluted. The remaining Irish ship limped away to the west. Felan had been thwarted but I had no doubts that he would return. Gwynfor had told me that the Irish had once conquered the whole of the island when the Romans had left and it took a mighty king of Cymri to remove them. So far I had seen little evidence of the King of Wales, Beli ap Rhun, but, perhaps, one day I would meet him. Whoever he was he was exerting little influence on his land.

Once back in my stronghold Brother Oswald organised the weapons and armour. The better pieces would be issued to new warriors and the pieces of poor quality used by the blacksmith. We always had need for iron.

Suddenly one of the guards shouted, "My lord! The beacons are lit!"

Garth looked at me. "The Saxons are here!"

"Get some men mounted. We are blind and they could be anywhere." I shouted over the sentry at the western end. "Have you seen any ships?"

"No my lord."

"I will head to the northern coast. Tuanthal would be able to find any at his end of the island." I saw Miach hurrying over. "Miach I want half of your archers on their horses now."

It was a pitifully small patrol I led out: ten mounted warriors, ten archers, Miach, Pol and Hogan. We were not going to fight a battle; we were going to find the Saxons. Even as we crossed the bridge the villagers and farmers were heeding the warning of the beacons. We questioned them all but they had only seen the beacons and not the Saxons. I headed directly for the coast. I reasoned that we would have seen them from Caergybi had they been close to that end of the island and the middle would afford me the best opportunity of spotting them.

Pol's sharp eyes saw them first. "There, Lord Lann. Down the coast."

I could see them about four miles away. There were six ships which meant anything from two hundred to three hundred men. I grabbed an archer. "Ride to the fort and tell Garth they are on the northern coast close to Amlwch." I pointed to a second. "Ride to captain Tuanthal and tell him to join me close to Amlwch."

Miach gave me a shrewd look. "You are counting on containing them with horses?"

"I am but I am also going to tempt them north towards the fort." I pointed at the furled standard. "That normally works." I raised my voice so that all could hear. "No heroics today. We annoy them and make them want to kill us." I paused. "They normally do that anyway!" They cheered. They were in good spirits and ready for a fight. Tuanthal had forty mounted men. Now that Mungo garrisoned his fort he had the freedom he needed for his horses.

The pall of smoke told us that they had fired the small cluster of huts. I led us slightly inland to cut them off and to see if any had escaped. This was where my scouts would have come in handy but they were now training to be warriors and we were blind without them. We found the first refugees a mile along the track. They were heading south to the bridge. I recognised one from Rheged, a one-armed farmer who had fought besides me against King Ida. He seemed quite composed whilst the others were almost hysterical. He carried his old sword in his good hand. "There are about five hundred of them Warlord." He grinned, "Although I didn't stop to count. They are a mile or so behind us. They spent too long destroying the huts and that gave us the chance to run."

"Well done. Keep heading along the track and tell Captain Garth your news. Tell him I will draw them on."

"I will do my lord." He turned to his party. "See I told you the Warlord would know how to handle it. Now let's get moving."

With old warriors like that my new land was safe. "We know where they are now. Let us lay a little ambush for them." There were few heavily forested areas on the island but there was a small knoll with a thin stand of trees ahead. "Miach. Take your men and hide in the woods. We will bring them to you. Five flights and then mount and get out of there."

"With pleasure."

We were now the bait; thirteen men against three hundred. As we rode I said to Hogan, "Do not get close to them. They will come for me so do not get in the way."

"But I am your squire."

"And I would like to see you a warrior. Pol, watch him carefully."

There was a small lake between them and my castle and I wanted them to take the northern route around the lake. We climbed a small ridge and saw the untidy yet well-armed warband. There were about three hundred of them. "Unfurl the banner. Let us annoy them." I fitted my bowstring as we trotted down the slope. We would be returning that way and I could tell that it would slow them down and tire them as they followed us.

We were three hundred paces away when they saw us. They just launched themselves at us. "Halt!" I fitted an arrow and aimed at the leading warrior. Even as my arrow plunged into his neck I had loosed a second and a third. The first three warriors fell dead. For my fourth arrow I chose a leader not in the front rank. He must have felt safe right up until the arrow struck him in the chest and he too fell dead. "Let us retreat now, but not too fast. We want them to catch us."

We rode at a steady trot which made the Saxons have to run after us. Had they not recognised me then I think they would have halted but seeing the Wolf Warrior they came on eagerly. Inevitably, the fitter warriors began to catch us and they became strung out. Nearing the wooded knoll where Miach waited I veered my patrol towards it as though we were seeking refuge and they took the bait. Twenty men ran at an angle to cut us off. Feigning panic I veered right almost straight away and when Miach launched his attack, most of the warband had their backs towards the archers. It was a bowman's delight and their fifty arrows all found marks. They wheeled to face the new threat; just in time to see Miach and his archers burst from the trees and head west, towards our bridge and fort. I too wheeled my horsemen to join up with them.

The Saxon leader halted. I could see the walking wounded being aided and those who would not survive having their throats cut. There was a debate going on. We reined in. "Well done Miach. It looked like every arrow found a home."

"Not quite my lord, I counted eight misses." He glared at three warriors who hung their heads. "I think we will have to have some extra practice sessions."

We watched as the debate went on and then they formed a column and set off after us. I suppose it made sense, if they were sent here to capture me, and I assumed that they were, they had to follow us. The leader showed that he suspected another trap and they walked this time; a depleted column of warriors. We skirted the lake on our left and even had time to, arrogantly, water our horses. When we reached the north western side, however, Pol shouted, "Saxons ahead of us!"

There was a second warband and they had tried to trap me. Where had they come from? Of course we could out run them but it meant that they had even more warriors on my island. "Head due north!" By heading north both groups would have further to go to entrap me. "Let us kick on a little." It was time to put a little distance between us. I was also acutely aware that I had to buy time for my people to reach their strongholds. We could all now see the second warband and it looked to be the same size as the first. They must have sailed out of sight of land

and landed on the southern shore. Perhaps they had sailed through the narrows and been seen by Tuanthal; in which case they would have damage to their ships. The time would come for us to find out the truth. For now we just had to react to their actions.

I hoped that Garth had reinforced the fort at the end of the bridge. I wanted the bridge whole and not destroyed. It had taken too long to build to throw the work away needlessly. By our own standards it was quite a primitive fort but it was still stronger than anything we had seen. There was a double ditch on three sides and the sea on the fourth. There were two gates; one over the bridge and one into the fort protected by a drawbridge over the ditch. Garth should have had time to move the onagers into place. They were not effective against lightly armed skirmishers but they could destroy a shield wall.

The light was fading behind us and I went a little faster. It was very easy to be deceived by movement in poor light and we were the ones highlighted in the setting sun. Our horses were now tiring but I knew that the Saxons would be wearier. "Miach take your men into the fort. Put your horses on the island and man the walls."

The archers, lighter armoured than we, kicked on and soon they were just a dark shadow racing west. Hogan glanced over his shoulder, "I think they are gaining."

Diarmid, the last warrior in the column shouted, "Don't worry young master, I'll let you know when they are close."

My men were all confident; it came from being undefeated. We were depleted but, as yet, undefeated. I turned and saw that they were less than half a mile back which was a safe distance but Hogan was right they had closed. I suspected now that they had not scouted out our base and only had Felan's description of the port. They must have assumed we would be heading to that side of the island. When they saw the fort they would receive a serious shock. The sun was setting rapidly and I saw the stark outline of the small fort loom up. Miach had warned the guards and the drawbridge was down. As we clattered over it I felt a sense of relief that we had made our sanctuary. As Diarmid trotted over the sentries raised and secured the drawbridge and the shut and barred the gate. It would be interesting to see how they fashioned a ram on this island of stunted trees. Once again we were besieged but this time there was no-one to come to our aid. We were alone ands outnumbered by more than two to one.

# Chapter 19

Garth and Myrddyn greeted me as I entered. My wizard handed me a water skin. "I think all of our people made the fort, my lord, and we moved two of the onagers. They are on the two corner towers and the others are facing the sea."

I looked at Garth, "The sea?"

"One of the sentries thinks he saw sails to the south but in the darkening sky he couldn't be sure."

"I am. It would make sense. They can move men around or they can take them off. I am afraid they are not just going to lie down and die." I ran up the steps to the walls and peered out. It was too dark to see anything. "Have we sown caltrops? Put traps in the ditches?"

"Yes Warlord. There is just the road free of caltrops but the onagers have the road covered."

"Good but they can advance down the road quietly if they wish."

I could see Myrddyn trying to come up with a solution. "Seaweed!"

"What?"

Before he could answer he had raced down the steps and crossed the bridge. I looked at Garth in amazement. "Do not ask me my lord, he is your wizard, but I suspect it will be a novel approach to defence."

We could hear the Saxons moving around but we could not see them. They would need to rest, eat and drink before they tried anything. Perhaps they wouldn't try anything in the night and wait for day. We could not take the chance and we would be the ones losing sleep. An hour later Myrddyn raced up with ten of the boys from the main fort. In their hands they held armfuls of seaweed. My incredulous face asked the question of Myrddyn. "The seaweed is slippery but it also has large bubbles in it. When it is stepped on it pops. It also stinks so it will annoy them and they cannot harm us if they throw it back."

Garth looked sceptical. "And how do we get it on the road?"

"I am sure that a huge warrior such as you can throw it the five paces to the other side of the drawbridge and your onagers can do the rest." He handed his bunch of slippery weed to Garth.

I grinned at my captain of warriors. "Well go on. Throw it."

I know he felt foolish but he did it. The solid plop told us that it had landed on the road we had built. Then we heard the whoosh of the Roman war machines as they hurled their cargo. It was maddening. We

200

would not be able to see the results until the morning. Garth pointed to Miach and me. "And now, Warlord. You have been riding all day. You sleep and we will awake you when, and if they come."

I might have argued but when I reached my hall Myfanwy was waiting for Hogan and me with arms folded. "Fancy keeping a young growing boy out all day without any food." She wagged an admonishing finger at me. "You should be ashamed of yourself. Now there is food on the table. I want it eaten and you two in bed as soon as the food is gone."

Hogan's mouth opened and closed and Pol chuckled. "I think I would sooner face the Saxons than get on the wrong side of that one!"

The food made me sleepy and, as soon as my head hit the bed, I was dead to the world. It seemed but a moment before I heard Myrddyn's voice. "Come my lord. They are trying something."

"How long?"

"You have been asleep for a few hours. I have risked Myfanwy's wrath to wake you. We heard noises a short while ago. It was the sound of the seaweed plopping which alerted us."

I sensed the smug satisfaction in his voice, "Yes Myrddyn, you are a clever wizard."

We reached the gatehouse and Garth pointed. "There is some movement out there but I can't see what.

Suddenly there was a sudden light as the Saxons launched some fire arrows at us. Miach snorted. "Well that is a bit rich; pinching our idea." Even as he was complaining he was taking aim. "Right lads, let's show them how real archers do it."

Garth had his men pour buckets of seawater on to the fire. We had them close by the onagers in case we needed to use fire ourselves. Miach's men did their job well and the incoming arrows stopped. "I could see what they intend my lord. When they launched their arrows I could see that they have faggots of wood to throw into the ditches."

"Then they will get a real surprise when they find the caltrops."

We heard the screams from the men as they stepped on the deadly weapon, designed to be used against horses but equally effective against Saxons. The rest of the night was a game of cat and mouse, as they tried every possible attack which did not involve a charge. We saw the dawn rise behind them and they were still in the same position.

"Ships! To the south!"

I ran to the southern wall and there were twenty Saxon ships. The two warbands had been landed to pin us down but my people were now

201

safe inside our wooden walls. The Saxons would find that I could defeat them, even with a tiny army. I looked around at the small fort. We had sixty warriors within while the other one hundred and the villagers were in the main fort. My archers were split between the two with plenty of arrows. The handful of slingers who remained was also equally split. Every man on the walls had a helmet and either mail or leather. The main problem we would have would be if they fired the walls. To counter that we had every container we could with sea water. It was easy to replenish.

"Garth you take command here. Do not risk your men. Fall back and destroy the bridge when all is lost. I will watch those ships."

"Very well my lord."

I hurried across the bridge to the second gate. The two guards there were more than enough. Their main task was to watch for those who might try to climb the cliffs. Once through there we ran the mile to the main fort. "Myrddyn, we will need fire before this day is out. When those ships close to land I want them set afire." When my two engineers had built the onagers they had fashioned the containers for the stones out of thin iron. It would not burn.

"Here Fa... er Warlord. Here is your helmet." I smiled at Hogan who gave me my helmet and the gleaming, freshly sharpened Saxon Slayer. Finally he gave me my wolf shield and I was ready.

I walked to the southern wall. The ships were closing in a line. The only place they could land was on the beach at Porthdafarch and that would aid us. They would have to bring in the ships just three at a time as the bay was narrow with high rocks on both sides. Once ashore they would have the rocks to climb. There were not especially high but they were jagged and irregular. A warrior would struggle to defend himself and climb at the same time.

"Onager crews prepare your weapons." Myrddyn had taken charge of the crews; Brother Oswald felt it went against his beliefs to cause death with his cleverly constructed weapons. Myrddyn had no such compunction.

I could hear the sound of battle from across the bridge. It had begun. The sound of the crack as the onagers loosed their rocks and the flights of the arrows contrasted with the screams and cries of the dying Saxons.

The ships were within range of the onagers but Myrddyn did not order the onagers to fire. The ships were fifty paces from the beach when he ordered them to begin their assault. There were only two onagers facing the sea but they were on the two corner towers and their strikes converged. The middle boat erupted in flames as the first two missiles struck. The Saxons threw themselves over the side of the ship as its bone dry timbers and sail became an inferno. The burnt timbers settled on the bottom as the two machines shifted their aim to new targets. The men who struggled ashore had to avoid the arrows and lead balls from the ramparts. Two more ships came in before the bay was filled with burning and sinking ships and the survivors were huddled amongst the rocks with their shields over their heads.

It looked like we had thwarted their first attempt at landing. One of the men from Caergybi was standing nearby and heard the men on the walls cheering as though we had won. "There is another bay just a mile away my lord. There are no cliffs and they can land there. It is this side of the bridge. Captain Garth will be cut off."

I suddenly saw that I had been outwitted. They had scouted out the island and my best warriors were in grave danger. "Send a rider to the bridge. Tell Captain Garth to destroy the onagers and bridge and get back here." I could rebuild the bridge; I could never replace Garth. "Miach, get rid of those men on the beach. We will have more at the front gate soon and we will need to move men around."

"You heard the Warlord. Aim well and kill every bastard Saxon who still breathes!"

The despatch rider would not take long to reach our bridge; I just hoped that Garth and his men could make it back on foot. "Adair. Mount ten men and cover Garth's retreat." My young horseman leapt down from the wall and raced to the stables. He might be young but he had a wealth of experience.

I had to hope that it would take time for the ships to sail down the coast and then land. "Myrddyn get the other two onagers moved to this wall and then bring the ones covering the beach. They can do no more good there. "

It felt eerily silent as the last of the men on the beach was killed. I sent down some men to bring back any wounded and weapons and stared out in the direction of the bridge just a couple of miles away. I wondered if I had doomed my warriors to a grisly death by trying to hold on to the bridge. I watched Adair and his horsemen gallop out of the gate. With luck they might just make the difference between life and death for Garth and his men.

203

"My lord! Smoke!"

I looked east and saw the smoke rising in the distance. I prayed it was the bridge. "Be ready. When Captain Garth reaches us there will be Saxons all over him. Archers I want you to aim like you have never aimed before. Hogan, my bow." Today I would need to fight alongside my archers. And then I saw the despatch rider waving his arms. "Open the gate."

He slid to a halt beneath us. "Captain Garth is coming. He set fire to the fort, the onagers and the bridge but there are Saxons coming from the south."

They had landed! I prayed that the gods of these lands who had been so kind to us would continue to do so. Myrddyn seemed to read my mind. "Do not worry my lord. The spirits of this holy place will aid us this day."

Suddenly our men appeared over the low rise to the south of us and Garth was leading them. "Get that gate open. I could see Adair and his horsemen behind but they appeared not to be under attack. I grinned at my deputy as he entered the gate. "I think we burned more than a few of them my lord. Thank you for sending Adair. The Saxons thought it was a larger force and went into shield wall. It bought us time."

Adair and his men trotted calmly through the gate, as though they had been for a pleasant morning's ride. "Well done Adair."

"Piece of piss my lord!" His little victory had made him cocky. I didn't mind, he deserved his moment of glory

I counted Garth's men and he had lost a third of his defenders. We now had a greater perimeter to defend but they could only attack from one side. The rest were protected by rocks and cliffs. The onagers had plenty of stones and Myrddyn smiled as he checked the tension on each machine. The three hundred Saxons formed a shield wall and marched resolutely towards us. Their comrades from beyond the bridge would take time to join them and the rest of the boats would not have had time to land yet. If I had been their leader I would have waited until I had all my men but he was eager to capture the Wolf Warrior.

"Myrddyn."

"Just a few more moments, my lord. There is a small rise and our stones will kill more this way."

He lowered his hand and four stones flew through the air. They struck four warriors and then continued to strike others. One of the stones struck a man's head and it disappeared but the stone went off at an angle and continued to fell men. Huge gaps appeared in their ranks. Myrddyn reloaded and launched again. The Saxons rushed forwards. All attempts at cohesion had gone as they ran to avoid the deadly rain. Then they came in range of my archers who did not miss the opportunity to strike at men who were no longer in a shield wall. The stones continued to strike although they were less effective now that the Saxons had split up into smaller groups. They fell into the ditch, lined with spikes without even seeing it and they lay writhing at the bottom. The archers slaughtered them and soon the Saxons were fleeing backwards towards the safety of the ridge. They left most of the warband dead before our walls.

While Myrddyn attended to the machines which already showed signs of wear and tear already my warriors went to empty the ditches. "I want two prisoners. Kill the rest." We needed the ditches clearing and the weapons would be useful. The onager crews reclaimed their best stones and when the Saxons, now reinforced, formed up again the ditches were clear and my men back in the fort. They came on in the same style and we struck them again in the same style. This time they filled their front ranks with other warriors who wore better armour and my archers did not have such easy targets. When they reached the ditch men from the rear began throwing flaming brands at the walls. Some of them were hit by arrows but others succeeded and we had to put the fires out. They also used their own archers to target the onager crews and I sent Pol with a shield to cover the brave Myrddyn. By the time they retreated they had lost many men but we had taken casualties too and one of the onagers was broken and would need repairs. Although the Saxons had lost many more than we they had more men to lose. In a warrior of attrition they would win. As the day ended the Saxons retreated to lick their wounds. I held a meeting with my captains.

"We did well today, my lord."

"Yes but we did not defeat the enemy, Ridwyn. Our archers killed many but each attack they made was more successful. We will be down to three onagers tomorrow."

"And they could easily break. They are a little fragile. If we had time we could make them more robust..." Myrddyn's voice tailed off.

"And remember they will be reinforced tomorrow by the men from the bridge. They will be eager to fight after they were singed by Captain Garth."

"That is it! The Dunum all over again." Myrddyn's face showed the excitement his idea had aroused.

"The Dunum?"

"Yes my lord, fire ships. We have the fishermen of Caergybi. They know these waters. They could sail around the headland and launch fire ships at the Saxon fleet. They will not wish to be stranded here without boats will they?"

I could see that it would work but I need Gwynfor to be willing to proceed with the plan. "Myrddyn come with me. Garth, Miach and Ridwyn you take charge here. If they break through the first wall then destroy the onagers and move back to the stronghold. Hopefully we will succeed but…"

"You my lord? There was shock in Ridwyn's voice and I could see that Miach and Garth were unhappy about my decision.

"Yes me, Ridwyn. If we have to improvise then Myrddyn and I are the most adept at that. I will leave Pol here and Hogan to give the illusion that I am still here. They will have watchers and if they see the banner then they will think I am here."

Pol and Hogan were equally unhappy but I was determined. Perhaps it was an arrogance bred from success. I do not know but each time I made a decision like this it normally worked. When we reach the port Gareth and Gwynfor were keen to know what had happened. Many refugees had made it to Caergybi, the Christians amongst them taking shelter in the small church of St. Cybi. I took the two men to one side. "I plan on setting fire to the Saxon ships but I will need your help. I need some boats we can set on fire."

Gwynfor looked alarmed. "The fishing boats are our livelihood!"

Gareth snorted, "If the Saxons come there will be no livelihood."

"Gwynfor is right. Tell me then, is there any way you can think of that we can float something close enough to the Saxon ships to fire them?"

"Coracles!"

Gareth and I did not understand the word but Myrddyn looked excited. "Of course. Have you any?"

"Aye my lord. Every hut has at least one and some have more. We use them to go out into the bay and collect crab pots and cross the water. We only use them rarely and we can easily build more."

Myrddyn turned to me. "Imagine an upturned bowl big enough for one man. You paddle with your hands. We can fill them with wood and straw and tow them." He turned to Gwynfor. "We would need to use your boats to tow them into position."

"Aye my lord," he grinned. "It means we keep our boats and that is good enough for me."

"Let us get started then. We have to sail around the headland be there before dawn or this will; not work."

"Where are they my lord?"

"I think someone said the Bay of Trearrdur."

"Then we can sail between the islands. It is narrow but my boat can make it. It will make for a much shorter journey."

"That will mean we will have to sail through their lines."

"Yes my lord, but they will not be looking at the sea."

Myrddyn was right. "Good then let us go."

It took longer to collect the flammable material than to get the coracles. They were all tied together looking like so many ducklings behind Gwynfor's duck. Myrddyn made a fire pot. It was the safest way to carry fire on a boat and would keep the flame hidden. It contained glowing coals from the blacksmiths and they would still be hot many hours later. One in each coracle would do the job. We took no armour and only short swords and my bow. The fishing boat was too small to allow me to swing Saxon Slayer and if I fell then it would go to Hogan. All of Gwynfor's crew wished to come but we needed as few men on board as possible and we set off with a slight breeze blowing from the west. It meant we could get there quickly but we would take longer to get home.

When I saw the gap between the islands it seemed quite wide but Gwynfor whispered that soon it would close upon us like walls of rock. He was right. I could see the glow from the burning fort and the remnants of the bridge. Gwynfor suddenly hauled down the sail. "What is the matter?"

"The bridge has partly blocked the channel we will have to edge around. Here." Myrddyn and I were given oars. "Fend off any wood that might stop us and I will steer."

We crawled through the debris sometimes having to go at right angles to the direction we really wished to go. All the time it was eating up the night and making it perilously close to dawn. Eventually we emerged into the open sea and we could see the fleet. We kept the sail down to lower our profile and rowed into position. I hauled the coracles up one by one. When the first one was alongside Myrddyn dropped the hot coal from the fire pot into the wood and straw and then pushed it off with his oar. We sailed a few more paces to the next ship and repeated it. The wind and the current took the little black blobs towards the silent, moored fleet. I wondered if the fire had gone out as the coracles remained ominously dark. As the last one was lit Gwynfor hoisted the sail. I could see the stern of the last Saxon ship less than thirty paces from me. "Give me the fire pot. Gwynfor sail as close to the Saxon ship as you can get."

Both men must have had misgivings but they obeyed. Before he gave me the pot Myrddyn sprinkled something inside. "A little magic from Myrddyn," he said.

As we passed within ten paces I stood and hurled the pot into the air. "Now get us out of here!"

The pot landed with a clatter and then a wall of flame sprang up. There were bright reds, blues, greens and yellows. It looked like a dragon had fired the ship. Even as we headed out to sea I saw the coracles begin to burst into flames. Some of them missed the boat nearest to them but they still posed a threat to all the ships. The Saxons on the boats reacted quickly and I saw sails being hoisted as they tried to run. Their only chance was to outrun the tiny coracles which would soon burn out and sink. The boat we had fired was aflame from bow to stern and the crew could be seen jumping into the water. We were edging quickly out to sea and soon we would have to tack to turn for home. The coracles had managed to set alight at least four ships. The Saxon ships were now desperately trying to avoid the coracles and each other. As the Saxon ships which were not on fire headed out to sea we were in danger of being caught by the bigger boats.

I notched an arrow. It would be like spitting in the wind but I could pick off the steersmen on one of the ships and give us a chance. The Saxons were highlighted against the burning vessels whilst we were a tiny black boat hidden in the night. As dawn broke, however, we would soon be seen. I peered over the side and saw that another four ships were on fire. The others, all ten of them appeared to be under control although I could still see small fires burning. It was then that they saw us and three boats turned to pursue us.

"Head for Porthdafarch!" I counted on the fact that my men in the fort would be watching for us and might be able to affect a rescue. I turned to watch the Saxons. They were three hundred paces behind us but gaining. The rocks at the edge of the bay jutted out into the bay giving Gwynfor the chance to sail closer to the shore than the deeper Saxon ships but they could cut the corner. It was a chance we had to take. When they were two hundred paces from us I chanced an arrow. The nearest Saxon boat was turning slightly to gain the benefit from the wind. I loosed and the gods were with me as the arrow thudded into the chest of the man on the tiller. Suddenly the boat yawed to the right and before they could do anything it crunched to its slow death on the deadly rocks.

We were still not safe for the two other ships were now less then two hundred paces away and gaining. They had a wall of shields around the vulnerable steersman and I would not be able to repeat my feat. It was with some relief that we rounded the headland. As we did the boat almost came to a halt as we tried to sail into the wind. Gwynfor quickly tacked and we crossed beneath the bows of the second Saxon ship. I loosed a speculative arrow and hit the man at the bow watching the rocks. The little spurt took us beyond the boat and they had to repeat the manoeuvre.

I pointed to the far side of the bay. "Head for a point over there."

Gwynfor looked confused but obeyed. It meant that the two Saxon ships would catch us. Myrddyn saw my plan and grinned. "I think someone else can be the bait next time!"

The leading ship was less than thirty paces from our stern when the first of the missiles from my fort struck it. The initial ones were stones but soon one of the onagers was loosing fire. They both tried to turn but the precocious and unpredictable wind did not help them; it veered a point or two. Soon both ships were slowly sinking. Gwynfor had time to turn for the centre of the beach where Garth, Pol and Hogan awaited me with warriors ready to finish off the Saxon survivors.

# Chapter 20

We hauled Gwynfor's boat onto the beach and were warmly greeted by my warriors. Dawn had broken and we see the smoke rising in the sky. The two Saxon ships in the bay had managed to turn and were wrecked on the rocks which divided the two bays. Some of the survivors would make it back to their comrades but many would have their throats slit- the penalty for failure. I headed for the gate. When I reached the top I could see that the Saxons were already beginning to withdraw out of the range of the onagers. They had edged closer under cover of the night and I suspect our early attack had thwarted their own attack. Ridwyn had done a quick count. "They still outnumber us my lord."

"Aye but the loss of their ships may make them reconsider the cost of this expedition."

"They may decide to gamble on winning all with one throw of the dice."

"Then, Captain Garth, let us hope that they do not do so otherwise I have got cold and wet for nothing."

This time they had thought their battle plans through. They had huge shields as high as a man and as wide as three men. They came behind these as they marched forwards. It was no wonder they had not seen us as we sailed between the islands. They must have spent all night building the twenty shields which they now used. Of course the three onagers punched holes in their attack but they did not kill as many men as we had previously. Our archers were forced to release their arrows blind and, again, the Saxon shields took many of the flights. First one, and then a second onager broke down and we were left with one. The Saxons reached the ditch and were able to lay the shields in the ditch as a bridge. Soon they were hacking at the wooden walls with their axes. The men on the walls killed many with their javelins, arrows and slings but still the relentless Saxons came on.

"Ridwyn, Garth, pull every warrior from the walls. Leave the slingers and archers. I want a double line shield wall here behind the gate."

I could see daylight through the walls as the Saxons succeeded in punching holes through the wood. We had our three lines and I stood in the second with Pol and Hogan. Garth and Ridwyn were in the fore.

"As soon as they come through we will run at them and throw them back! Do not become reckless and follow them. When we have thrown them back then we retire behind our walls and their dead!"

When the section of wall went, it went quickly. "The gate had held but the wall to the right had been breached and thirty men poured through. The fifty men of our front rank struck them as one line and Garth and Ridwyn carved a swathe of death through the centre. When one of the warriors in our front rank fell then another took his place. I was not needed as I was following my two captains. In a very short time we were at the breach and the men and boys on the walls decimated the survivors. They ran back to their lines and we retreated.

"Brother Oswald, get some men to shore up the gap."

As they did so Myfanwy and the women came with water and food for the men on the walls. She personally handed me a water skin and some fresh bread. "I know that you will not have eaten." She sniffed, "and you have had another night without sleep!"

Much to my discomfort, my men, and especially Pol and Hogan found this very funny. Their laughter, however, showed me that they were still in good spirits despite the perilous position we were in. The walls had been roughly repaired when the shout from the walls came, "They come again."

"Time to rotate." I stepped into the front rank with Pol and Hogan just behind me and they, in turn, were flanked by Gareth and Ridwyn. My son had the best protection of any of my warriors. They came at the same place they had destroyed. That was their first mistake. Although easier to break down we had not removed the bodies and, as they smashed through and rushed forwards, eagerly, they tripped and fell over the bodies of their own dead. The javelins on the walls made short work of those who flailed on the ground.

"Hit them!" We half ran forwards and hit them in a solid line. Saxon Slayer smashed through the helmet of the first warrior as though it had been parchment. Hogan had sharpened it well. I used a backhand stroke to sweep across the faces of the warriors before me but a spear darted out and stuck me in the thigh. The warrior who had struck the blow gleefully twisted it before Hogan's seax slashed across his throat and he died. I could feel the blood seeping rather than gushing from the wound. I would live. My men were spurred on at the wound inflicted on their Warlord and they fought ferociously, driving the Saxons back once again. As soon as they had retreated Garth shouted, "Myrddyn!" while

Ridwyn tried to organise the repairs to the walls. This time we had nothing left with which to repair them and the Bernician brought his men back to our thin shield wall.

Myrddyn used a knife to widen the breech in my breeks made by the spear. He washed it in water and then dabbed it with a sweet-smelling potion. "Bite on your dagger, my lord. This needs stitching."

"Just do it! I have had stitches before." With Hogan gripping my hand, Myrddyn quickly stitched the wound and bandaged it.

"They come again."

"I know it will do me no good to ask you to go to your chambers but, Hogan, keep your father from fighting again!"

The infuriating healer then went off to see to our other wounded. Garth and Ridwyn had formed the men up in a smaller formation. We had lost warriors. Helped by my son and Pol I dragged myself to my feet and with sword and shield stood beneath the Wolf Banner. The fight was even more frenetic and closely fought than before. The Saxons were throwing everything into this attack. When they were thrown back I saw that just fifty of my men remained. Both Garth and Ridwyn had new scars.

"The next time will be the last my lord. We cannot hold them anymore."

"Here they come again!"

Despite Myrddyn's words my place was with my men and I limped forwards to stand in the thin line of warriors awaiting the attack. The Saxon line was just about to step through the breach when a cry went up from the ramparts. "Horsemen!" And we heard the sound of the Dragon Standard wailing in the distance.

The Saxons paused; this was our chance, "Charge!" We struck them in an improvised wedge but the heart was gone from them. Tuanthal's men poured down the hill and my archers, slingers and the last onager rained death upon them as we struck them. They ran. They hurtled towards their ships in the nearby bay and Tuanthal and his men chased them all the way into the water. By the time my weary men and I reached them, the Saxon ships were edging out to sea. They would not return.

I took off my helmet and grinned up into the face of Tuanthal. "Well met, my friend."

"I am sorry that I am late but we had three ships to deal with. They landed near the Narrows and it took us some time to persuade them to return home."

"So it seems they tried to land in four places. They must really want me. Thank you anyway. We were about to be defeated. Did you suffer many casualties?"

"Fifteen men dead, but none of my horsemen."

"Let us go back to the fortress. Brother Oswald can collect the booty and dispose of the bodies. I could sleep for a week."

Garth laughed, "And Myfanwy will ensure that you do."

"Myfanwy?"

"We have much to tell you Tuanthal."

When we entered the gates our people and those of Caergybi had gathered to cheer us in. Their smiling faces told us how much it had meant to them. As I limped to the warrior hall Myrddyn said, "We will repair the walls and deal with the dead. What do you want to do with the prisoners? Do you still need them?"

I had forgotten my ten prisoners. "We will eat and then I will question them."

Ridwyn shrugged, "They can tell us little now my lord."

"They can tell us who led them and what they hoped to achieve."

"I would have thought that was obvious. They want to capture the island."

"They would have captured the mainland first. If they are at Deva then there is little in their way. No, we will question them and then begin to rebuild."

Food after a battle, no matter what the quality, always tastes as though it is a new food from the gods; the food Brother Osric used to call ambrosia. Certainly, we all ate well and enjoyed ourselves. After the meal I took Myrddyn and my four captains to question the prisoners. All of them had wounds but Myrddyn had tended to them. One had a torc and I knew him to be a chief. I left him for last.

I pointed to one young warrior, "Him!" They dragged him to his feet and held him before me. "You know who I am?"

"The one they call Wolf Warrior."

"Then you know my reputation. Speak the truth and you will have a warrior's death. If not, we will geld you, blind you and throw you to the fishes."

He was brave and defiant but Garth's knife next to his testicles brought forth tears and a torrent of information. Their leader was another Aella, unrelated to the one we had killed. They had been sent by King Aethelric to kill or capture the Wolf Warrior and bring back his people as slaves. He gave us an accurate count of the ships and the men and we knew that we had defeated the whole force. Garth put a sword in his hand and Ridwyn cut his throat. We did the same for them all but the chief. His eyes had been filled with anger and hatred and more, he had a self satisfied smirk upon his face. He knew more than his men.

"Do I now get the warrior's death my men did?"

"No you get the same questions the brave young warrior had and the same threats. What do you know?"

He put on a bland smile. "I know many things. What do you wish to know?"

"Geld him!"

Ridwyn pulled down his breeks and Ridwyn sliced off his testicles in one clean move. He screamed in pain and anger and his face infused with rage. "What I know, Lord Lann, Warlord of Rheged and king killer is that every Saxon in the land is coming to get you and we have your brothers surrounded. Prince Pasgen is a prisoner in Civitas Carvetiorum and Saxons come from all over the land to kill the Wolf Warrior. When King Aethelric comes he will dangle your brothers' heads before you. Is that enough?"

I was never angrier than at that moment and I did not behave well. I was too shocked to think like a leader. "Throw him from the cliffs!"

"My lord!"

"Stay out of this Brother Oswald." My men were frozen like statues. "I will do it myself."

Ridwyn and Garth nodded and picked up the bleeding and still defiant chief and left the room. I heard his voice as he was taken, "I will wait for you in the Otherworld and I will tell them that you have no honour! You are a nithing! We will all be waiting!"

Myrddyn, alone of all of them knew the pain I was feeling and knew why I had acted as I had. "They are both resourceful and brave. They will find a way out of the trap… or he could have been lying. And Prince Pasgen, we escaped and he might too."

"A gelded man does not lie." I slumped into a seat. "It is not just that Myrddyn. While they remained free then there was a chance we could go back some time but now there is no chance for there is no Rheged, just a Saxon England!"

# The End

# Glossary

Characters in italics are fictional

| Name | Explanation |
|------|-------------|
| *Aedh* | Despatch rider and scout |
| Aelfere | Northallerton |
| Aella | King of Deira |
| *Aelle* | Monca's son and Lann's step brother |
| Aethelric | King of Deira (The land to the south of the Tees) |
| *Aidan* | Priest from Metcauld |
| Alavna | Maryport |
| *Ambrosius* | Headman at Brocavum |
| Artorius | King Arthur |
| Banna | Birdoswald |
| Belatu-Cadros | God of war |
| *Bhru* | Bernician warrior |
| *Bladud* | King Urien's standard bearer |
| Blatobulgium | Birrens (Scotland) |
| Brocavum | Brougham |
| Caergybi | Holyhead |
| Civitas Carvetiorum | Carlisle |
| Cynfarch Oer | Descendant of Coel Hen (King Cole) |
| *Delbchaem Lann* | Lann's daughter |
| Din Guardi | Bamburgh Castle |
| Dunum | River Tees |
| Dux Britannica | The Roman British leader after the Romans left (King Arthur) |
| Erecura | Goddess of the earth |
| Fanum Cocidii | Bewcastle |
| *Felan* | Irish pirate |
| *Freja* | Saxon captive and Aelle's wife |
| *Garth* | Lann's lieutenant |
| *Gildas* | Urien's nephew |
| Glanibanta | Ambleside |
| Halvelyn | Helvellyn |
| Hen Ogledd | Northern England and Southern Scotland |
| *Hogan* | Father of Lann and Raibeart |

| | |
|---|---|
| *Hogan Lann* | Lann's son |
| Icaunus | River god |
| King Gwalliog | King of Elmet |
| King Ywain Rheged | Eldest son of King Urien |
| *Lann* | A young Brythonic warrior (Lann means sword in Celtic) |
| Llofan Llaf Difo | Bernician warrior-King Urien's killer |
| Loge | God of trickery |
| Loidis | Leeds |
| *Maiwen* | The daughter of the King of Elmet |
| Metcauld | Lindisfarne |
| *Miach* | Leader of Lann's archers |
| *Monca* | An escaped Briton and mother of Aelle |
| Morcant Bulc | King of Bryneich (Northumberland) |
| *Mungo* | Leader of the men of Strathclyde |
| *Myrddyn* | Welsh warrior fighting for Rheged |
| *Niamh* | Queen of Rheged |
| Nithing | A man without honour |
| Nodens | God of hunting |
| *Osric* | Irish priest |
| *Oswald* | Priest at Castle Perilous |
| Pasgen | Youngest son of Urien |
| *Pol* | Slinger and Lann's squire |
| *Radha* | Mother of Lann and Raibeart |
| *Raibeart* | Lann's brother |
| Rhydderch Hael | The King of Strathclyde |
| *Ridwyn* | Bernician warrior fighting for Rheged |
| *Roman Bridge* | Piercebridge (Durham) |
| Sucellos | God of love and time |
| *Tuanthal* | Leader of Lann's horse warriors |
| Urien Lann | Son of Lann |
| Urien Rheged | King of Rheged |
| Vindonnus | God of hunting |
| *Wachanglen* | Wakefield |
| wapentake | Muster of an army |
| *Wide Water* | Windermere |
| Wyrd | Fate |

# Historical Note

All the kings named and used in this book were real figures, although the actual events are less well documented. Most of the information comes from the Welsh writers who were also used to create the Arthurian legends. It was of course, *The Dark Ages*, and, although historians now dispute this as a concept, the lack of hard evidence is a boon to a writer of fiction. Ida, who was either a lord or a king, was ousted from Lindisfarne by the alliance of the three kings. King Urien was deemed to be the greatest Brythionic king of this period. He was succeeded by Aella.

While researching I discovered that 30-35 was considered old age in this period. The kings obviously lived longer but that meant that a fifteen year old would be considered a fighting man. If the brothers appear young then I suspect it is because most of the armies would have been made up of the younger men without ties.

The Angles and the Saxons did invade towards the end of the Roman occupation and afterwards. There appear to be a number of reasons for this: firstly the sea levels rose in their land inundating it and secondly there were a series of plagues in Central Europe. This caused a mass movement towards the rich and peaceful lands of Britannia. Their invasion was also prefaced by the last Roman leaders using Saxon mercenaries to fight the barbarians to the north and the west. At the same the time Irish and the Scots took advantage of the departure of the Romans and engaged in slave raids and cattle raids. It was not a good time to live in the borders.

Carlisle, by all accounts, was a rich fortress and had baths and fine buildings. The strong room in the Praetorium is a fact. There is an excellent one at Corbridge, which is what gave me the idea. There are steps down and it could accommodate ten men; three would have not posed a problem. Carlisle exceeded York at this period as a major centre. Rheged stretched all the way from Strathclyde down to what is now northern Lancashire. Northumbria did not exist but it grew from two British kingdoms which became Saxon, Bernicia and Deira. This eventually became the most powerful kingdom in Britain until the rise of Alfred's Wessex. Who knows what might have happened had Rheged survived?

Morcant Bulc was king of Bernicia and he was jealous of King Urien who was considered the last hope of Romano-Britain. All of the writings we have from this period come from Wales which is distance from Rheged and perhaps they were jaundiced opinions. In the years at the end of the Sixth century the kingdoms all fell one by one. Rheged was one of the last to fall.

In terms of the names I have used the historically correct names. Bryneich and Bernicia are the two names for the same place. As Lann is reporting this after the event, as it were, I have used the Saxon spelling (Bernicia) in the book. As the only reports and written evidence we have comes from the Welsh I have anglicised many of the names. If there is confusion please accept my apologies but it is a fascinating, if complex, period to research!

I do not subscribe to Brian Sykes' theory that the Saxons merely assimilated into the existing people. One only has to look at the place names and listen to the language of the north and north western part of England. You can still hear anomalies. Perhaps that is because I come from the north but all of my reading leads me to believe that the Anglo-Saxons were intent upon conquest. The Norse invaders were different and they did assimilate but the Saxons were fighting for their lives and it did not pay to be kind. The people of Rheged were the last survivors if Roman Britain and I have given them all of the characteristics they would have had. This period was also the time when the old ways changed and Britain became Christian but I have not used this as a source of conflict but rather growth.

There was a battle of Chester, when the Saxons finally claimed the whole of England but this was fifteen years after my story. Beli ap Rhun was king of Gwynedd at the end of the sixth century. Asaph was the bishop at the monastery of St. Kentigern (Aka St. Mungo) and they named the town after him. Julius Agricola swam horses and men across the straits between Wales and Anglesey four hundred years earlier and I thought that Lann could do the same. There is no evidence that Ywain succumbed to the Saxons but Prince Pasgen did rule, briefly in Rheged.

I mainly used two books to research the material. The first was the excellent Michael Wood's book "In Search of the Dark Ages" and the second was "The Middle Ages" Edited by Robert Fossier. I also used Brian Sykes book, "Blood of the Isles" for reference. In addition I searched on line for more obscure information. All the place names are accurate, as far as I know and I have researched the names of the characters. My apologies if I have made a mistake.

*Griff Hosker June 2013*

# Other books

# by

# Griff Hosker

If you enjoyed reading this book, then why not read another one by the author?

**Ancient History**

**The Sword of Cartimandua Series** (Germania and Britannia 50A.D. – 128 A.D.)

Ulpius Felix- Roman Warrior (prequel)
Book 1 The Sword of Cartimandua
Book 2 The Horse Warriors
Book 3 Invasion Caledonia
Book 4 Roman Retreat
Book 5 Revolt of the Red Witch
Book 6 Druid's Gold
Book 7 Trajan's Hunters
Book 8 The Last Frontier
Book 9 Hero of Rome
Book 10 Roman Hawk
Book 11 Roman Treachery
Book 12 Roman Wall
Book 13 Roman Courage

**The Aelfraed Series** (Britain and Byzantium 1050 A.D. - 1085 A.D.

Book 1 Housecarl
Book 2 Outlaw
Book 3 Varangian

**The Wolf Warrior series** (Britain in the late 6th Century)
Book 1 Saxon Dawn
Book 2 Saxon Revenge
Book 3 Saxon England
Book 4 Saxon Blood
Book 5 Saxon Slayer

Book 6 Saxon Slaughter
Book 7 Saxon Bane
Book 8 Saxon Fall: Rise of the Warlord
Book 9 Saxon Throne

**The Dragon Heart Series**
Book 1 Viking Slave
Book 2 Viking Warrior
Book 3 Viking Jarl
Book 4 Viking Kingdom
Book 5 Viking Wolf
Book 6 Viking War
Book 7 Viking Sword
Book 8 Viking Wrath
Book 9 Viking Raid
Book 10 Viking Legend
Book 11 Viking Vengeance
Book 12 Viking Dragon
Book 13 Viking Treasure
Book 14 Viking Enemy
Book 15 Viking Witch
Bool 16 Viking Blood
Book 17 Viking Weregeld
Book 18 Viking Storm
Book 19 Viking Warband
Book 20 Viking Shadow

**The Norman Genesis Series**
Rolf
Horseman
The Battle for a Home
Revenge of the Franks
The Land of the Northmen
Ragnvald Hrolfsson
Brothers in Blood
Lord of Rouen

**The Anarchy Series England 1120-1180**
English Knight

Knight of the Empress
Northern Knight
Baron of the North
Earl
King Henry's Champion
The King is Dead
Warlord of the North
Enemy at the Gate
Warlord's War
Kingmaker
Henry II
Crusader
The Welsh Marches
Irish War
Poisonous Plots

**Border Knight 1182-1300**
Sword for Hire
Return of the Knight
Baron's War

**Modern History**
**The Napoleonic Horseman Series**
Book 1 Chasseur a Cheval
Book 2 Napoleon's Guard
Book 3 British Light Dragoon
Book 4 Soldier Spy
Book 5 1808: The Road to Corunna
Waterloo

**The Lucky Jack American Civil War series**
Rebel Raiders
Confederate Rangers
The Road to Gettysburg

**The British Ace Series**
1914
1915 Fokker Scourge
1916 Angels over the Somme

1917 Eagles Fall
1918 We will remember them
From Arctic Snow to Desert Sand
Wings over Persia

**Combined Operations series 1940-1945**
Commando
Raider
Behind Enemy Lines
Dieppe
Toehold in Europe
Sword Beach
Breakout
The Battle for Antwerp
King Tiger
Beyond the Rhine

**Other Books**
Carnage at Cannes (a thriller)
Great Granny's Ghost (Aimed at 9-14-year-old young people)
Adventure at 63-Backpacking to Istanbul

For more information on all of the books then please visit the author's web site at http://www.griffhosker.com where there is a link to contact him.

Made in the USA
Columbia, SC
13 August 2021